T.M. CROMER

ENCHANTED MAGIC Copyright © 2021 T.M. Cromer

All rights reserved.

ISBN: 978-1-7352032-1-8 (Digital)
ISBN: 978-1-7352032-4-9 (Paperback)

No part of this book may be reproduced in any form or by any electronic or mechanical means, including information storage and retrieval systems, without written permission from the author, except for the use of brief quotations in a book review.

This is a work of fiction. Names, characters, businesses, places, events and incidents are either the products of the author's imagination or used in a fictitious manner. Any resemblance to actual persons, living or dead, or actual events is purely coincidental.

Cover art: Deranged Doctor Designs
Editor: Trusted Accomplice

To Jeannie H. - thanks for understanding how my brain works and being patient about your dedication. You knew I'd get there eventually. :)

CHAPTER 1

Mackenzie hadn't really expected to see Sebastian Drake again this soon. After all, they didn't run in the same circles. He was the British elite and the newest ranking member of the Witches' Council. She was a rebellious Thorne and an empty-headed American model—or so it was rumored by those who only saw an exquisite face and didn't actually know her or that she held a master's degree in nanoscience.

Yet there Sebastian was, across the room, looking sexy and smart in his very expensive tuxedo jacket and kilt. James Bond in warlock form. His thick black hair was combed neatly, with a single errant lock falling in such a way to make a woman want to smooth it back into place.

Well, this woman anyway.

She took a measured sip of her champagne and maintained a pleasant neutral expression. It would never do to show her interest in Sebastian despite her cousin Alastair's desire to match the pair of them. If a man saw a woman was attracted to him, he immediately assumed she wasn't worth the chase and looked elsewhere. Sure, sometimes he'd bed her, but then he'd implement the slow fade and eventually ghost her. But if a woman played it cool and was reserved, it would whet the male's appetite, and he'd pursue her to the ends of the earth.

Clearly a fault in the male design.

Her gaze dropped to the red plaid kilt. Sebastian had legs the size of small tree trunks, and when he shifted, Mackenzie was able to catch a glimpse of those mighty fine knees. A smile tugged at her lips. Oh, what she wouldn't give to see what he really wore under that skirt of his.

She let her eyes leisurely trail upward and linger where his package resided underneath the low-slung leather sporran around his waist. Like many of the lust-struck women she'd overheard discussing the incomparable Sebastian Drake, Mackenzie wouldn't mind spending a night or thirty in his bed. Sighing deeply, she drained what remained of her drink and placed the glass on the tray of a passing waiter. Hell, she'd spend her life in his bed if he gave her any encouragement.

When she glanced back one last time, it was to meet the intense gaze of the ruggedly handsome Sebastian. For the count of five chest-thumping heartbeats, they locked eyes. His slow, knowing smile brought with it a searing desire to close the distance between them and plant her mouth firmly on his. In her mind's eye, she saw them tangled, naked and sweating, going at it like sex-starved fiends. She wasn't sure if the image was his or one of her own. Such was the way with psychics.

He winked.

She blushed.

What the hell?

She, who *never* blushed, felt the heat of embarrassment rush up her neck and heat her cheeks. Somehow, he'd either guessed at the torrid thoughts crowding her mind, or he'd put them there. Now, she had an obsessive need to touch him.

Damn him!

With a tilt of her chin skyward, she pivoted on her stilettos and headed for the closest exit. The cold, crisp air would cool her overly warm skin and clear her head of images involving the horizontal mambo with that "English playboy"—as her cousin was so fond of calling him.

Mackenzie had just cleared the doorway when her internal warning system went haywire. A tingling started between her shoulder blades, and goose bumps broke out along the exposed skin of her arms and neck. Hands raised to strike, she spun back around and faced the oncoming threat.

Only it wasn't a threat, not in the truest sense of the word. Certainly not a hazard to her health—more along the lines of a danger to her heart.

Sebastian.

And based on the amorous look in his dark eyes, he was coming to claim the kiss she'd been fantasizing about since she met him three months ago.

"Leaving so soon, Ms. Thorne?"

Crap on a cracker! The husky, teasing quality of his voice made her insides a quivering mass of jello. "Of course not. Not before the dedication for Georgie Sipanil. I simply required air." There, that sounded like a legit excuse, right?

"Mmhmm." He placed his palm flat against the bare skin at the small of her back and guided her toward the railing.

Her mind blanked. Like literally all the words and thoughts rolling around in her head went south, and in their place, something darker, more sinister took root. She violently shuddered from the kaleidoscope of images she received from his simple touch. Her body's reaction had nothing to do with here and now, but everything to do with future events involving Sebastian.

He quickly removed his hand.

"I'm sorry. I didn't expect you'd find my touch abhorrent." His voice had taken on a coolness and held an edge of discomfort. Here was a man who respected boundaries, and Mackenzie appreciated the hell out of that type of guy.

"Oh, no... I... it's not that... you..."

The ridiculousness of the moment suddenly struck her, and she laughed. Here she was, one of the most sought-after models of all time, with nearly every member of the fashion world clamoring for her attention in some way or another. Women wanted to be her. Men wanted to bed her. Corporate heads wanted to make money off her looks. But all she could do was act like a stammering virgin when confronted with the magnificent Mr. Drake.

"I'm sorry, Sebastian. It wasn't you. It was..." What could she tell him? It actually *was* his fault, but only insomuch as his fate would play out in the coming weeks.

His eyes warmed, taking them from near-black to a milky chocolate. "So now we are on a first-name basis? I'd hoped to get there soon."

Aaannnd they were back to his patented panty-dropping charm.

She sighed her disappointment. While she didn't mind dropping her panties for this man, she wanted the genuine guy she'd witnessed only a minute before. Not *this* guy. Not the one who was practiced and suave. Not the one who gave all his potential conquests the same cool, sexy smile but failed to offer anything more lasting than a few hours in the sack.

"Look, Mr. Drake, I'm sure you're nice and all, but this..." She waved a hand up and down to indicate his gorgeousness. "Yeah, it's going to be a hard pass from me."

He frowned his confusion but remained silent. Watchful.

"Haven't been told no before, have you?" she asked, her voice dripping with faux pity.

He laughed. Not just an indulgent chuckle, but a full-bodied amused bark of laughter. "You remind me of GiGi," he finally said. "Same sarcastic wit, same ability to put a person in their place. Well done."

GiGi.

Yes, for a brief second, she'd forgotten he had a thing for her cousin. Disappointment rode her hard. At most, Mackenzie would be second-best since Sebastian was probably still in love with GiGi. And didn't that beat all? The guy she was crushing on wanted someone else.

"She's taken," she snapped. Her irritation wasn't a result of jealousy or because she didn't wish her cousin well. It was because she *did* want GiGi's happiness that Mackenzie was irritated. As long as she was around, no one was going to screw up GiGi and Ryker's marriage but them.

"I'm well aware." Sebastian's eyes took on a quizzical light as he studied her.

"Good. Have a nice evening, Mr. Drake." She gave him a brief nod.

When she would've moved away, he held up a hand. "What have I done to give you such a low opinion of me, Ms. Thorne?"

With a concerted effort, she pasted a smile on her face. "I don't have any opinion of you. I don't think of you at all."

Liar, liar, pants on fire.

His eyes narrowed.

She arched a brow. "If you'll excuse me, I don't want to miss the dedication."

"By all means." He swept his arm toward the door. An indication for her to precede him. She'd only taken two strides when he said, "I believe you do think about me, Mackenzie Thorne. You think about me a lot."

She met his mocking gaze in the reflection of the doors. He was right, but she'd never admit it. Not to this arrogant version of the man she wanted him to be. "Keep telling yourself that, *Mr. Drake.* In the meantime, you should go soak that big fat head of yours. It's matched only by your ego, and *that* should be deflated, too."

His amused chuckle set off the butterflies in her lower abdomen.

Dammit!

As Mackenzie rushed away, Sebastian allowed himself a small smile of satisfaction. She wasn't immune to him despite what she claimed. The high color in her cheekbones and the spark of interest in her eyes belied her words.

She'd been wrong when she assumed he nursed unrequited feelings for GiGi Thorne-Gillespie. Oh, without a doubt, he'd desired her, and had they explored a relationship, they'd have been happy enough as partners. However, GiGi's heart had always belonged to her husband, Ryker, and everyone knew a Thorne only loved once.

Sebastian would likely never admit it aloud, but he wanted someone to love him with that same all-consuming passion.

Taking his time, he sauntered back into the ballroom. He sought out the scarlet-haired Mackenzie and found her speaking with an old school chum of his, Hugh Cunningham. A feeling akin to irritation rippled through him. He wanted nothing more than to plant Hugh a facer and hurry Mackenzie away. In more than twenty years, that slimy prick, Hugh, hadn't changed much. Although he'd retained his blond good looks, Hugh's eyes had grown paler, and no amount of glamouring could reduce the bags underneath them. His long nights of excess were clearly stamped on his puffy features. Still, he regarded every woman as a conquest to be bedded and abandoned with undue haste, uncaring if they found him attractive or not. It was the singular thing Sebastian hated about him.

At that precise instant, his friend locked eyes with him across the distance and winked. It was an indication that the bloody wanker intended to make a move on Mackenzie. Wasting no time, Sebastian cut a path to her side. He'd be damned if Hugh would try to seduce the woman he wanted for himself.

"Baz! Have you met the lovely Mackenzie Thorne? You have? Brilliant. Brilliant." Hugh smiled widely.

How had Sebastian never realized how annoying Hugh was? Always repeating the last word of his sentence. Always grinning like a demented jackal. Always… yeah, well, now that he thought about it, Hugh was a great waste of space, and an irritating one at that.

"I was just trying to convince her to have dinner with me. What? What?"

When Sebastian glanced down into Mackenzie's laughing blue eyes, the tension in his neck and shoulders eased. Obviously, she had no intention of being charmed by Hugh.

She gave him a slight nod when Sebastian lifted a brow in silent question. Their gazes remained locked for an extra few seconds—

mainly because he found it impossible to look away. Finally, as the sound of another person clearing their throat penetrated, he faced Hugh.

"Sorry, but the lady has already agreed to give me a go of it. I'm sure if she ever tires of me, she'll look you up." On that note, Sebastian ushered her away, cutting off any protest Hugh might have.

"Give you a 'go of it'? What, precisely, does that mean?" she asked as he handed her a new flute of champagne.

He tapped his glass to hers. "I intend to wine and dine you."

"Just so long as you don't throw the sixty-nine in there," she muttered as she took a sip and turned away.

Sebastian was sure she'd never intended for him to hear the low-spoken words, yet he did, but only because the orchestra had died at that precise moment. Leaning in close, he whispered, "Why? You don't like to sixty-nine?"

She spewed her drink and proceeded to cough as if her lungs were afire.

Wordlessly, he handed her his handkerchief.

She mopped up her chin and dress, her cheeks a vivid shade of pink. "I can't believe you said that."

"Because all Englishmen are expected to be refined?"

"Are you saying you aren't?"

Sebastian let a cheeky grin answer for him.

Color flooded her face for the second time. She surprised him when she said, "I think I like you better unrefined, Mr. Drake."

"He's technically an Earl. That would make him Lord Kilbride," inserted a female from behind them. "And he's half Scot. So, yes, completely unrefined."

He twisted slightly to glance over his shoulder at his sister.

"Arabella!" Mackenzie kissed her on each cheek. "You are looking lovely tonight. I'm glad you could make it."

"It's nice to see you again, Ms. Thorne. I hope I'm not interrupting?"

"Not at all, and I thought we were on a first-name basis? Please, call me Mackenzie or Mack." She waved a waiter over and retrieved two more flutes of champagne, handing one off to Arabella.

"So you're on a first-name basis with my sister, but not me?" Sebastian asked, curious how Arabella ranked such familiarity when he'd been in Mackenzie's company more. Keeping his gaze focused on Mack, he directed his next comment to his sister. "Actually, you *are* interrupting, Bella. I was about to ask Mackenzie to—"

Expression bordering on panic, she was quick to slap her palm over his mouth.

Sebastian didn't know who was the more surprised of the three of them. He suspected Mackenzie herself, based on the way she jerked her hand away and hid it behind her back.

"To have dinner with me," he concluded with a smirk.

Although he never looked her way, he could feel his sister's speculative regard bouncing between the two of them.

"Oh, do say yes, Mack," Arabella urged. "Better yet, you should be our guest for the weekend. You and I could get to know each other better."

Mackenzie turned her dazzling blue gaze on his sister. She seemed to understand the offer of true friendship because she smiled her agreement.

"Wonderful." Arabella linked their arms and steered her toward the front of the room. "We are going to be great friends," she declared. "I just know it."

Sebastian followed the women at a slower pace, watching as Arabella leaned in to impart some tidbit of information here or there as they walked away. He hadn't realized how lonely his sister was all this time, but the hint of desperation she'd shown when she invited Mackenzie to their home spoke volumes.

As for himself, he could freely admit to his own loneliness. It had been too long since he had anything resembling a relationship. The siblings guarded a life-altering secret, and it made them overly cautious of the outside world. Yet they still longed for friendships in general.

Mackenzie Thorne might be the Drakes' salvation.

CHAPTER 2

The Drake estate was magnificent by anyone's standards. Four stone stories crowned with a smattering of towers made the place majestic. As she stared at the exterior of Sebastian's home, Mackenzie couldn't help but gape. The windows were a good foot and a half taller than her host, who stood at six-four, and she could just imagine a lady of old staring wistfully out over the drive, waiting for her long-lost love to return.

"This place is amazing!" She craned her neck to see the domed towers better. "Is it just you and your sister living here?"

"We have two aunts haunting the halls, but otherwise, yes."

She gave Sebastian a sharp glance. "Haunting?"

He grinned but said no more.

"He's teasing you, Mack. They are alive and well." Arabella bit her lip. "Or mostly well, if you disregard the fact they are both madder than a March hare."

"I don't know what to say to that," Mackenzie admitted with a laugh.

"No need," Sebastian assured her. He kept his hands locked behind his back and nodded toward the now-open door. "After you."

Today, Mackenzie was wearing flats, and although she was on the tall side, she barely reached Sebastian's chin. As a result, she had to tilt her head back a bit to meet his dark, dancing eyes. "You think I'm going to be the first to walk into a house with creaking doors and haunted halls?"

He chuckled and held out an arm for her to take. And oh, how she wanted to, but she was afraid of what she'd see again. Just as he was about to lower his arm, she placed her hand in the crook of his elbow. She released a relieved sigh when no visions slammed into her.

"Is everything all right, Mackenzie?" His charming veneer dropped to show legitimate concern.

"Yes, I…" She gave a self-deprecating laugh. "Sorry. I don't touch many people. I don't always care for the feelings I receive."

His eyes met hers, and he nodded. "Last night makes more sense now. What did you feel?"

"Nothing that made any sense, really," she hedged.

"You're not being completely truthful with me," he said. "But your secrets are your own to keep. I understand all about the need for such things."

"Thank you, Sebastian."

"Baz. All my close friends call me Baz."

"I don't know that I'd classify us as close friends."

He smiled at her teasing tone. "I would, because it won't be long now."

Her breath stalled, and she found it difficult to take in air.

The intent behind his comment was clear; Sebastian Drake desired her and would do everything within his power to make her his lover. Mackenzie's ability allowed her to feel his seriousness. The want in those mocha eyes was plain for anyone to see.

The two of them were locked in the moment. Each lost in the magic of the other's gaze and the possibility of becoming lovers.

Arabella cleared her throat, and the spell was broken.

Or mostly.

Sebastian's hot-eyed gaze dropped to Mackenzie's lips, and he shifted as if he intended to kiss her.

"*Sebastian!*"

Arabella's scold had done the trick. He jerked slightly and shook his head. "Right." Once again, his eyes met Mackenzie's. "Right."

Placing his other hand over hers where it still rested in the crook of his arm, he guided her toward his sister at the top of the stone stairs.

Trying not to attract notice, Mackenzie inhaled deeply to restart her lung function. Goddess, the man was sex on a stick. All yummy and tempting, making her insides gooey.

He was correct; they'd become lovers. But that didn't mean she was going to make it easy for him.

She suppressed a grin at the thought.

"What has you so amused?" he asked in a low voice.

"You. Me. Us."

He paused in the entry hall to stare down at her. "The idea of us amuses you?"

"The upcoming dance does."

The light of challenge sparked a fire in his dark eyes, and an appreciative smile eased the hardness of his rugged features. "Me, too." He leaned in until his lips were a mere inch from the shell of her ear. "You should know, I'm a master dancer."

Removing her hand from his, she stepped away. "I've no doubt. But you should know, I can dance circles around you, Baz."

His grin widened to encompass half his face.

"What has you so amused?" she parroted his earlier question.

"You. Me. Us." He had replied as she expected he would.

"Care to elaborate?"

"You called me 'Baz.' It shows you're already warming to me."

She gave him an arch look and turned away to admire the hall. "Your home is gorgeous."

"Not nearly as gorgeous as you," he said smoothly.

"First, if you want to charm me, Lord Kilbride, I suggest you discard the practiced-flirt routine. I don't like it, and for each time you lay it on thick, it will set you back by at least ten steps and kill your game."

"I'll make a mental note of it. And second?"

"Pardon?"

"You said 'first,' which implies a second."

The twinkle in his eyes was genuine, and it derailed her thought process. "Yeah, I got nothing."

His deep laughter was like a thick blanket on a cold day. She wanted to snuggle down and get comfy.

"I like you, Mackenzie Thorne."

Raw honesty shone on Sebastian's face, and Mackenzie's heart unlocked enough to crack the door to possibility. It wasn't necessarily an open invitation for him to step through, but she wasn't shutting him out either. Maybe he'd taken her at face value and decided to be himself instead of some over-the-top Lothario. She'd like him so much more if he was genuine.

Because she feared her face displayed her longing, she glanced away, looking for a distraction, and realized Arabella was missing. "What happened to your sister?"

"Her first action is always to check the welfare of the aunts when we return."

"Arabella is such a lovely soul."

"You can tell that after such a brief acquaintance?"

"Call it a gift."

"Ah."

She stopped her inspection of his home and spun back around to face him. "Your 'ah' holds a wealth of meaning. What are you thinking?"

"Simply that you're insightful. It explains why you dislike it when people put on an act with you."

She gave him a single nod to acknowledge he'd guessed correctly.

"Tell me, Mackenzie. Are you like your cousin Alastair?"

"In what way?"

"An empath."

"Somewhat. My ability goes deeper."

He placed a hand lightly on her shoulder to gain her attention and direct her toward another room, but just as quickly removed it. "In what way?"

"I have psychic visions." She'd turned back around when she said it so she could see his reaction.

He nodded thoughtfully. "What did you see when we were on the balcony last night?"

"How did you know?"

"When I touched you, you had a visceral-type reaction and responded with a shudder. You then said it wasn't me. That leads me to conclude you had a vision. So again, I ask, what did you see?"

"They were more impressions, really. Nothing concrete."

His eyes narrowed, and his mouth curled down with distaste.

"I'm sorry, Baz. My line of work doesn't allow for confidences." She shrugged and gave him a rueful smile. "I'm constantly on guard against the world because of who I am. It wasn't meant to make you feel bad."

The hardness in his features softened. "Forgive me. As I said, you're entitled to your secrets."

"There's nothing to forgive. When I've had time to decipher what I saw, I promise to share."

He nodded and held out his hand. "Come. Let me show you my home."

SEBASTIAN COULD SPOUT FACTS REGARDING THE ESTATE WITHOUT lending much thought to the conversation, but he remained silent whenever Mackenzie stopped to admire a painting, an antique, or the room in general. Because he knew a simple brush of her fingers along the surface told her more than he ever could, he gave her time to absorb the energy from the object or space.

"You're awfully quiet," she said, giving him a curious look.

"I didn't think you needed me to regurgitate unnecessary details when you could simply touch an object to know about its history."

She bit her lip to hide her smile. The gesture irritated him because he wanted to enjoy the pleasure of her wide grin. When she relaxed enough to tease or flirt, her eyes sparkled and her lips curved, showing her mischievous side. A side Sebastian would dearly love to see more of.

"You're stunning when you smile," he blurted. The comment surprised both of them. Perhaps him more so than her. She was, in all likelihood, used to constant compliments, which was why she detested them.

Instead of grimacing or turning away in distaste, she laughed. "Genuine compliment. I'll take it and thank you for it."

"Good. I'm glad you recognized it for what it was."

The fun light in her eyes disappeared, and she looked as if she wanted to ask him something. A slight frown came and went, and she started to turn away.

He stopped her with a hand on hers. "You can ask me anything, Mack."

"Now who's the insightful one," she teased with a light laugh.

He recognized her desire to divert his attention from her seriousness a moment before. Remaining silent, he lifted his brows in question.

"Last night, you mentioned my cousin GiGi." She met his gaze head-on. "Do you love her?"

"No."

"Did you?"

"No."

Her shoulders dropped, and he imagined her sigh was one of relief.

"Would it bother you so much if I had?" He asked the question to quench his curiosity and found himself eagerly awaiting her response.

She studied the vase of fresh flowers next to her. With a slight shrug, she said, "Yes. I suppose it would."

"Mackenzie." His tone commanded attention.

When she looked up, Sebastian said, "Your aunt is a beautiful woman. Both inside and out. I found her attractive, and I flirted shamelessly when I believed she was going to divorce Ryker." He shifted forward and brushed a lock of her outrageously red hair from her face. "I hadn't met you yet, but I can tell you now, I didn't feel half of the desire for her that I do for you."

His heart rate increased as he waited for her to process his comment and respond. Her happiness brightened her eyes, and again, she bit her lip to hide her smile.

"Don't do that," he ordered softly, touching the pad of his index finger to her lower lip. "Don't hide all your loveliness from me. Please."

Anything she would've said was forgotten as his aunts, Gwendoline and Theodora, scuttled into the room.

"Oh, dear me. She's perfect, wouldn't you say?" Aunt Gwennie said, her hands fluttering the black lace veil she still insisted on wearing sixty years after her husband's death.

"I'll say," Aunt Teddie agreed, her voice a whisper compared to Gwennie's commanding tone. In contrast to her sister, Teddie tended to wear all white. A symbol of her unmarried state from a time when debutantes wore light colors to denote their innocence.

"Perfect for what, or don't I want to know?" Mackenzie asked in an aside.

"Who really does with these two?" Sebastian murmured. "Just smile, but never nod. Otherwise, you'll encourage them, and no one wants that."

She shot him an admonishing glare and crossed to the elderly women. "How do you do? I'm Mackenzie Thorne."

She had held out her hand, but quickly drew it back when Gwennie hissed her displeasure.

"A Thorne? Oh, dear. Oh, *dear!*" Teddie cried as she wrung her hands and ping-ponged her head back and forth between her sister and Mackenzie. "What do we do, sister? What do we *do?*"

The oddest thought occurred to Sebastian that Teddie and his now ex-friend Hugh might somehow be related based on their speech patterns alone. Before he had time to form a sentence to convince Mackenzie everything was fine and this was the norm, Arabella skidded into the room. Apology in every line of her body.

"They escaped. I'm sorry, Baz."

"Escaped? I beg your pardon!" Gwennie snapped.

"And this is why we never invite guests back to the estate," Sebastian whispered into Mackenzie's delicate ear.

A sparkle lit her eyes, and she smothered a laugh. "They're delightful," she countered.

"Not in the least. You'll see. You'll see." He'd purposely mimicked Teddie to draw another giggle from Mackenzie.

Her eyes flared wide, and she did the thing where she bit her lip to hold back her amusement.

Sebastian wanted nothing more than to lean in and taste those plump pink lips, but he figured he'd send the aunts the rest of the way into madness.

"Tea is served."

They all pivoted toward the far end of the drawing room, where the Drakes' ancient butler proudly stood with his tie askew and one stocking bunched around a painfully thin ankle. The poor old bugger still dressed as if he belonged in the time of carriages, balls, and bustles. The only thing out of the ordinary—or maybe it wasn't—was the bright-pink lipstick peppering his jawline.

Teddie and Leopold had been at it again.

Sebastian closed his eyes and sighed.

Of course this was happening when he wanted to impress Mackenzie. Why wouldn't it? Such was his life.

"Tea? Oh, I don't think I've ever had proper tea." She practically danced in her eagerness.

"Don't get too excited," he told her in a low voice. "The scones are always rock hard and the milk curdled. Do play along, but be sure to replace what's in your cup with something consumable and not likely to poison you, won't you?"

Hearing her choked laughter brought heat to his cheeks. He didn't have the courage to see if she found all this a lark or whether she was secretly appalled, unable to get away fast enough.

Tucking her arm through his, she tilted her head to stare up into his face. "Should we work out a signal? Something to let me know what's edible and when I should pull the old switch-a-roo?"

Releasing a pent-up breath, he chuckled. "I'll tap a finger to the side of my nose if you need to swap out the food or drink. Although, I must say, you'll probably want to with everything that crosses your plate. It's what Arabella and I both do."

"I think I'm going to love it here."

Sebastian drew her to a halt and let the others go on ahead. When they had the room to themselves, he said, "Thank you. I truly hope you do."

CHAPTER 3

*L*ater that afternoon, as Sebastian attended to business and Arabella wrangled the aunts down for a nap, Mackenzie escaped to the gardens with their maze of herbs, boxed hedges, and large oak trees.

She truly loved this place.

The temperature consistently sat in the mid-seventy-degree range, or as any country other than the States registered temperature: twenty-three degrees. Although she'd traveled extensively for her modeling career, she still needed to stop and think about the conversion from Celsius to Fahrenheit when she was in a foreign country.

Laughing at her own silliness, she swirled a hand in the air to kick up the currents. The trees around her danced, and the wind through their branches whispered her name. The fallen leaves rose and formed in the shape of a heart before morphing into something entirely different.

A child's giggle came from behind one of the trees bordering the garden.

With a slight grin, Mackenzie swirled her hand to gather more leaves. This time, she formed the words, "Hi, I'm Mack."

A dark-haired sprite of a child peeked from around the tree. The smile slowly died from the girl's face as she looked at her. "I'm sorry."

"For what, honey?"

"For what my grandmother will do to you."

This precious girl's sincere apology struck Mackenzie's psyche like a physical blow. Her blood turned to ice, and her heart hammered double-time to pump the frozen sludge through her veins as a feeling of doom struck her. "Who's your grandmother?" She wanted to ask why the hell the woman would target her, but she didn't want to frighten the child.

Before she could answer, an instantaneous flash of light split the space between them, and a black-haired, black-eyed man appeared in front of the girl. Obviously her father, based on the resemblance. He looked a bit harried, and irritation turned his full mouth down at the corners as he gave Mackenzie a once-over.

Dismissing her, he faced his daughter. "What did I tell you about leaving the estate, beastie?" he ground out.

With his hands on his lean hips, his muscular upper body was displayed to advantage. His stance triggered a memory.

"You're Damian Detheridge. The Aether," Mackenzie blurted. She'd seen him years ago when she was younger. And holy hell, the man never seemed to age. With his power, he probably could glamour into the divine creature before her.

"She was making the leaves dance, Papa," the child said, coming out from behind the tree and skipping toward her. All sense of worry for her grandmother's impending deeds seemingly gone as a mischievous grin took the place of her somber frown. "Will you show him, Mack?"

Unbidden, a wide smile formed on Mackenzie's lips. This little girl was too precious for words. "Of course. Tell me what you wish to see?"

"A dragon!"

"Huh. Well, now we know why your papa calls you a beastie. Seems as if you like the darker side of nature," Mackenzie teased as she called forth all the fallen leaves from the ground. She moved her hands as if she were sculpting a great work of art, careful to get the proportions of the dragon's head and body correct for what she had in mind. The darker crinkly leaves formed the scales of the creature's chest and the triangular tip of the tail. For the claws, she used broken twigs.

"There. I think that about has it, don't you?" she asked the girl.

"Make him growl!"

From the corner of her eye, she saw Damian shake his head with an indulgent half smile. Obviously, he was used to the girl's precocious ways and adored her.

"Of course. What's a dragon without a fierce growl?" Mackenzie bit her lip to hide her amusement and, once again, waved her hands about. "Abracadabra! A growling dragon you shall be!"

She was careful to soundproof the garden so any mortals in the surrounding area didn't crap their pants at the echoing roar.

The child's eyes flew wide in delight, and she ran forward as if to hug Mackenzie. She was stopped short by her father's hand on her shoulder, but it didn't kill her enthusiasm. "Oh, thank you! *Thank you!*"

"Well done, Ms. Thorne," Damian said with a deep chuckle. "Sabrina will live on this for a week."

By calling her Ms. Thorne, the Aether basically told her he'd known who she was from the moment he set foot in the garden. Interesting. She wanted to question him, but Sabrina interrupted her train of thought.

"Will you make an elephant? Will you, Mack? Please?"

"I believe we've taken up enough of Ms. Thorne's time, beastie," her father admonished gently.

"But she won't be able to do it when the darkness gets her, Papa."

Again, a cold sensation swept through Mackenzie's cells. She squatted in front of the child. "Should I be aware of something I'm currently not, honey?"

Sabrina frowned and looked toward the back of the property. Her face tilted up to meet her father's cautious gaze.

ENCHANTED MAGIC

"What do you see, Sabrina? Best tell us now, my love."

"The Darkness wants her, too, Papa," she said forlornly.

Mackenzie could feel the blood drain from her face. She didn't know what the hell the Darkness was, but this was the second time the girl mentioned it, and Mack was beginning to freak the fuck out. Because she was in serious danger of falling over, she sat back on her rump and placed her palm flat against her chest, hoping to calm her thudding heart. Her skirt would need a magical laundry booster to remove the grass and dirt stain that was bound to be on the seat after she'd connected with the damp ground.

"Ms. Thorne, are you all right?"

Damian squatted beside her. Underneath his concerned mask was a grimness. As if his daughter's words had disturbed him as much as they did Mackenzie. He didn't reach a hand to her, and she was curious why such a gentleman wouldn't extend that simple courtesy.

"I'm a little thrown by this conversation, if we're being honest." She met the tearful eyes of Sabrina. "What's the Darkness?"

The little girl shrugged, and she looked much younger than she had mere minutes ago.

Damian twisted slightly to look at his daughter. He gently pinched her chin to tilt her face up. "The Darkness will *never* get you, my love. The woman who conjured it is gone now." He tapped her nose. "I promised you I'd protect you always, and don't I always keep my promises?"

Sabrina nodded and patted her father's face with a worshipful look. "Yes, Papa."

The two shared a bond that turned Mackenzie's heart to mush. Theirs was a father-daughter relationship to be treasured. With the easing of Sabrina's fear, Mackenzie's own trepidation dissolved. Perhaps the warning was only a child's flight of fancy?

"How old are you, Sabrina?" she asked.

"Six."

Mackenzie smiled and nodded. That was it then. The girl was doing what children all around the globe did—letting her imagination take flight. Maybe the worried look she sent her father had been for the trouble she might get into. What Mackenzie couldn't shake was the Aether's initial reaction to the word "Darkness." As if he'd suddenly wanted to scoop his daughter up and lock her away from any danger. His eyes had sharpened as his body tensed. Alert. Prepared for danger.

At her first opportunity, she decided to corner Damian and discover what this was all about. To have him fill her in on the witch who'd conjured the evil to begin with. For sure, it wasn't anything serious if the Aether was no longer worried, and maybe Sabrina's fear was due to residual danger to a past experience, but Mackenzie had to be sure.

"So you wanted an elephant, huh?" she asked brightly, hoping to dispel any remaining pall hanging over the day. "Any particular color?"

Sabrina sat down beside her, crossed her legs, and rested her palms on her skinny little knees. "Sit, Papa," she ordered, not bothering to look at him to see if he complied. "A pink elephant."

The girl was queenly in her gestures, nodding her head at the place beside her in the dirt, ordering her father about. Damian, who looked like he'd rather eat glass than sit on the damp ground, tugged up his black slacks and complied without a word of protest.

Mackenzie couldn't help it; she laughed. "A pink elephant for a pretty little princess. Got it."

Gathering up the leaves, she pulled them to her and ran a fingertip over the bunch. They turned various shades from bubblegum to fuchsia. Next, she sorted them by color. Recalling her cousin Summer's perverted rescue, Eddie, Mackenzie solidified the image in her mind. A flick of her wrist, and the leaves began building Sabrina's elephant. With a little smirk, she drew a few of the green leaves from the mighty oaks, giving them a silent apology and a boost for growth, then formed an outrageous top hat.

"Do you want to see him march around?"

"Yes, please." Sabrina's voice trembled with excitement.

The elephant pranced about, tooting an off-key tune with its trunk. Sabrina's laughter triggered Damian's, and he reached to ruffle his daughter's hair.

"Mack? What are you doing?"

Glancing over her shoulder, her smile widened to welcome Sebastian.

"Hi, Baz. I was just entertaining our guests—" Her words died in her throat when she turned toward the Dethridges. Mainly because they weren't there, and the grass beside her was undisturbed. Not a flattened blade to be seen.

The dancing leaves returned to their former colors and shape and settled on the ground as she visually scanned the area, searching for a single sign of her previous company. "I don't understand. They were right here."

"Who was, Mack?" Sebastian's tone was smooth and neutral, as if dealing with a dangerous mental patient.

She frowned in his direction. "Damian and Sabrina Dethridge."

He paled and cast a wary glance around the garden. "We should go."

"Do the Dethridges often pop into your garden?"

Sebastian lifted his head to stare at her. Behind the question, Mackenzie heard her own tremor of uncertainty. Because he hadn't seen either Damian or his daughter, it was possible she'd imagined the entire incident. Perhaps she'd enacted a future event yet to unfold. Sometimes that happened with psychic witches, and anyone witnessing her talking to herself might look as Sebastian did now.

"I've spoken with Damian on occasion, but he's never crossed the property line. Or rather, he hasn't in quite some time. I've not heard of a daughter."

She slowly nodded. "So, their appearance could be all my imagination?"

"I didn't say that, love."

Casting him a sad little smile, she said, "You didn't have to."

He opened his mouth, but no words came forth.

The well-known truth was that clairvoyant witches tended toward madness. They couldn't maintain both the visions and their abilities together in the long run. The Witches' Council had many documented cases where members of the magical community had had to have their powers bound or they went completely insane.

Sebastian would know that, which would explain his current reaction.

"Let's not let it spoil our afternoon, Baz." She wanted to wrap her arm through his, but he had a wary don't-touch-me vibe about him. "How about you show me the maze? I've never seen one so extensive, and I fear I'll be lost if I try it on my own."

His expression eased, and he led her toward the break in the hedges. "Through here."

LATER THAT EVENING, AS THEY WERE ALL SITTING DOWN TO DINE, Sebastian recalled their earlier conversation in the garden. Mackenzie had been so earnest in her claim the Dethridges had been on the property. He supposed it was possible, since their land bordered his, but Sebastian doubted Damian would set foot in the Drakes' gardens if he could help it.

There was no love lost between the two men.

Also, he'd never heard tale of a daughter being born to Damian and his wife, Vivian, but Sebastian surmised they'd want to keep it hidden if possible. A child of such a powerful magical couple might attract unsavory characters looking to cash in on unlimited magic. If they could find a way to tap into the Aether's source, they'd do it in a second.

Sebastian watched Mackenzie as she laughed and interacted with his family. She appeared to be perfectly normal, but madness didn't always show on the outside.

As a psychic witch, she would be shunned by others of their kind, because not many witches with her ability lasted into their dotage with their mind intact. His own feelings about her were mixed. For a fact, he knew she'd never even appeared as a blip on the Witches' Council's radar. Although she might not if she was sheltered by the mighty Alastair Thorne—who was feared by all.

As his cousin, Mackenzie had most likely been protected. No one would dare challenge the most powerful of all the families. Even before, when it was only the Six, the Thornes had the greatest power.

Sebastian had grown up on stories of their greatness. Once upon a time, he'd believed by taking down Alastair, he could secure a seat for himself on the Council. He silently scoffed at his own naiveté. Going head to head with the patriarch of the Thorne family had been the stuff of nightmares. His own arrogance had nearly earned him a formidable enemy. Yet now, after peace had been brokered with a portrait and a defeated enemy, they were friends of a sort.

Someone at their table cleared their throat, and Sebastian jerked his attention from the contents of his wineglass.

"Forgive me, what did I miss during my woolgathering?"

"Aunt Gwennie said she saw the Dethridges from the window overlooking the garden," Arabella said then took a dainty bite of roasted duck.

A glance at his aunt confirmed his sister's comment.

"So Damian Dethridge *was* in our garden," he murmured. The Aether venturing anywhere remotely close to the secret garden at the back of the property ruined Sebastian's relief regarding Mackenzie's sanity. But he raised his voice to a more moderate level, showing no sign of his inner turmoil. "Which one?"

"The one with the maze," Gwennie volunteered.

"Is there a problem with having them visit?" Mackenzie asked between bites of the vegetable medley on her plate.

Hell, yes!

"No, I suppose not." Sebastian shoved down his unease. Damian knew the risks. If he'd come here, he was confident everything would be fine.

"His daughter is darling." She sipped her wine with a thoughtful frown.

"But?"

"No buts. I was simply thrown by her odd comments peppered throughout our conversation. I imagine it's because she's a child and they have such active imaginations."

"What did she tell you, Mackenzie?"

She'd been about to cut a piece of her duck, but she must've caught the edge to his tone because she halted her action. "I'm not sure I could quote it verbatim, but it was something along the lines of 'the Darkness' wanting to get me."

Sebastian stilled. Everyone at their table did, too. His family knew what it could potentially mean. "Are you sure she said 'the Darkness' and not something else?"

"Positive."

He forcefully shoved back his chair and strode from the room. When he got to his study, he pulled out his phone and rang Damian.

"Dethridge."

The smooth, cool tone of his neighbor's voice set Sebastian's teeth on edge. "Were you here today? *In my garden?*"

"You may want to introduce yourself instead of immediately going on the attack. You forget who you're talking to, son," came the acerbic reply.

"I haven't forgotten anything, Dethridge. Not Vivian, not the fact we have to babysit your psychotic mother, not—"

The line went dead at the same time a golden rift split the night outside on the veranda. His study doors were slammed back on their hinges, glass shattering and raining down on the old, English-oak floors.

The Aether had arrived, and he was bloody furious.

CHAPTER 4

"*You dare?*" The impact of Damian's rage was in the form of a wall of energy that smacked into Sebastian and shoved him back three feet.

"*Yes!*" he snapped in return, stalking forward until he was within a foot of the Aether. "You showed up in my garden, interacted with Mackenzie Thorne, and left as I arrived without any indication you'd been there. That poor woman thought she was losing her bloody mind, Dethridge."

Regret simmered in the dark depths of Damian's eyes. "It was exceedingly bad form. My apologies."

"You should apologize to *her*."

"My apologies, Ms. Thorne."

Sebastian pivoted to see her hovering in the doorway of his study. "Mack."

"We heard the breakage and grew worried," she said by way of explanation. "I didn't mean to intrude."

"You're not. Intruding." Why did his tongue always seem to tangle around her? For the love of the Goddess! He was a forty-two-year-old man. He should be able to form a coherent sentence in her presence. Except when she looked at him with those wide, shining eyes, his tongue thickened, his mouth went dry, and thoughts flew from his mind, leaving him dull-witted and wanting.

"It seems your heartbreak over Vivian is all healed," Damian murmured.

Jaw clenched, Sebastian faced his neighbor. "It doesn't make what you did right."

A regretful smile, bordering on sad, tilted Damian's mouth on one side. "True. But she's my wife now."

"For all the good the gold band does." Sebastian leaned in to sneer. He couldn't resist a dig. "Rumor has it she left you, and I imagine it was a smart move on her part."

The temperature in the room dropped to freezing, and Sebastian had to make a concerted effort not to shiver from the bitter cold. All the plants in the room lost their color and shriveled. His bollocks had the same idea. Still, he didn't have it in him to back down.

The rapid tapping of Mackenzie's heels signaled her approach and was the only sound that broke the tense silence between him and Damian. The air around them returned to normal, and life was restored to the indoor plants.

"What's going on?" she asked, practically wedging herself between them. "Is this about earlier today in the garden?"

A wicked light entered the obsidian eyes staring Sebastian down. "This is about *fourteen years ago* in the garden, my dear."

Sebastian saw red. He'd be damned if Damian stole another woman from him. "You stay away from Mack, Dethridge."

"Careful, Drake. I might consider your attitude as hostile. There's no telling what I will do if I feel threatened."

A loud crack echoed outside the window, and a three-hundred-year-old tree on the other side of the balcony toppled to the ground with a thundering boom. It resulted in the room shaking.

"Mr. Dethridge, please," Mackenzie implored.

"I'm afraid it wasn't me, Ms. Thorne." His hard stare never left Sebastian's challenging glare. "You can thank your new beau for that impressive display of temper."

Her head whipped around, and she stared at Sebastian in open-mouthed wonder. "You?"

"I believe you would call him 'salty.'" Damian smirked. "Which is completely understandable since I married his betrothed."

"I see."

Sebastian could've easily throttled Damian when the light died from Mackenzie's face and her radiant eyes darkened from a bright, sky-blue to a murky blue-gray. Her changing irises were a clear indication she was upset or hurt. "Mack—"

"I apologize for the interruption, fellas. I'll take myself off to bed and leave you to your posturing."

Before she could leave, Damian's hand shot out and gripped her forearm. "Ms. Thorne..."

"Take your bloody hand off her, or I'll sever it at the wrist!"

Everyone froze, even Sebastian. His threat hung in the air and couldn't be called back. Without a doubt, the Aether would end his life, because Damian wouldn't allow a threat to his person to stand. Sebastian's entire body went clammy, and he took a silent moment to say goodbye to the world around him.

Damian laughed. And not a simple chuckle, but a highly amused guffaw that shook his frame and filled the cavernous room.

Neither Sebastian nor Mackenzie joined in.

As for himself, Sebastian figured Damian's sanity had taken a holiday from his body. Mackenzie was most likely frozen from the fear she was about to bear witness to a murder.

With a shaky hand, Damian wiped his eyes. "Good one, Drake." His smile turned downright arctic. "I'll let this one go because I imagine you are still smarting from Vivian's defection, but never threaten me again. The consequences will be dire."

The urge to challenge him was strong, but Sebastian clamped his jaw shut. If one had excellent hearing, they were sure to notice the sound of his teeth grinding together.

After a long moment of assessing him, Damian faced Mackenzie. "As I was saying before we were so rudely interrupted... I'm deeply sorry for any upset I caused you today. I wanted to avoid a conflict like the one just now, so I felt it was better to simply disappear."

"Of course. I understand." Her smile was polite, but there was a distinct coolness in her manner. "Good evening, Mr. Dethridge." Her expression softened marginally. "Please give Sabrina a hug for me. She's a lovely girl."

As she once again attempted to leave, Sebastian stopped her. "Mackenzie, wait, please." He faced Damian and sucked in a deep breath, releasing it slowly on the exhale. The humble pie he was about to partake wouldn't sit well on his stomach. "I owe you both an apology for my temper. The underlying cause was my worry. Mackenzie mentioned 'the Darkness' at dinner tonight. Can you tell us what your daughter knows, Dethridge?"

With a troubled expression, the Aether shook his head. "Sabrina wasn't forthcoming when I asked about her prediction this afternoon. The only thing I do know is there have been attacks against my daughter." He rubbed the back of his neck. "When we foiled Josephine Champeau's plan earlier this week, we assumed the Darkness had been eliminated. It wasn't. Or rather, not completely, anyway. Sabrina told me she felt her grandmother was trying to 'reach her through her mind.' Whatever that means."

Mackenzie gasped, and Sebastian frowned his concern for Sabrina. Shelving the animosity, he asked, "What can we do to help?"

"So these attacks would've been earlier in the week, when the Thornes' magic went down as a whole?" Mackenzie looked between the two of them. "When Alastair called me and told me all was well, I thought we were in the clear."

Both men grimaced. The similarity in their coloring was remarkable, but where Sebastian stood at an imposing height and had a ruggedness to his handsome features, Damian was shorter, thinner, and more elegant in form.

The Aether was beautiful for a man. His nose was straight and perfect—not too long, not too short, and without a bump on the bridge to speak of. Every feature on his face was symmetrical, from his almond-shaped eyes to his full lips to his chiseled cheekbones and jaw. It was as if the Goddess had taken all of the best features a human had to offer and rolled them into one, creating this incredible dream of a man. He had a panther-like grace. Every gesture, every step, an economy of movement. Pure elegance. Yet, the undeniable power was there, ready and available should he decide to strike.

While absolutely hypnotic, Mackenzie had no need to fight the Aether's pull, because her attraction to Sebastian was far stronger.

When Damian turned his attention on her, the knowing in his eyes convinced her he could read her thoughts. And when he winked, she knew it to be true.

Crap on a cracker!

That meant he had a good idea of her feelings for Baz. Was it why he'd said what he had earlier? Was he trying to warn her Sebastian's heart would never be hers?

"Dethridge?" The hard edge was back in Baz's tone, and Mackenzie shot him a sharp look. "What are we dealing with? Is it Isolde?"

"Who's Isolde?" Their grim expressions had Mackenzie's nerve endings dancing. She was missing something important, and she didn't like it.

"My mother," Damian informed her.

"Sabrina said she was sorry for what her grandmother would do to me. I get possibly hurting a stranger, but why would she attack your daughter? Her own blood? This makes no sense."

He sighed deeply and rubbed the back of his neck again, as if to relieve a building tension. With a shake of his head, he walked to the doors and stared out into the night. Mackenzie received the distinct impression he could see what no one else could. The inky blackness didn't affect him in the least. He'd have made a wonderful vampire. Dark, mysterious, powerful... sad.

Sad? Why had *that* thought occurred to her?

"I don't know what this all means at the moment. When I learn more and can put all the puzzle pieces in place, I promise to be forthcoming. For now, Isolde is still contained," he said. "Please enjoy what's left of your evening."

"Wait!" Mackenzie rushed forward to stop him from leaving and placed a hand on his upper arm. "I got the feeling your daughter was trying to warn me of the inevitable today. Won't you tell me if I should be worried?"

He turned his head to meet her eyes, and in those near-black depths, she definitely witnessed a silent request for forgiveness. "What happens will be fate's design, Ms. Thorne. I cannot stop a train once it's in motion. I can try to prevent my mother from escaping, but I can make no guarantees. She's strong and mad as a hatter. If she finds a way to break free of her stasis, it will take more than just me to prevent the path of destruction she'll create." He shook his head and grimaced. "I can only assume this is what Sabrina is talking about unless the Goddess sends me a vision. I hope you understand."

"And do you believe it has been set in motion, Mr. Dethridge?"

"I'm afraid it may be so. If you're what I suspect and possess the powers you do, you may have triggered it by setting foot on this estate."

Goose bumps peppered her skin, and it wasn't from the cold. Unable to withstand his intense stare, she dropped her gaze to where her palm came in contact with his arm. She caught a brief glimpse of his recent past, but no clear future.

"If you're trying to, you'll be unable to read me, my dear," he said in a low tone. "It's by design because of what I am. You are the psychic Thorne, are you not?"

She gave a single short nod. "The only one I know of. But Cousin Alastair could be holding out. He's a wily one."

Damian chuckled. "He is at that. But no, he's not psychic. I've known him a long time."

"Tell me something, Mr. Dethridge. If I leave here, tonight, will it at least help Baz and Arabella?"

Respect shone in his eyes, and he allowed himself a small smile. "I don't have the answers you seek. *Yet*. Follow your heart, Mackenzie." He nodded toward a watchful Sebastian, who stood a few feet away. "I think you know where it leads. Don't we all deserve happiness, even if it's for a short while?"

"Is that all I'm allowed?"

"It's all within your grasp, dear, but nothing is worth having without a fight. Remember that, won't you?"

She cocked her head and tried to figure him out. Damian Dethridge was a strange duck, but damned if she didn't like him. "Since I suspect your cryptic response is all I'm going to get, I'll say fair enough."

His smile bloomed wide and unfettered. "I think you're going to give him a run for his money. But don't run too fast or hard. You still want him to catch you."

Her laughter filled the space between them. Before she could say another word, a rift opened in front of him, and she could see the child standing on the other side. The worry eased from the girl's obsidian eyes when she saw her father wink in her direction. Damian left without a backward glance, and the last thing Mackenzie saw was Sabrina flinging herself into her father's arms.

The picture was heartbreakingly sweet.

After the portal sealed shut, she crossed to Sebastian. "I believe we need to talk, Baz."

"Indeed, we do."

"I'll let you get your apology out of the way first."

To give him credit, he didn't wince, grimace, or otherwise make a face. Remorse shone in his warm brown eyes. "I'm sorry, love. For all of it. Storming from the dining hall, summoning Damian, threatening him, and acting like a complete ass." His mouth pulled down at the corners. "I may have gone slightly mad when he touched your arm."

"And why is that? Vivian?"

"In small part." He crossed to the sideboard and poured himself a drink. "Would you care for one?"

"Sure. Brandy if you have it." She sunk onto the settee in the center of the cavernous room and studied the shattered doors. Closing her eyes, she visualized them as they had been the first time she saw them and waved a hand in their direction. With only the slightest clink of glass, all the pieces fused together as they had been prior to Damian's forceful entrance.

"Nice party trick. I should have you restore the oak tree."

She accepted her drink from Sebastian and took a small sip. "I can if you'd prefer."

"No, I'll do it. Come, let's go out to the terrace."

He escorted her outside with a hand hovering at her elbow as if he feared she'd bolt from the room and never return. Sebastian offered her his glass with a small smile and crossed to the massive downed tree.

He ran his fingertips down the length of the trunk, and had Mackenzie not been watching closely, she'd have missed the healing green light. Lifting both arms, with palms facing skyward, Sebastian channeled his magic to raise the tree back to its original position. Mackenzie waved a hand to part the earth, helping as a sign of goodwill.

Once the mighty oak was firmly back where it belonged, with the dirt packed around the base, Sebastian joined her by the low stone wall and accepted his glass. "As I was saying, I'm sorry for my behavior. Vivian was my fiancée prior to her meeting Damian. In *my* garden." He looked toward the maze of hedges and shook his head. "Perhaps I still hold a bit of animosity for them both."

She snorted. "No perhaps about it, Baz. You've got issues."

"Not because of Vivian, Mack." He frowned down at her. "But because his brand of charm is lethal. He tempts all manner of people, unknowingly or not, and it's fueled by what he is. The Aether's power is enticing to others, and they find it nearly impossible to resist."

"And you're worried I'll fall under his spell?"

"I'd be lying if I said no."

"You do me a disservice."

"Do I?" He shrugged and stared moodily into the depths of his drink. "Perhaps."

"I'm not Vivian, Sebastian. I'm a woman who knows my own mind." To gain his undivided attention, she placed her hand over the top of his glass. When he raised his gaze to hers, she said, "He doesn't hold a fraction of the appeal for me that you do."

His dark eyes dropped to her lips, but he didn't kiss her as she'd hoped. Instead, he turned away to stare out over the darkened landscape. "I'm glad. Good night, Mack."

CHAPTER 5

"*Hello*, child. I've been waiting for you."

The woman standing in the center of the garden was easily the loveliest person Mackenzie had ever seen. Her long wavy hair hung to her trim waist, and as the air around them picked up speed, her blue-black locks lifted and danced with a life all their own. Her face was thin, but not painfully so, and her high sculpted cheekbones would make anyone in the modeling industry green with envy.

Mackenzie included.

"Who are you?"

Displeasure swept across the woman's stunning face before she could smooth her features into a serene mask. "I'm Isolde de Thorne."

Isolde.

Mackenzie recalled the earlier conversation between Sebastian and the Aether. A small shudder swept her, and she got her first sense of unease. "You're Damian's mother."

"Yes." Triumph shone in Isolde's eyes.

Wait! De Thorne? Was the name a coincidence? Did that mean they were related? Mackenzie needed to remember to ask Damian the first chance she got. "What do you want?"

"It's not what I want that matters. It's what you want, and I can help you gain it. Sebastian Drake."

Mackenzie barked a humorless laugh. Funny, but even in dreams, people underestimated her intelligence. "I wasn't born yesterday, lady. Whatever you're selling, I want no part of."

"You'd be a fool to make an enemy of me, child." Isolde narrowed her obsidian eyes, and the wind around them picked up. "I will destroy you and all those you love."

Odd how those near-black eyes looked mysterious and sexy on Damian, yet on Isolde, they were flat. Devoid of light and humor. Dare she say demon-like?

"Meh." Mackenzie shrugged. "I'd be a little more worried if your son was concerned, but since he's assured me you're out of the picture, I think I'll end this little dream here and now."

Isolde surprised her when she laughed. The sound was full-bodied and seductive. Even Mackenzie was drawn by it. She was disconcerted to witness Isolde's unguarded humor.

"You have courage, child. I like that in an adversary."

"Do we have to be enemies? Can't you just leave me in peace, and I'll do the same for you?"

For an instant, Mackenzie thought she detected real regret in the other woman's gaze. But her eyes hardened, and the coldness in them would chill anyone to the bone.

"Until next time, child."

A HAND CAME OUT OF THE NIGHT AND TOUCHED HER SHOULDER.

A scream was ripped from her soul.

"Mack! It's me. Sebastian." He bent slightly to look into her eyes. Worry clouded his. "Are you all right?" At her shaky nod, he asked, "What are you doing here in the garden, love? It's freezing out here." He frowned as if he'd just realized the temps were ridiculously cold for the time of year.

Mackenzie rubbed the skin of her bare arms and focused her magic in an effort to ward off the bone-chilling air temperature.

Although her body heated marginally, her teeth began to chatter from the fear associated with her conversation, and she wanted to wake from this god-awful nightmare.

Sebastian scooped her up, and with long, smooth strides, he ate up the distance to the terrace. His body heat began to permeate her icy skin, and she felt toastier than she had moments before.

"I'm not dreaming? We're really in the garden?" Her unease from earlier returned.

"Yes. Mack, why are you walking the gardens in a tank top and shorts?" Worry was heavy in his voice.

"I'm not sure. I thought it wasn't real." She glanced back over his shoulder to the spot she'd seen Isolde. A faint red glow pulsed at the center of the garden. Her heart rate kicked up a few notches, and it wasn't all from Sebastian's nearness. "Um, is that a normal occurrence here?"

He turned to look.

"No." His arms tightened. "No. It's not."

He wasted no time getting her inside. After depositing her on the settee in his study, he wrapped her in a throw blanket and poured her a tumbler of brandy.

From their seats on the sofa, they watched the red light fizzle out.

"Who were you talking to, Mack?" His tone was low and urgent, causing her stomach to clench.

"Isolde."

His head whipped around, and he stared at her in horror. *"You summoned her?"*

"No!" She was at a loss to explain how she'd come to be outside when less than a half hour ago she was sound asleep in her four-poster bed, dreaming of him. "No, Baz. I can't explain it. One second, I was in bed, and the next, I was in the garden, and she was trying to make me her ally." She shrugged. "For what, I don't know."

"Her ally? What exactly did she say?" His intent dark gaze was hyper-focused on her, and Mackenzie felt like she'd opened a can of worms just by being here at his estate.

"She said she'd been waiting for me," she admitted weakly.

Sebastian jumped to his feet and swore up a storm.

"I thought the English were supposed to be more reserved," she said. "Nothing fazes you. Stiff upper lip and all that."

"I'm only half English, and all that flies out the window when the Enchantress decides to use you for her personal agenda."

"The Enchantress?" She had no idea what he was talking about. Since the moment she'd arrived here, it seemed everyone was talking in code, and Mackenzie couldn't seem to break it.

"Damian's mother was the last one."

"I think you need to start at the beginning because I'm so lost it's ridiculous."

Sebastian ran his hands through his hair and huffed out a breath.

For a brief second, Mackenzie was distracted by his masculine appeal. In his haste to get to her, he'd failed to button his shirt, and it hung open, exposing all his delicious muscles. She'd never wanted to touch anyone more. "All those beautiful ridges and tempting skin."

When she lifted her gaze to his face, he was staring at her. Wry humor curled his lip. "Do you normally blurt out whatever's on your mind?"

"Sorry." She bit her lip, fighting the urge to flee. She'd thoroughly embarrassed herself by revealing her innermost thoughts all willy-nilly-like. When had she last done that? When she was twelve? For the love of the Goddess! She was a thirty-five-year-old woman with plenty of experience under her belt. Yet, around him, her brain cells took a vacation. "You were saying?"

"I wasn't saying anything. You were." His smile transformed into a breath-stealing grin. He ran his palm over his exposed chest and abs. "You were admiring all my beautiful ridges and tempting skin."

"The Enchantress," she ground out. She scowled, trying to offset the blazing heat in her cheeks.

The humor dropped from his face, and he cast an uneasy glance back at the garden.

"Baz?"

"Right. The Enchantress was born in the year fourteen fifty-four. She—"

"Wait! What? How is that possible? And how can she be Damian's mother if she's that old?" The math didn't compute—which was saying something for a woman with a degree in nanoscience.

"An enchantress can live hundreds of years. As can the Aether. In Isolde's case, she was both."

He paused for her to process the information.

"Are you fucking with me?" Mackenzie was finding it difficult to comprehend. Yes, she knew witches had a longer life span than the average bear, but close to six hundred years seemed impossible.

"No. Trust me, if I were fucking with you, you'd know. I take my fucking *very* seriously." His lips twitched as if he was fighting a laugh.

Despite the seriousness of their situation, a tidal wave of lust swept over her. She wasn't sure if they were his feelings, hers, or a combination of both. All she *did* know was she wanted him to get super serious about it right now. Overly warm, she shrugged off the blanket. To occupy her mouth so she didn't regurgitate her desire to surf that particular crest all the way to the sex shack, she sipped her brandy.

He joined her on the sofa—the picture of casual sophistication as he crossed one leg over the other and rested his arm along the back of the settee. His cool elegance, paired with his amused smile, turned Mackenzie on as nothing else could. It was as if he could read her churning thoughts and knew exactly what effect he was having on her.

"The Enchantress," she blurted in an attempt to focus on the subject at hand.

"Right." All teasing left him. "By all accounts, she was a horrid woman. Her main goal in life was to amass power, not caring who she hurt or killed to get it. Isis gathered the strongest family members of the Six to stop her reign of terror."

"The Six?" Mackenzie was irritated with herself for not paying more attention to the history of the witch community. She'd been content with her science books, choosing to ignore everything else. Now, she felt like she was out of the loop and didn't care for the experience at all. Her cousin Spring would've known and been able to drone on for hours about all this crap.

"The Six were the founding families: the Thornes, Dethridges, Champeaus, O'Malleys, Carlyles, and my family, the Drakes. Yours has always been the strongest, with the exception of Damian. It's why few want to incur Alastair's wrath." He removed the forgotten tumbler from her fingers, sipped her brandy, and held the glass to her lips. After she swallowed a little, he lowered his hand and continued his explanation. "Just shy of two hundred years ago, Isis crossed from the Otherworld with some of the deceased members from all those lines. Her intent was to have them join with their descendants to neutralize Isolde's power and stop her from hurting anyone else."

"Apparently, they succeeded. The Aether said she was 'contained,' so it would indicate she is no longer a danger."

"Yes. She was entombed in a magical box."

But was she?

Mackenzie looked out the window toward the center of the garden. "How was Isolde able to get to me tonight?"

"I don't know, but I intend to find out. I'll call Damian in the morning and see if he has any insight."

"You're going to willingly call Damian?" she taunted. "Will wonders never cease?"

Sebastian dropped his gaze from hers, looking decidedly uncomfortable. "I owe you a more in-depth explanation than the one I offered earlier tonight. Damian Dethridge is my trigger."

Mackenzie no longer felt like teasing him. It hurt her to think Sebastian was pining for Vivian after all this time. Needing more to drink for this particular conversation, she retrieved the tumbler from Baz and concentrated on the smidgeon of brandy left at the bottom, visualizing it tripling.

After taking a fortifying gulp, she fanned her eyes to stop them from tearing due to the alcohol's burning trail down to her stomach.

She blew out a breath and faced him. The sardonic smile he sported tempted her to kiss the hell out of him, if only to see if he was experiencing the same emotions and feelings as she.

"Okay, shoot. Tell me all the gritty details of your hate-hate relationship with Damian."

"Hate-hate relationship?" he asked with a chuckle.

"Well, for sure there is no love lost."

His lips twisted into something resembling a grimace. "Vivian and I knew each other growing up. Her family and mine have been intertwined throughout time. Our parents wanted to arrange a match, and neither of us was opposed, because the attraction was there."

He stared off into space as if trying to recall the past. A small frown marred his forehead, and Mackenzie suppressed the urge to smooth it.

"I loved her."

The bottom of her stomach fell out. "And now?"

"I suppose I'll always hold affection for her because of our shared memories, but no. She transferred her love to Damian so quickly, I was left wondering if what we had was ever real." Sebastian met her inquiring gaze head-on. "I won't lie and say it didn't cut me to the core, but it was a long time ago. I think the residual anger is the lack of closure."

"She never apologized?" she asked, shocked anyone could throw him over. From everything she'd seen, he was attentive and caring with his family, a pillar of the witches community, and did everything in his power to walk the proper path. Add to that his killer body, and Mackenzie had to wonder what was not to love about him.

"She tried. I wasn't in a place to hear her excuses. I was too devastated." He snorted and took the glass from her hand. After a long swallow, he said, "Looking back, I believe it was mostly ego on my part. I had it all, didn't I? Looks, money, a sparkling wit." He rolled his eyes at his own arrogance. "Vivian was right to leave me, Mack. I was an arrogant prat. And an assuming one at that. She didn't deserve my cockiness or the assumption I was the Goddess's gift to all women."

"You cheated on her?"

"No! Never. I merely strutted about, acting as if I were the best thing since sliced bread. I'm sure, for her, the act got old." He smiled slightly. "I believe you called me out on it a time or two."

"But it's all an act, isn't it?" Mackenzie said knowingly. "To hide the caring man inside. The question is, why?"

"I'm not sure. I suppose if I reflected on it more, I could figure it out, but the simple answer is most likely I don't care to be hurt again."

"It's hard to reconcile who you describe with the man sitting next to me." She smoothed back a stray lock of hair from his forehead. "You are kind, Baz. I see it in the way you treat everyone around you. Perhaps it's why I called you out on your 'act.' I sensed it wasn't the real you. The you I like."

He captured her hand and kissed her fingertips. "Thank you."

"But why do you hate Damian so much if you understand why Vivian defected?"

"Habit, I suppose. He was everything I wasn't. Suave, intelligent, powerful, and he has the ability to seduce with a look."

She smiled. "You want to seduce with a look?"

Sebastian shot her a smoldering glance. "It would be helpful."

"Mm." Mackenzie took the glass from his fingers and sipped. "You can totally seduce with a look."

He laughed and kissed her cheek. "You're adorable, Mack."

"So I'm told. But you should set aside the animosity for Damian, Baz. You're a better man than that, and you have all the things you envy about him. You're highly intelligent. You're a powerful warlock. As for suave, you may be a little rougher around the edges than he is, but it's nice and a whole lotta sexy. It makes a woman feel protected."

"Thank you."

"For what?"

"This little counseling session. You've made me see I'm holding on to emotions I should've let go of a long time ago. Perhaps it's time to call Vivian and apologize."

A small swirl of jealousy danced about inside Mackenzie's mind. "Perhaps it isn't a bad idea if you wish to move forward."

Sebastian narrowed his eyes as he watched her. "You hate the idea?"

"No. Not at all. I was wondering if it would drag up old feelings to talk to her, is all."

"Maybe I should let sleeping dogs lie?" he teased as he ran a finger along her upper lip.

She bit him. "That's on you either way. Just don't poke the bear in the cage." She leaned closer until their lips were mere inches apart. "The bear is the Aether, in case you were clueless. He's got a powerful love for his wife."

Sebastian closed the distance between them. His lips just shy of brushing hers. "To make it perfectly clear, I'm no longer interested in Vivian, Mack."

"Good to know," she whispered.

She kissed him. Tentative at first then with more aggression as she felt his arms come around her and tug her to his chest. Desire exploded inside her, and she wanted to climb onto his lap, humping him until his eyes rolled back in his head and he lost all control.

But the timing was off. She had yet to receive a vision of where a relationship with Sebastian would lead, and a quick tumble between the sheets wasn't her style. She wouldn't place her money on a risky bet. Not at this early stage.

With a great deal of regret, Mackenzie pulled back and took a sip of her drink. If her hand shook a little and sloshed the liquid inside the glass, it was understandable. There was a lot of passion at play between them. Unfulfilled passion that would keep her awake the remainder of the night.

She took a deep breath to cool her ardor and recalled why they were sitting here to begin with. "Back to the Enchantress. What do you think is happening?" She couldn't keep her nervous tremble from her voice. "Do you think Isolde wants to drain my powers?"

She jumped up and hugged herself against the cold trying to invade her soul as the hint of a premonition swept her. "That had to be what Sabrina was trying to warn me about. She said the Darkness wanted me, too. What I thought was a little girl's imagination might be a prediction."

Sebastian got to his feet and crossed to where she stood, staring out into the night. Placing his hands on her shoulders, he squeezed gently. "It would make sense if she's a seer. Most Aethers are to a degree. We should probably call Damian right now."

Mackenzie looked at the grandfather clock. "Baz, it's three in the morning, and as big a crisis as this feels to me, I'm a little leery of waking the Aether—a man I don't know well—in the middle of the night."

"Mack, if this pertains to Isolde, he should know. If there's even a remote possibility she's been resurrected—or is about to be—we can't wait on this." As he picked his phone up to make the call, it rang. He frowned down at the screen and turned it to face her.

Alastair Thorne.

She gave him the universal *"What are you waiting for? Answer it!"* sign by rolling her hand. Leaning forward, she prepared herself for bad news.

"Drake, I know Mackenzie's staying with you. Is she within hearing distance?" Alastair sounded grim, and it didn't bode well.

She met Sebastian's concerned gaze. She had the foolish desire to inch closer to his large body and have him ward off any impending disaster on her behalf. "I'm here, cousin."

"Good." A heavy sigh sounded on his end. However, it couldn't be good if he was stalling.

"What is it, Alastair?" Sebastian's tone was brisk. "We're already dealing with one crisis here."

"Let me guess. The lovely Mackenzie is having visions of the Enchantress." There was no question in Alastair's tone. He acted as if it was a foregone conclusion.

She took the phone from Sebastian. "How the hell did you know that?"

"Sabrina Dethridge just woke Damian in a panic. She is insistent the Enchantress is about to possess you."

Sebastian's eyes flared wide in disbelief. *"Bloody hell!"*

"I don't understand. How can she possess an unwilling vessel? Should we summon Isis?" Mackenzie asked.

"I'll see to it." Alastair sighed again. "In the meantime, you should leave the Drake estate. Come here, where we can watch out for you."

"She'll stay here."

Mackenzie shot Sebastian a surprised look. "It's too dangerous for your family if she intends to target me, Baz."

"We can hold our own, and I'm not sending you away until we know for sure what this is and how to combat it."

Before she could protest, Alastair's smug voice came across the line. "Excellent. I'm thrilled you're willing to help, Drake. Keep her close, won't you, son?"

An amused smile twisted Sebastian's lips at the same time Mackenzie rolled her eyes.

"Could you be any more obvious, cousin? If I didn't know better, I'd say you called so you could play matchmaker." She jerked when Sebastian wrapped an arm around her waist. "What are you doing?" she squeaked, jumping sideways.

"Keeping you close."

Alastair's deep chuckle came across the line. "We'll be in touch in the morning. Try to get some rest."

"Oh, no you don't—! *He hung up on me!*" Mackenzie tossed the phone on the settee in disgust and glared around the room. As surely as she drew a breath in her lungs, her wily cousin was scrying even now. "Alastair is never satisfied unless he's meddling in someone else's life. Jerk."

Sebastian rested against his desk, hands gripping the wooden edge and ankles crossed. His white shirt hung open, and half-curled forward as he was, his abdominal muscles were on full display. The man didn't have an ounce of fat covering that mouth-watering stomach, and Mackenzie was hard-pressed not to drool. As it was, she found her concentration wandering at inappropriate times.

When she saw his contemplative expression, her nerves got the better of her. "What?"

"I didn't say anything." He grinned. "But I find myself unopposed to Alastair's games this time around." Sebastian pushed off the desk and stalked to where she stood, gaping, by the sofa. "Come on, let's get you to bed."

Her jaw dropped even more.

He tapped it closed with a chuckle. "To your bed. *Alone*. I need to remain awake and enforce the wards on our home."

She finally found her wits enough to ask, "What about Isolde and Damian?"

"I'll call him as soon as I'm confident the estate is secure. Don't worry, Mack. We'll get this sorted."

Her mind careened from one worrisome thought to the next on the long walk to her room. Sebastian remained quiet by her side, and Mackenzie assumed he was locked in his own private hell. For sure, calling Damian would eat at him, but what choice did they have?

After they reached her suite, he opened the door and gave the room a cursory glance. Turning to her, he smiled. "All safe and sound."

Whenever he flashed those pearly whites in a genuine grin, Mackenzie wanted nothing more than to jump his bones. To feel skin on skin and melt into him until she didn't know where her body ended and his began.

"If you keep looking at me that way, love, I'm going to say the hell with it and tumble you into bed." His voice dropped, low and raspy, as his eyes took on a hot gleam.

Mackenzie bit back a sigh. Even if she was being cautious, a woman could dream, couldn't she? "Sorry. I—"

He didn't wait for her to finish. Sebastian swooped in for the kiss Mackenzie had been fantasizing about since the moment she saw him. It put their kiss in his study to shame.

Her knees went weak, and if it hadn't been for his steely arms wrapped around her waist, she'd have been a puddle on the floor.

Her low moan seemed to echo in the corridor, but she didn't care if anyone heard it or not. Doubtless they'd heard a lot more from the ghosts haunting these old halls.

Sebastian slowly eased back, looking as shell-shocked as she felt.

She released a girly sigh. *"Dude."*

His sputtering laughter triggered her giggle.

With an engaging grin and an unholy gleam in his mocha eyes, he traced her jawline.

"Good night, Mack. Sleep well."

CHAPTER 6

Sebastian's grin lasted all the way to the Drakes' magical stronghold, located in the east tower. He couldn't have wiped the smile from his face for all the tea in China. Mackenzie Thorne made him feel things he'd never experienced before. Primarily, the desire to laugh at inappropriate moments.

She'd also opened his eyes to the residual hurt and anger he felt toward Vivian, which should be resolved posthaste. If he intended to pursue Mackenzie, and he most definitely did, then he needed to clear his mind and heart of the past. With a lighter step, he opened the door to the tower room. And promptly halted in his tracks.

"Aunt Gwennie, what are you doing up here?"

"I saw the Thorne chit in the garden." She lifted her troubled gaze from the family grimoire to fix him with a penetrating look. "There was something off about her. It was as if she was sleepwalking. Never blinked. Not once. And she walked straight into the red mist."

"You saw the mist, too?"

"I did."

"Alastair Thorne called tonight."

"What did that wily old fox want?" Gwennie's mouth curled downward to show her distaste.

Sebastian was suddenly hesitant to reveal tonight's discovery. Not that he didn't trust his beloved aunt, but the fewer people who knew Mackenzie might be the one vulnerable to the Enchantress, the better.

"He was concerned for our family with Mackenzie being in residence. He suggested we need to fortify the wards on the estate as a precaution." The lie came smoothly, and he didn't question why. Part of him knew he'd do whatever it took to protect her because in the span of forty-eight hours, she'd brightened his life in a way no one else ever had.

Gwennie's narrow-eyed stare made him uncomfortable as hell. She'd seen right through his antics as a boy, and he suspected she did so again now. Just when he was ready to confess all, she smiled and tossed back her black veil. "Come, dear Baz. I've the perfect spell."

She held out a frail hand, and he clasped it with great care and a relieved grin. "You always do, Auntie."

Sebastian delighted in Gwennie's indulgent chuckle. It took him back to the past when he was a small child. She'd been constantly amused by his tomfoolery and always slipped him sweet treats when his parents weren't looking.

Gwennie directed Sebastian to gather the twelve-inch ceremonial crystals. He placed them on the five points of the pentagram engraved in the wood floor beneath his feet. The symbol was thirteen feet in diameter and took up half of their ritual room. Next, he set candles along the perimeter of the circle surrounding the pentagram, roughly a foot apart.

Together, they cast a protective ring and lit the candles required for the ritual. In the air, Gwennie drew the tyet sign to represent Isis. She repeated the gesture for north, south, east, and west to pay homage to the Goddess.

"Dear Goddess, hear our plea and assist us in our time of need." Gwennie lifted her arms toward the sky, and the ceiling rolled back on the built-in metal tracks, parting to allow the moon to shine down upon them.

"Goddess, we ask you to ward our home from the rising evil and protect those within our property's border." Sebastian knelt to pay homage.

Gwennie joined him at the center of their circle and clasped his hand. "And protect the children of this household—Sebastian, Arabella, and Mackenzie—so they will have the strength for the trials to come."

Sebastian almost broke his neck, whipping his head around to stare at her. He didn't dare interrupt the ceremony, but his aunt had some explaining to do when it was over. Because his mind had blanked at the idea of "trials to come," Gwennie took over the rest of ritual, added a few more heartfelt requests for the powers that be, and closed the circle.

He doused the candles with a wave of his hand.

"Care to tell me what that was about, Auntie?"

"We both saw the mist, dear boy. The Enchantress was never going to be contained forever. We all know the prediction."

Sebastian stumbled back. He'd forgotten until this precise moment. There was some prophecy in their grimoire about a psychic Thorne becoming the vessel for evil. He gripped the book and thumbed through the pages, looking for the entry. "What have we done by bringing her here?"

"You set Fate—that capricious wanker—in motion."

"Arabella must've also forgotten." Never mind that his hundred-and-nineteen-year-old aunt knew the term wanker; Sebastian's mind was reeling from his stupidity. "She couldn't have known Mack was a clairvoyant."

"I can't say if Arabella realized Mackenzie was the psychic Thorne, but I can tell you, your sister knew well what the prophecy foretold. We've discussed it at length." Gwennie patted his arm. "Perhaps Arabella brought your Mack here because she believes it was the only way for you to find true love. She doesn't want you to be alone."

"I'd have gladly gone through life alone to spare the world of Isolde's evil." Terror for his family and for Mackenzie took up residence in his heart. He paused his search of the spellbook and hugged his aunt tightly to him. "I'm scared for you all, Aunt Gwennie."

"Both Teddie and I have lived a full life, dear boy. No need to fear for us. It's Arabella and Mackenzie you need to protect now."

"I'll protect *all* of you or die trying," he swore. Trepidation for the inevitable ratcheted up his pulse.

"No need for that, darling."

"I'm sorry, Baz." Arabella's regret-filled voice drifted to him from the doorway. "There was no other way for you to get to know her. You rarely leave the estate unless it's for business."

He stalked to his sister, struggling against the urge to hug her and physically harm her at the same time.

"How could you, Bella? You should've spoken to me first." He swore and ran a hand through his hair. "Do you know what you've done? Mack's psychic ability makes her a sitting target for Isolde, and my guess is she has no ability to fight it. *None!*"

"What?" Both Gwennie and Arabella stared at him, their eyes wide with shock.

Sebastian fisted his hands and began to pace, shaking his head at the mess in which they now found themselves embroiled.

"Alastair Thorne called a short while ago after speaking with the Aether." He stopped in front of Gwennie and gave her a rueful look. "What I didn't tell you was Sabrina Dethridge has had a premonition. It coincides with whatever Mack is experiencing."

"What?" Arabella screeched again.

"Right. By bringing Mack here, we may have destroyed them all. If anyone gets wind of this..." He rubbed his brow. "I dread to see how this mess unfolds. When the Enchantress wakes, I doubt any of us stands a snowball's chance in hell of surviving."

"It's been over two-hundred years, Baz. Yes, we are the Keepers of the Gate, but be honest, did you ever think Isolde was a true threat after all this time?"

"Not really. Not if I'm being truthful. I suppose I felt we'd never have to deal with her other than to maintain the wards on the property." He grimaced and shrugged. "But we can't pretend she's not a threat anymore. Not after tonight."

Arabella wrung her hands and gave him a semi-hopeful look. "She may never go after the Six. She may simply be happy to start over."

"Revenge, Bella," he retorted. "Not to mention what she will do to us, her gaolers."

He hugged his sister when her devastated expression became too much for him to bear. "We'll figure it out. But I want you to take the aunts and staff away from here. As far and as fast as you can."

"What about you and Mack?"

"It's too late for her, and we all know it. So I'll stay to protect her and do what I can to mitigate the damage. Maybe Dethridge has an idea."

Her arms squeezed him and nearly cut his waist in two. "I'm not leaving you, Baz. You're my brother, and Drakes stand together."

"We'll die together if you don't go," he snapped, untangling her from his person. "I'm still Laird of our rag-tag clan. You'll go."

"Pfft. Laird in name only, dear boy. Remember, Teddie and I changed your nappies. It's difficult to take orders when we've seen your dangly bit, weeing all over your cradle."

Sebastian's face burned hot. He shouldn't be embarrassed by his aunt, but Mackenzie happened to enter the room behind her.

She bit her lip but failed spectacularly to hide her grin.

He closed his eyes against the humiliation and sighed. "Goddess save me from the women of this family," he muttered. Lifting his lids, he met Mackenzie's amused gaze. "I thought you were sleeping."

"Mmm, well, I was having a difficult time, what with my being a catalyst for the Enchantress to make a reappearance and all."

Arabella frowned. "How did you find this tower? It's enchanted. Only our family should ever be able to locate it."

"I followed the light." Mackenzie looked at each of them in turn.

With a hesitant smile, she gestured over her shoulder. "It was so bright, and it lit the way."

Sebastian, Arabella, and Gwennie all traded wary looks. There should be no guiding light. He stepped forward and took Mackenzie's hand in his. "Show me. Please."

She tugged him into the hallway and turned her head left then right. She spun in a slow circle, a confused frown puckered her brow. "I don't understand. It was like a trail of yellow light, but it's gone now."

"Like the yellow brick road?" Aunt Teddie asked from the shadows, giving them all a fright.

"For the love of the Goddess, Teddie!" Gwennie snapped, slapping a hand over her heart. "Are you *trying* to scare us into the Otherworld, you daft cow?"

Sebastian peered closer into the dark corner of the corridor and sighed. Where a tarted-up Teddie was, their butler was sure to be found. "You can reveal yourself now, Leopold."

The butler stepped farther into the hallway, frantically working to fasten the buttons of his nightshirt.

Sebastian felt queasy. *As if he didn't have enough on his plate!*

RESIDING AT THE DRAKE ESTATE WAS LIKE HAVING A FRONT-ROW SEAT at a comedic theater production, and Mackenzie absolutely loved it. Although she did have to wonder if anyone slept around here. One would assume the Drake aunts and Leopold would've gone to bed early due to their advanced years. But here they lurked, making out in the shadowy corridor.

She bit back a smile.

The Drakes' butler was a mess. The only hair he possessed, encircled his head, leaving the top bald as a cue ball. The remaining thin gray strands stuck straight out at ninety-degree angles from his scalp. A bright pink smear of lipstick colored his drooping mouth and played hide and seek in the folds of his wrinkled neck. As he hurried to fasten the buttons of his nightshirt, he missed the proper holes, resulting in the uneven hem of his clothing and showing one boney knee in the process. Once again, his striped sock pooled around his skinny ankle. Unfortunately for him, the other was missing, and his toes curled as if to hide the tufts of hair on his big toe joints.

Mackenzie was certain she saw some type of writing on the side of the sock, but she'd be damned if she could read it in the low light.

Despite it all, poor Leopold had a proud air about him. Currently, his chin was lifted as if he were determined to take his punishment like a trooper, but the expression in his eyes said he feared the noose, as if he'd been caught stealing the family's silver.

Mackenzie adored him.

"Leo! Or do you prefer Leopold? So good to see you again. I forgot to tell you how wonderful dinner was last night. You must give me the recipe for the Duck à l'Orange." She stepped forward and hid Leopold's front from view as she quickly reworked the mess of buttons. Reaching up, she straightened his collar and used her thumb to wipe away the evidence of Teddie's lipstick from the corners of his mouth. She twiddled her fingers to remove the vivid color that had found a home in the creases of his neck. Anything Mackenzie did was like closing the barn door after the horse got out, but still, if she could preserve his dignity, she would. "My cook simply *must* attempt to recreate your masterpiece when I get back home."

A grateful light came into his rheumy eyes, and his lips twisted in a semblance of an affectionate smile. "Of course, Miss Thorne. I'll write it down first thing for you."

"Sweet! You're the best, Leo." She kissed his weathered cheek. "Thank you."

"No, miss. Thank *you*."

She stepped back and linked an arm with Sebastian's. His inscrutable expression made her nervous, and she wondered if she'd overstepped.

"Mackenzie, may I speak with you privately?" His tone gave no indication as to his thoughts or intent.

She pasted on a bright smile, and perhaps she was channeling old Leopold, but she felt like she, too, was heading for the hangman's noose.

Sebastian escorted her to an abandoned room, took one look around, and did an about-face with an expression of such abject horror Mackenzie was sure there was a dead body on the floor. Although he tried to usher her from the bedroom, she was able to get a clear view of the rumpled bed and the butler's missing sock.

Finally, she was able to see the design: a fat pickle with the words *"Kind of a big dill"* beneath it.

She laughed.

She couldn't have contained it if she tried. Tears of mirth rolled down her cheeks as she struggled to breathe. For a brief second, Sebastian looked put upon, but he, too, began to laugh. Soon, they were doubled over, using each other for support.

"His sock!" she sputtered. "Do you see what's on his sock?"

Sebastian snorted. "Do you think he was advertising his *pickle?*"

Mackenzie fell back on her butt, holding her sides as a second wave of laughter struck.

He joined her on the floor and rested his head back against the door, a wide smile firmly in place.

"How do you do it, Baz?" She fanned herself, trying to stop giggling like a prepubescent girl. "How do you keep a straight face twenty-four-seven? It's like living in the midst of a sitcom."

His smile dropped, and he looked uncomfortable.

It didn't take a genius to realize she'd offended him. "I didn't mean it as an insult." She shifted to touch his arm. "Please know, I'm not making fun of your family. I think they're absolutely wonderful. I have to resist the urge to hug Leo every time I see him."

"It's his pickle and his animal magnetism. I'm sure it's why Aunt Teddie can't keep her hands off him." A grin tugged at his firm, full mouth. "Now, I have to fight him for you?"

"Well, he *is* adorable."

"My reputation will be in tatters if it gets out that my thousand-year-old butler was able to steal the woman I've been wooing."

Mackenzie sucked in a breath. "You're wooing me?"

"What the hell do you think those kisses were about earlier?"

"Hmm." She fought a smile and lost. "You're going to have to up your game if you want to beat out Leo, ya know."

"It's not widely known, but my *pickle* is also a bit of a big dill."

"Oh, believe me. It's *so* widely known."

CHAPTER 7

Sebastian was torn between horror and laughter. Yes, he had a reputation of sorts, but he hadn't expected Mackenzie to wave it merrily in his face.

"You can't be surprised, Baz. Women talk."

"Yes, well." He cleared his throat. With anyone else, he wouldn't be flustered. What was it about Mack? With a wave of her hand, a knowing smirk, and a perfectly arched brow, she made him feel like a gauche boy on the verge of puberty.

"Look at you!" she crowed. "You're embarrassed." Mackenzie's laugh was naughtiness personified. The husky sound wrapped around his dick and squeezed. "How delightful!" Rising to her knees, she closed the distance between them and gave him a light peck on the cheek. "And sweet."

Sweet?

He didn't realize he'd said it aloud until she nodded.

"Yes, sweet. It means you aren't just a player, out for a random hookup."

"I wouldn't go that far." He chuckled when she leaned back and frowned. "I mean, I'm happy to randomly hook up with you, if you so choose. Multiple times a day, in fact." He stared into her narrowed blue eyes and felt his smile grow. "For the rest of our lives."

The last bit was a surprise to them both, and they froze, gazes locked.

With a swiftness that floored him, Mackenzie straddled his lap and grasped his head between her palms. She latched on so deeply, he felt she could see into his soul, and he was helpless to look away. Shutting her eyes, she swayed, and when she lifted her lids, there was a distinct golden glow reflected back at him. The light was holy and somehow pure.

"Okay."

"What?" He was baffled by her response and a whole lot of aroused by her lithe body in his lap.

"Okay. For the rest of our lives." She grinned. "Let's get married. Tonight. Right now."

"Wait, what? What was this all about?" He placed his palms over hers where they still cupped his head.

"Would you believe me if I said I saw our ceremony? There was an old ivory handfasting cloth, binding our wrists together." She bit her lip, and a teasing glimmer shone from her eyes. Mackenzie rose and drew him up with her. "Either we intend to have kinky sex, or there's a ceremony in our future. I won't rule out either."

Part of him wanted to backpedal. Tell her it was too fast. They'd known each other all of a heartbeat. But her spontaneous suggestion felt right, and who the bloody hell knew what tomorrow would bring. Most likely the Enchantress to kill them all.

"Tonight," he agreed. "Who should we have officiate our spontaneous wedding?"

"Leo." A twinkle entered her eyes. "But he has to wear his pickle socks. You can conjure him a matching green vest and tie."

Sebastian laughed and tugged a lock of her hair. "This is pure madness and won't hold up legally. We'll have to make it official at some point."

"I know, but it will be fun. And I'm game if you are."

"Yes." He'd never been so certain of anything in his life.

Sealing her lips to his, she stole his breath with her passion. As their tongues became intimately acquainted and his desire flared white-hot, he ran his hands under her shirt to cup her breasts. Exploring them to the fullest.

She moaned into his mouth.

He pulled back and gave her jaw a light nip. "Let's save this until after." It killed him to suggest it, but again, he knew it was right.

Her smile rivaled the sun on a clear day, when it was at its highest point in the sky. So bright. So warm. So—for lack of a better word—*sunny*.

"Goddess, you're beautiful, Mack."

Some of her happiness faded. "Is that all you see in me? Beauty?"

"Not all. Without a doubt, you're exquisite, but it's the *way* you smile. The way you seem to find joy in each moment, regardless of who you're with. The way you look at *me*, the man, as if I can do anything. You make me want to be a better person."

The light in her eyes was soft, and as he spoke, she caressed his jaw.

He was almost afraid to ask, but what was fair was fair. "And me? What do you see?"

"Everything. I see a strong, loving man who adores his quirky family. I see a stand-up guy who always does what's right. When you shed that ridiculous worldly persona you present to those on the outside, you are sweet and caring. Genuine and a bit shy. But I get a deeper sense of loneliness. Am I wrong?"

"No. You're not wrong, Mack." He couldn't believe she saw his true self this clearly when no one else ever had. Not even Vivian. "You're not wrong at all."

"Are you holding onto any unrequited feelings for another woman, Baz?" They both knew she meant his ex-fiancée, even if she didn't say the name. "I don't want to give you my heart only to end up with it broken in the end."

Behind her inquiring gaze, he could see caution and maybe a little fear. But he sensed it wasn't of him so much as getting hurt. "No one holds my heart. And while I can't claim to love you on such short notice, I can honestly say I've never felt this swept away by anyone. I can't stop thinking about you. I'm jealous of anyone you give your attention to. And all I want to do is touch you, make love to you, feel you pressed against me as I sleep. I can't wait to hear you laugh or see you flash that incredible smile." He leaned in and gave her a light, lingering kiss. "Whatever that feeling is, I want to hold onto it forever."

"Can I tell you a secret, Baz?"

"Of course."

"That feeling you have? That *is* love. Or rather the beginning of it. It's exactly what I'm experiencing. And we all know a Thorne only loves once."

"Perhaps." He grinned and kissed her more thoroughly. "I can't believe we're considering this." He almost gave into the urge to tumble her back on the Aubusson carpet and make love to her as he'd been fantasizing about since the moment they were introduced. Just as he was inching up her top, he caught sight of Leopold's discarded sock.

Yeah, he'd wait.

The idea of getting down and dirty where his butler most likely just had, turned his stomach.

Sebastian glanced down into Mackenzie's sparkling eyes. She knew exactly what he was thinking. He didn't know how she did, but he was certain of it. "Are you ready to get married, love?"

"I believe I am."

"Then let's round up Leopold, the aunts, and Arabella to make this official." He grimaced slightly. "Or as official as it can be without a Council member overseeing the ceremony."

"Let's!" She grabbed the pickle sock and waved it in the air like a prize. "This is going to be such fun!"

He couldn't prevent his laugh. Just as he was about to turn the doorknob, he remembered why he'd dragged her into this chamber to begin with.

"Bloody hell." He sighed and turned back around. "Mack, before we go. We should talk."

"Already having doubts?"

"Not at all, but *you* might when you hear what I have to tell you."

MACKENZIE'S STOMACH TIGHTENED AS SHE REGISTERED SEBASTIAN'S pained expression. She knew exactly what he wanted to tell her. A few minutes before she'd made herself known, she stumbled upon him speaking to his aunt and sister.

Somehow, Mackenzie was going to be the catalyst for the Enchantress's escape from her prison. Damian had hinted at her predicament. But he'd also suggested she grab onto happiness for whatever time she had left because once the wheel was set in motion, there was no turning back.

She believed in living for today. As a Thorne with a never-ending number of enemies, she'd learned to seize whatever life had to offer at any particular moment. This was one of those. But lest Sebastian think she didn't take the threat seriously, she said, "You don't have to tell me, Baz. I know."

"Everything?" One black brow lifted.

"Enough. And maybe I don't care to hear the rest. If we can't change Fate's design, perhaps we should just enjoy what time we have left."

"What else did you see a few moments ago when you touched my face?"

"How did you...?" She shrugged away her question. Sebastian was more perceptive than people gave him credit for. "You. Me. Happy. For a while."

Concern lit his dark eyes. "What else?"

"I'd rather not say." How could she tell him she'd seen herself with a wicked-looking athamé in her hand as she knelt over his unconscious body? She could see her two faces flashing back and forth; one twisted with hate and the other fearful. They represented the two forces within her, each fighting desperately for control. One to kill him. One to save him. Beyond that, there was nothing but darkness.

The thing she sensed the strongest was the love they would share. Knowing it existed, she was sure she'd never hurt him.

"I want to take you away from here, love."

"It's too late, Baz. The Aether said as much. Even if he hadn't, I can sense it. You can, too, I think." The devastation on Sebastian's face tore at her heart. "But if you don't want to do this. To become invested in us, knowing our world could come crashing down at any moment, then I get it. I truly do."

"This is mad. *We're* mad."

She waited him out, giving him the space he needed to make a decision that could—and would—affect the rest of his life.

"Fuck it. Let's do it."

Mackenzie laughed her joy and clasped his hand. "How American of you!"

"Your family is rubbing off on me."

"It's good to be fluid. To dismiss the rigid structure guiding your life."

"You live a bohemian lifestyle, don't you?" His expression was indulgent and on the verge of teasing. Mackenzie adored it.

"I do, indeed, Lord Kilbride."

"Then I shall endeavor to join you by living my life the same way, my future Lady Kilbride."

Pausing in the act of tucking her arm through his, she stared. "Oh dear Goddess! I never thought of the responsibility involved in being a peer of the realm. Is that the right wording?" She waved a hand and hugged his bicep. "Perhaps we should simply be lovers and leave it at that."

"While I'm not opposed to becoming your lover, Mack, I can promise there are no great trials in being my wife."

"Well, I'm game if you are." She soaked up his warm regard and bathed in the yumminess of it.

"Oh, I'm game." Sebastian shifted to cup her neck and urged her closer. "I'm definitely game."

His kiss robbed her of her wits and her will to do anything but savor the flavor of his tongue as it swept across hers. Teasing. Tasting. Caressing.

After he pulled away, she frowned up at him. "When did you have chocolate, and why didn't you share?"

"I don't share my chocolate with anyone but my wife."

"Well, we'd better tie the knot soon. I have a craving." And it wasn't for sweets. Or at least, not the candy kind.

"I'll import only the best from all of the world's greatest chocolatiers for your sampling pleasure."

Mackenzie grinned and rose on tiptoes to brush her mouth against his one final time. She really liked kissing him. "I don't understand why some smart woman hasn't scooped you up by now. I guess it shows my brilliance far exceeds everyone else's."

"Or your foolishness," he murmured. "I'm not convinced I'm the prize you believe me to be, love."

"Let's break this down." She pretended to think about it, although she already knew she didn't need to. She began ticking points off on her fingers. "First, you're hot as hell." She smothered a giggle when he huffed out a breath and rolled his eyes. Clearly, Sebastian didn't feel his looks were all that important. He was wrong. "Second, you wear a kilt."

"Mack. You're being completely shallow."

"I know, but it bears saying. Now hush. I'm getting to the good parts."

"As long as you realize looks and a kilt aren't the good parts." His tone dipped into suggestive, and she struggled to keep a straight face.

"Don't play those down, Baz. They weigh heavily in my decision to marry you. Where was I?" Frowning, she put a fingertip to her lip and tapped.

He laughed and flung an arm around her shoulders. "I'll let you list the rest after the ceremony and *after* I've had my way with you."

"Ohhh! I'm sure there will be many, *many* things to add by then. Tongue, hands, penis."

Sebastian jerked to a halt and glared down at her. The humor in his eyes gave him away. "Behave!"

"Never!"

CHAPTER 8

The planning of the ceremony was frivolous and fun, as Mackenzie had hoped it would be. Arabella was delighted to be her maid of honor and took her role a bit more seriously than Mackenzie assumed she would.

"Really, Bella, you're going overboard."

Both women gave Sebastian the stink eye. It wasn't that Mackenzie didn't agree, but she didn't want to steal her future sister's joy either.

He held up his hands and sighed. "How about I wait by the altar?"

"Perfect. Thank you, Baz." She grinned when he caught her eye and winked.

As soon as he disappeared, her future sister-in-law became all business. "Okay. We need to create an exceptional gown for you. One designed to melt Baz's brain matter."

Mackenzie laughed. "You'll have to do the conjuring, Fairy Godmother. I'm afraid I'm like Cinderella. I've nothing to wear for the ball and no great sense of style."

Arabella's happy expression turned skeptical. "You are a world-famous model. How can that be?"

"Other people dress me in their latest creations. I'm essentially a doll. Besides, I trust your exquisite taste in clothing. I've seen you at social functions, and you're always impeccably dressed." Mackenzie cheered inwardly when Arabella's smile returned, tinged with pride.

"White?"

"Well, I'm no Aunt Teddie, but I think I can rock it."

Arabella laughed. "Oh, please don't begin haunting these halls and kissing our butler."

"I don't know. Leo is awfully cute."

Soon enough, Mackenzie was decked out in a confection of form-fitting lace and flowing organza. The A-line silhouette accentuated her curves, and the embellishments on the sleeveless bodice shimmered in the candlelight. "Is this V-neckline a little too plunging?"

"Not at all. Baz will love it." Arabella stepped back and fluffed the floor-length ruffles. "He won't be able to lift his jaw from where it drops to his chest."

"Thank you, Arabella. This means the world to me."

"You make a stunning bride, Mack." She did a head-to-toe scan. "Hair upswept, I think. But no veil. Oh, and a single red calla lily in place of a bouquet."

Once Arabella magically transformed her into the perfect bride, she kissed her cheek and rushed away.

Part of Mackenzie wished her family could be here, but she understood it was impossible as last minute as this ceremony was. When she would've stepped from the shadows to walk the aisle, the air around her shifted and a pale-pink light formed beside her.

"Sabrina! What are you doing here, sweetie? It's the middle of the night."

The girl's eyes sparkled as she touched a ruffle on Mackenzie's dress. "May I be your flower girl?"

"You had a vision of this, didn't you?"

Sabrina nodded, and a shadow crossed her tiny elfin-like features. Refusing to allow the child to bear the weight of the world, Mackenzie leaned down and hugged her. "I'd be honored to have you as my flower girl. How about you conjure a princess dress in your favorite color and a basketful of matching petals?"

The girl's eyes flew wide, and excitement shimmered in their obsidian depths. Before Mackenzie could catch her breath at the beautiful sight of Sabrina's blissful expression, the world around her froze. She knew it had because Leopold stopped mid-snore and Teddie's chirpy chatter ceased echoing in the chapel.

Sabrina looked scared, and Mackenzie couldn't swear she wasn't as terrified as the girl. She only knew of three family members who could freeze time, and one was dead. Whatever was coming had powerful magic. "Go. Hide in the shadows."

"It's Papa," Sabrina said in a small voice.

A blinding gold light split the room in two, and the Aether crossed to them. He was less than thrilled, and his thundercloud expression proved it.

A shiver of fear ran through Mackenzie. Pissing off a badass of his ilk was not good.

"What have I told you about leaving our estate, Sabrina?" His voice sounded like an avenging god and practically shook the rafters.

Despite Mackenzie's trepidation, she stepped between father and daughter. "Mr. Dethridge—"

"No excuses, Ms. Thorne." He held up a hand, and she could swear it trembled. Here was a scared father, not a furious one. "She cannot leave the estate without supervision. She *knows* this. The danger involved is *limitless.*"

"Of course." Mackenzie turned and squatted in front of a contrite Sabrina. "I'm sorry. I would've loved to have you as my flower girl."

Sabrina lifted tearful eyes to her father, her lower lip trembling.

Damian was no match for her tragic little face, and the added little sniffle did him in. "Fine. You can do this one thing, beastie, but then it's back to bed for you."

"I understand, Papa."

Mackenzie bit back a grin, wondering if it hadn't been the girl's plan all along. She was certain of it when Sabrina turned away to hide her smile and to conjure her princess dress.

"I've never seen a more stunning creature in all of existence, my darling girl." Damian's praise made his daughter beam. He leaned in close to Mackenzie and lowered his voice. "I'm well aware she just manipulated me. I'm putty in her tiny hands."

Holding back her laughter at that point was impossible. "How about you restart time and allow us to get on with this little shindig?"

"Shindig? Hmm. Yes, how appropriate." He cleared his throat and tugged on his cuffs. "For what it's worth, Mack, I'm happy to see you seizing the day."

"That's me. If carpe diem wasn't already coined, it would've been our family's motto."

Damian released a genuine laugh. One so wholehearted and encompassing, Mack could see why Vivian had fallen for him. When he sobered, he gazed down at her with something akin to affection. "You're one in a million, Mackenzie Thorne. Enjoy your wedding, dear."

"Why not come in and sit down? I imagine you aren't leaving your daughter here alone anyway. No sense skulking in the alcove here."

"Oh, I'm sure Drake would be *overjoyed* to have me attend. It almost makes me want to sit in the front row."

She laughed, reached for Sabrina's hand, and positioned the girl to walk down the aisle. "Sit in the back, Damian. It's more menacing and will make Baz sweat."

"Don't mind if I do." He hurried around her and came to an abrupt halt. A confused frown clouded his countenance. "Is that old Leopold at the altar?"

"You know him?" Mackenzie blinked a few times and stared harder at Leo. "Did he just move?"

"Doubtful. Frozen time and all, remember?" Damian coughed into his hand and hurried away.

She glanced down at Sabrina. "Why do I have the feeling he was lying?"

"Because he was."

Before Mackenzie could comment, the girl was skipping down the aisle, tossing flowers up and following them with a light burst of air to make the petals dance on the current. Apparently, she wasn't aware she was supposed to throw them on the ground.

Sabrina stopped, looked over her shoulder, and grinned.

Okay, the mischievous little "beastie" absolutely knew the proper way to throw them. She just chose to march to her own tune. Mackenzie could appreciate that.

Leopold officiated between bouts of sleep, and the aunts bore witness, bickering through it all. Sebastian desperately wanted to question Mackenzie on the arrival of the Dethridges, but he kept his thoughts to himself. If he had to guess, he'd say Sabrina had divined their intent and decided to see for herself what a wedding was all about. He felt sorry for the girl. Being the child of an Aether would be lonely at the best of times.

"Do you, ah… um… do you…" Leopold looked to Sebastian in panic.

"Mackenzie Thorne," he supplied.

"What?"

"It's the name you were after, Leopold. Mackenzie Thorne."

"Why's that?"

"Because you were in the middle of the vows."

Leopold scratched his ass and sniffed. "Don't know why the gel's family ain't present."

It appeared too much for Mackenzie as she dissolved into a fit of giggles. Beside her, Sabrina echoed the sound. Sebastian was hard-pressed not to join in.

"If you'll allow me." Damian stepped up to the altar and, in a show of great kindness and patience, guided Leopold to sit beside

Aunt Teddie. "You did a smashing job of it, dear fellow. I'd like to add my own blessing now, if you don't mind."

Leopold nodded, but Sebastian wasn't positive the poor old sod wasn't in the process of dozing off, rather than agreeing. The short snore cemented Sebastian's belief.

Mackenzie's grip on his arm tightened.

He glanced down into her sparkling eyes and found himself grinning. "He was your choice," he reminded her.

"As Damian said, Leo did a smashing job."

"If finances ever grow tight, we can rent him out," Sebastian deadpanned.

A muffled snort from Damian sent Sabrina into another fit of giggles.

She was a precious girl, and Sebastian was left to wonder, had things been different and had Vivian married him, if they would've had a child about Sabrina's age.

"It was never how it was meant to be," Damian spoke quietly from beside him. "You're on the proper path now, Drake. By the by, you know if I officiate, it's legal and binding as per the Council bylaws."

"I know." And he did. The rightness of this moment couldn't be denied. His differences with the Aether seemed to dissolve, and Sebastian was happy to set aside the old animosity. "I suspect Mack knows, too. Regardless, I'd like to be married before the sunrise. So if you'd care to get on with it."

Damian smirked. "Of course."

The rest of the ceremony was nothing short of magical.

The Aether lifted the Drake family's metal wedding bowl, twirled a finger, and released the fragrant herbs into the air around them. He gave a brief speech about love, trials, and how they should face them together as a couple. The white candles behind him flared brightly as if to emphasize his words. Damian encouraged them to honor their commitment throughout time with no exception.

Next, he picked up an ivory handfasting cloth threaded with

silver. The wispy metal reflected the light and gave the illusion of glowing fabric.

The ancient material had been gifted to the first couple of the Drake line by the Goddess herself. Although gossamer and delicate in appearance, it contained ancient magic and would never deteriorate due to the rigors of time.

"Mack, if you will?"

She placed her left hand in Damian's.

"Sebastian?"

He mimicked the action.

Damian took their wrists and placed their palms together, weaving the cloth around them and tying it off.

Sebastian smiled when he felt the tingle between his palm and Mackenzie's. The Thorne blood was right powerful, but she had magic all her own, and it spoke to him. His gaze locked with hers.

"Mackenzie Thorne, I bind thee to Sebastian Drake in this, a holy union. You shall honor and love him throughout all your days and beyond. Do you pledge to do so?"

"I do."

"Sebastian Drake, I bind thee to Mackenzie Thorne in this, a holy union. You shall honor and love her throughout all your days and beyond. Do you pledge to do so?"

"I do."

Damian nodded and covered their joined hands with his. "I ask the Goddess to bless this joining of souls. I ask her to protect and watch over them when they need it the most. And I ask her to grant them many years of wedded bliss."

The room filled with a radiant light for the span of ten seconds.

As it faded, Damian closed his eyes and whispered, "Blessed be."

"Blessed be," they echoed.

"Sebastian, I encourage you to kiss your bride." Damian smacked him on the shoulder and laughed.

Every person, every sound, faded into the background as Sebastian gazed down into the deep-blue pools of Mackenzie's eyes. The realization struck him that he never wanted to be anywhere else but with her.

Leaning in, he touched his mouth to her glossy lips and kissed his new wife. She opened under his gentle persuasion, and he slipped his tongue inside. The touch was butterfly-light. A flitting about, to taste, tease, and savor the sweetness of their first kiss as man and wife. When he drew back, he gave her one last clinging kiss, noticing the stars in her eyes. He imagined his reflected the same.

Damian turned them to face Sebastian's family. "Ladies and Gentleman, I present to you, Lord and Lady Kilbride."

Seeing the tearful gazes of his sister and aunts turned their way, Sebastian felt his own tears well up. They all knew how temporary this could be, but he would channel Mackenzie's zest for life and live it to the fullest for whatever time they had left.

He inhaled a deep, cleansing breath. "If anyone is still awake enough for a celebration, there will be cake." He placed his mouth next to her ear. "And for you, chocolate and me in a kilt."

"Can you *be* any more perfect?"

"Probably, but then you would take me for granted."

CHAPTER 9

"I'm thrilled to finally catch you alone. You're a difficult man to pin down."

Damian fought a smile as he turned to face Mackenzie. She was here to ask him about Leopold, and her determined expression said she wasn't leaving without answers.

"About Leo..." Her brows clashed together when he laughed. "What?"

"I'm not at liberty to reveal secrets, Mack."

"But there *is* a secret?"

He felt his lips twitch despite his effort to curb another laugh. "Perhaps."

"*'Perhaps.'* You must spend a lot of time with Alastair. Because I swear to the Goddess, your mannerisms and avoidance tactics are exactly the same."

"As a matter of fact, we've been friends for an entire lifetime." Damian wasn't more forthcoming regarding their familial connection, and he half expected her to stomp her foot in frustration.

She narrowed her eyes instead.

"I can see why Sebastian is so taken with you." His gaze traveled from the top of her shockingly red hair to the tips of her pointy shoes. "Not only are you stunningly beautiful, but you are wickedly intelligent. I don't expect much escapes your notice. *Not* that it's going to help you where I'm concerned. However, you're more than welcome to keep trying. It's providing me with endless entertainment."

"I swear, if you weren't the Aether, I'd zap you."

He chuckled. "I suppose you could say Alastair and I are cousins, although distant. I trust you to tell no one. It may be dangerous to be related to me."

"No worries here." She shook her head. "De Thorne. When I first heard the name, I wondered. How is it your last name is Dethridge if your mother was a de Thorne?"

"Actually, she married her second cousin, Damarius Dethridge. She was a Thorne through her father's line, and when the Dethridge family disowned her for her crimes, she went back to her maiden name."

Fixing his gaze on her, he stepped closer and clasped her hand. "I'm sorry, Mack. If I had it within me to stop Mother, I would. It's not to say I'll leave you and Sebastian to face this alone, because I absolutely won't. I intend to work day and night to prevent what is to come, but you need to know, if I fail and she succeeds in her plan to use you against the rest of us, I'll have no choice but to destroy you."

He felt her trepidation through his empathic ability and through the physical connection of their joined hands when she shivered.

"Your daughter predicted this. This is what she saw in the garden and again in the church."

Mackenzie hadn't said it as a question, but he confirmed it anyway. "Yes."

"Do either of you know why this is happening? Why me in particular?"

"Not yet, but as soon as I know anything, I'll inform you straight away."

"I would never willingly hurt any of you." She shot a worried glance across the room at Sebastian. "Mr. Dethridge—"

"Damian."

"Damian," she conceded as she pulled her hand back. "Is Baz's family in danger because of me?"

"You love him?" As an empath, he'd already picked up on her feelings, but sometimes other people needed a nudge in the proper direction.

"Love? I don't know this early in the game, but I believe so. His light is brighter than any I've ever seen. With the exception of yours, but you don't hold an attraction for me like he does." She shook her head and finally dragged her attention from him to meet Sebastian's steady gaze from across the room. "It's strange, but I want to cling to him and never let go."

"Then I urge you to build on your mutual feelings. It will serve you well when the time comes," Damian said.

She looked up into his face, and he was positive he couldn't hide his sadness. "I'm scared."

He had no words to soothe her. Mackenzie was the witch the Goddess had foretold would be the catalyst to wake Isolde. When or how was a mystery, but Damian didn't believe it would be long.

"What have you seen so far?" he asked.

She hesitated, the picture of indecision.

"Don't hold back, Mack. This is important." He narrowed his eyes as he studied her, searching for what, he couldn't say. Perhaps he needed a sign she wasn't intentionally going to bring about the destruction of the magical world as they knew it.

"I have two faces. One wants to hurt people; the second is terrified of the first." Mackenzie wrapped her arms around her waist as if to chase away a chill.

He couldn't make heads nor tails of her vision, but he suspected possession. Sure, it would be a different tactic for Isolde, who was prone to steal a person's magic and leave a broken shell in his or her place, but it didn't mean she wouldn't take over another's body completely if she needed to. "We'll figure this out, my dear."

"Sadly, I think we're screwed."

Silently, he agreed, but he smiled to reassure her. "Remain positive, all right?"

He wasn't expecting her fierce hug or the influx of feelings and visions that came with it. When she pulled away, his mind was still churning with all the possible outcomes for the future. Each showed the resurrection of his mother. Somehow, he had to find a way to sort through them and find the best solution to stop her forever.

"Mack?"

She must've heard the heaviness in his tone, because her worried expression deepened. Damian wanted to send calming energy her way, but it would be a waste. She, too, knew what was on the horizon.

"If you had a choice, would you take your life to save the others?"

Her eyes flew wide, and she sucked in her breath. "Is that what I have to do?"

"No!" Sebastian's shout startled them both. Caught up in their conversation, they hadn't heard his approach. "That is not an option." He pulled Mackenzie into his tight embrace and glared at Damian. *"Get the fuck out of my house."*

"Baz—"

"No, Mack. Just *no.*"

If ever there was a man more tortured, Damian was unlikely to see it. "Sebastian, you're a Keeper of the Gate. You should know the prophecy well enough, and you definitely know what Isolde can do."

"I said, *no,*" Sebastian snarled. "How dare you suggest Mack end her life? *How dare you?*"

The small reception room was eerily silent, with all eyes turned in their direction. For maybe the first time in his life, Damian grew nervous under everyone's wary stares.

"I didn't suggest she do it," he said softly. "I merely asked if she was *willing* to."

"I don't see a difference."

"But it's there."

Sebastian frowned and loosened his hold enough to look down

into Mackenzie's anxious face. "Don't ever do it, Mack. Promise me," he said hoarsely. "Promise me."

"I won't promise, Baz. I can't if it means saving your family. Saving you."

"None of us want to live with your death on our conscience, love. Not a single one."

Damian shrugged when she looked his way. "I wasn't advising you do it, Mack. I was simply trying to determine your level of commitment to stopping Isolde." He sighed, weary down to his soul. Moments like these made him remember his advanced age and how young this couple was in comparison. "But we have time to work out a plan yet. I'll collect Sabrina and leave you to your celebration."

"Please stay, Damian." Mackenzie arched a challenging brow toward her new husband. "We *both* want you to."

"Not true," Sebastian retorted. A teasing smile curled his lips as he made what Damian considered a valiant attempt to shrug off his righteous anger. "I want everyone to leave so I can get you alone, wife."

"On that note, I'll bid you adieu," Damian said with a forced chuckle. "Enjoy your honeymoon." He started to go, but turned back. "If either of you need me, day or night, call me. This is more than your issue now. This problem belongs to all of us."

SEBASTIAN WANTED TO DISMISS DAMIAN'S WORDS AS QUICKLY AS THE man left, but he couldn't. For the remaining half hour of their small reception, he was plagued with the sickening fear Mackenzie would take it into her head to end this problem of Isolde with a bottle of witchbane or a poisoned blade to her wrists.

He watched her as she interacted with his family. Although she was quick to smile, the strain around her eyes was apparent to him. When he could take no more, he swept in to hustle her off to bed. "Sorry, all, but it's well past time for everyone to be in bed." He smiled down into her upturned face. "And I want some alone time with my new bride."

She smiled through her fatigue.

Resting his brow against hers, he said in a hushed voice, "To sleep and to hold you, Mack. Everything else can wait until you're a little more awake."

"I'm down for anything. Tired or not."

"I'm honestly going to love having you for my wife."

"I should hope so," she replied, her tone sassy and full of herself.

Sebastian laughed as he spun her toward the door.

She stopped in her tracks. "Wait! I thought newlyweds were supposed to have a first dance."

"I thought I'd leave that for a more formal reception with your family, but if you desire dancing, dancing you shall have, love."

Closing his eyes, he mentally thumbed through songs that might be good for a waltz. Deciding on one, he withdrew his phone from his tuxedo pocket and scrolled until he found what he was looking for. He placed his cell in the center of the floor, pressed play, and held out his hand. "May I have this dance, Mack?"

Her beaming smile was his reward, and she stepped into his embrace.

Sebastian spun them in wide circles worthy of the finest ballrooms, and when the music concluded, he brought them to a halt by the device on the parquet floor. The adoration in her eyes stalled the breath in his lungs. Never had anyone looked at him the way she did now, as if he'd hung the moon and stars for her alone.

I love her.

He didn't know how it happened this quickly, but he recognized his soulmate in the woman before him. "Remind me to thank Damian the next time I see him," Sebastian murmured as he drew her closer.

"Why's that?"

"He did me a favor the day he absconded with Vivian." He drew back slightly to meet her curious gaze. "Had she and I been married, I'd have never met you or had this perfect moment."

"Oh, Baz."

He detected the sheen of tears but suspected, like him, her

emotion was based on pure happiness. "Let's go to bed. The sooner we get some sleep, the sooner I can wake and make love to you properly."

"I appreciate that you're thinking about my needs, but unless you're completely exhausted, I have *other needs*."

Sebastian couldn't stop his wolfish grin. "Hold on tight, love. We're taking the speedy route to our bedroom."

Within seconds, they were standing by the foot of their bed. Someone had thought to fill the room with lit candles and to add rose petals atop an ivory bedspread. Gossamer netting hung over their bed, suspended by a wreath of red and pink roses. Crystal flutes sat on a bedside table and contained a bubbling champagne to complement the chocolate-covered strawberries on the china plate next to it. A true honeymoon suite.

"Oh, Baz," Mackenzie gushed after taking it all in. "When did you have time to do this?"

"I'm ashamed to admit I didn't think of it first. This must be Arabella's doing."

"Remind me to thank your sister for all she's done tonight."

He took off his suit jacket, hung it over the back of a chair, and tugged at his tie. "How about we don't think about my sister or anyone else for a few hours?"

Mackenzie's smile turned decidedly wicked. "I'm cool with it." She approached him and replaced his hands with hers so she could unbutton his shirt. "I've wanted to do this since the first time I saw you."

"Really?"

"Oh, yeah."

"I remember how reserved you seemed at our first meeting."

She smirked but didn't look up. "You don't say."

"Mackenzie Drake! Were you putting on an act?"

"Absolutely. And every time we met afterwards."

He halted her dexterous hands, mainly to get her attention. "You wily, little minx. You made me think the attraction was one-sided."

She pulled a hand away to press to the opening of his shirtfront.

Her clever fingers explored his exposed skin, trailing small circles as she stood, absorbed by their progress.

"Mack," he growled. "Tell me it wasn't only one-sided."

"It was never one-sided, Baz." She finally raised her gaze to his, and Sebastian was able to see the burning emotion she fought to hide. *"Never."*

"Thornes only love once," he murmured.

"Yes."

"Why didn't you tell me? I feel like we wasted so many months."

She shrugged and traced the column of his throat. "I suppose I was afraid to care. Afraid you would never love me back. My track record with relationships is crap."

"Because they weren't *me*."

Her smile was so sudden and wide, it stole his breath. "Thank the Goddess for that. Now, help me out of this dress. I can't wait to be with you."

He obligingly unzipped the gown, not surprised to see his hand shook. Their joining would be monumental for them both. For him, this was the last woman he ever wanted to make love with, the only one he wanted to give his name to, and to be able to share this perfect moment with. This night was a gift he would treasure always. Because he loved her and intended to show her exactly how much when he finally had her naked in his bed.

Sebastian eased open the sides of the dress and allowed it to drop, pooling at her feet. Instead of assisting her in stepping out, he swept her up into his arms and deposited her in the center of the bed. Following her down and covering her body with his.

Their gazes locked, and he let his eyes communicate for him all the things he couldn't say past the emotion locking his throat. She smiled her understanding and raised her arms.

Kissing her, knowing this time they wouldn't be rushed or interrupted and, knowing they had the rest of the night and into the morning to explore one another's likes was heaven on earth. She tasted of champagne and sweet dreams.

"The sweetest of dreams," he murmured against her silky throat, repeating his thoughts.

"Mmm." She arched her neck to give him better access, and he blazed a trail of kisses down to her breasts.

Taking one beaded nipple into his mouth, he moaned in his pleasure and reveled in the sound of her echoed agreement. He could spend hours tasting her skin, suckling her breasts, but Mackenzie was impatient and gripped his hair to draw him level with her so she could plant her lips on his.

Passionate and panting, she pulled back after ravaging his mouth and said, "Time to see what's under that kilt, darling. I've waited way too long."

Sebastian took her hand and placed it directly on his dick. "This. And I've had a permanent erection since the first moment we met."

"Mmm. We have to do something about that."

"Christ, I was hoping you'd say that." He rolled onto his back and spread his arms to his sides.

Mackenzie grinned as she lifted the hem of his plaid. One excruciatingly slow inch by one excruciatingly slow inch. He could feel the cool air hit his bollocks first, but it did nothing to dampen his ardor. It would take a whole lot more than a brisk room now that his gorgeous wife was hovering over him, with her exquisite breasts brushing tantalizingly across his thighs.

He heard the catch of her breath as she finally caught sight of him.

"I hope that's a good thing," he teased.

"Well, let's just say the rumors are all true. You are a big dill."

He laughed and tugged her more fully on top of him. "I don't know that I've ever laughed in the middle of sex before."

"We're not in the middle," she said with a sassy smile. "We're just getting started."

He rolled them over and pressed a kiss to her lips. "Goddess, I love you."

"Just you wait. After tonight, you'll worship the ground I walk on."

"I have no doubts."

He kissed her more fully then, too impatient to taste her, touch her, and be buried deep inside her to play anymore. The snap of her fingers was loud in the room, but not unexpected. And the feel of skin on skin made them both sigh their pleasure as she melted into him.

He gave into his unrelenting need and stroked her core, pleased to feel her wet and ready for his entry. Sitting back on his knees, he spread her legs wide and used the head of his penis to caress her folds. Running the tip up and down until her body wept with desire.

Sebastian bent and touched his tongue to her, sweeping it along her opening and stopping only when he touched her clit. When she arched into him, he smiled and sucked on the tiny bud.

"Oh, Baz," she cried out. "Yes."

He inserted his fingers; first one, then the other. Working her, making her ready for him. Her quickening breath was the only warning of her orgasm. He continued to kiss her most intimate area as the walls of her vagina pulsed around his fingers.

Her scream of pleasure brought with it the power to raise the rose petals off the ground and sent them swirling in the air around them. As she came down from her release, so did the petals, settling lightly on his back. Little, fluttering kisses along his spine and buttocks. The sensation wasn't unpleasant, and the idea of using magic to enhance their lovemaking made him smile.

Once again, he sat back on his heels, but this time to position himself between her thighs to take her. She lifted her legs and rested her heels on the mattress to open herself up to him further.

Sebastian took a mental picture of her like this. Bold-red hair spread around her. Cheeks flushed. Mouth slightly open as she panted and fought to catch her breath. Nipples tight and beaded. The picture of wanton.

Her glowing eyes met his, and she practically growled as she reached for him.

He couldn't wait, and in one smooth thrust, he buried himself to the hilt. Their mingled moans turned him on like nothing ever had before. And he began to move, stoking the fire within. Deepening his thrusts until the only sounds she made were little grunts of pleasure and pleas of "faster" and "harder."

His hips pumped in time to his heart, and he thought it was in imminent danger of bursting. His orgasm was building; he felt it in the tightening of his balls. Reaching between them, he used his thumb to bring her to completion. As she shattered in his arms, he thrust one last time and followed her over the edge.

CHAPTER 10

*A*s Mackenzie traversed the pebbled paths of the Drakes' garden, she turned her face to the sun. The beauty of the fine English day wasn't lost on her. Unlike her small hometown back in the States, the weather here tended to be cooler and, at times, overcast.

Because Sebastian had been pulled away first thing this morning to deal with a last-minute business matter, he'd encouraged her to entertain herself for a short time until his return. With a lascivious look, he'd promised they'd find the perfect spot to enjoy their breakfast picnic, going so far as to suggest round four under the open sky.

Mackenzie smiled and stretched. Her body tingled when she thought about what they'd done last night and again before he'd had to dart off this morning. Making love with Sebastian was all she could've hoped for and more.

Now, as she waited for Baz to finish and join her, she explored the estate's extensive grounds. "Beautiful," she murmured to herself. "I could live here forever." She grinned because now that she was Lady Kilbride, she most likely would.

At the end of a northbound walkway, tucked behind an overgrowth of trees and rosebushes, she discovered a weathered garden gate with a handful of timeworn symbols carved into the framework. The grass around the entrance had turned to a dingy yellow as if it were on the verge of dying.

Unfortunately, the gate had a dilapidated lock and required a skeleton key.

Mackenzie frowned down at the handle. Although her cousin Preston had taught her to pick locks for fun when she was a small child, she hadn't retained anything except the basics. As rusted as the keyhole looked, she doubted the mechanism inside could be moved without a barrel of lubricant. She wasn't getting in that way anytime soon.

"Well, hell."

Backing up, she eyed the height of the wall, judging it to be a good eight-feet tall if it was an inch. She could levitate, but if a non-magical human happened to be present and glancing out the window, they'd be in for the shock of their lifetime. Granny Thorne's cloaking spell could work for that little issue, but then Baz wouldn't find her.

Mackenzie grinned at the mental image of him walking right past her.

Deciding to scale the wall, she focused on a massive oak tree on this side. It would allow her to look like a normal, everyday mortal —albeit a crazy one—climbing a tree, should anyone happen upon her.

Unfortunately, there were no low-hanging branches to grab onto. With a quick look around, she swirled her hands in the air and created a thick, rope-like vine to aid her.

"Perfect."

As she wrapped her hand around the climber, a shiver of awareness danced along her skin. She almost backed away, but when no immediate vision of the future appeared to her, she shrugged off her unease. In mere seconds, she was at the top of the wall, peering over.

The sight filled her with a sickening dread.

The secret garden was nothing like she'd imagined it would be and was nothing but a wasteland of dead foliage. Any grass had long-since shriveled and died, and tree remains were blackened and bare. The only explanation could be a fire had swept through.

She'd have believed it to be so if it weren't for a single rosebush flourishing at the center of the destroyed area. The bush was no more than three-feet high, but it had runners along the ground in every direction. Long, fat vines unlike any rosebush she'd ever seen.

But it was the sight of the roses themselves that chilled her. They were a black so void of light, they looked like mini black holes dotting the landscape, ready to consume anything coming into their orbit.

Mackenzie shifted her grip on the wall slightly and peeked over the edge, straight down. Even as she watched, the runners grew in length and started climbing the brick wall faster than she would've thought possible without magical intervention. The thorns were at least three inches in length. The tips, wicked and threatening.

She knew she was being fanciful, but so much death and darkness was off-putting.

"What the bloody hell are you doing?" boomed a furious voice from below her.

She almost lost her grip on the wall and nearly wet her pants from fright. She'd have grabbed her pounding heart if her position wasn't so precarious.

"Dear Goddess, Baz! You nearly gave me heart failure." She peered down at him and, in doing so, missed the fact the rose runner had reached the top of the wall.

"Mack, *look out!*"

She whipped her head around in time to see the vine poised to shove one of those three-inch spikes directly into her neck. Throwing up a hand to protect herself, she deflected the plant's trajectory, but not without injury to herself. Her palm now sported a deep gash, and blood flowed freely, dripping down the secret garden's side of the wall.

The rosebush wasn't done with its attack on her person and coiled up, arching like a viper ready to strike.

"Let go, Mack. I'll catch you," Sebastian shouted up. *"Now!"*

As the vine stabbed at her a second time, she released her hold on the wall, calling on her air element to slow her descent and not be such a burden to Baz when he caught her. She was exceedingly glad when the wind kicked up. Even with the air as a cushion, Sebastian grunted at the impact.

He stood her on her feet and gave her a single hard shake. "That garden is forbidden, Mackenzie. Do you hear me? *Forbidden.*"

"I'm sorry, Baz." Never had she witnessed such a strong reaction in another person, and she'd seen everything from fear to fury to murderous rage. Where this overwrought emotion came from was anyone's guess.

"You don't understand the dangers it holds." The fingers gripping her shoulders dug in on the word "dangers."

"Please calm down." Although she could've easily broken his hold with magical force, she realized he needed the physical contact. Not to intimidate, but to stress the importance of his worry.

She stroked his exposed wrist. *"Please."*

As if he'd woken from a dream, his wide-eyed gaze locked onto where his hands clutched her. His chin jerked as if the sight shocked him, and one by one, Sebastian loosened his fingers. "I'm sorry, Mack. Please forgive me."

"There's no need to apologize. We both got a scare."

"Every time I turn my back, you find something to get into." The heavy irritation in his voice was based on his concern for her safety—she was wise enough to recognize that much.

"I like to explore. It's one of life's little pleasures."

He lifted her hand to examine the wound. "And this?" he asked dryly. "Is this one of your life's little pleasures?"

"Comes with the territory," she teased. The sight of his pale face as he stared down at the deep cut gave her a little pang of conscience. "I didn't mean to frighten you. I'm truly sorry."

He met her steady gaze, and in his dark, soulful eyes, Mackenzie saw worry.

"Baz? What is it?"

Glancing up toward the top of the wall, he grimaced. "I don't know how you found this place. It's been cloaked for as long as I can remember." His grim expression made her nervous. "We shouldn't be here."

"What is this place?"

"The Garden of Death."

"That's terrifying," she quipped, only half joking. With a look back at the gate, she noticed the pale glow of the symbols. "Um…" She pointed. "Has that ever happened before?"

"Fucking hell!"

"I guess this means it's time to call Damian?"

He shot her a dark look as he conjured a cloth to wrap her hand. "Let's get antiseptic on your wound."

As he ushered her toward the manor, he whipped out his phone and dialed. "Dethridge, it's Sebastian. I think we may have a serious problem."

ON THE OTHER SIDE OF THE WALL, THE BLOOD FROM ITS VICTIM trailed down the considerable length of the rose climber. When it got to the ground, the liquid re-formed into droplets and ran toward the base of the bush, picking up speed as it neared the center of the garden. From there, it was sucked into the roots and converged to tunnel through the poisoned soil until it connected with the six-by-three Carrara marble casket located ten feet below the ground's surface.

The earth rumbled as it received the nutrient it so craved —*magic!*

Inside the cold interior of her coffin, the Enchantress rested in a forced stasis. But the moment the blood drops fell upon the sigil etched into the stone lid, she opened her obsidian eyes, waking from her one-hundred-ninety-two-year slumber.

Isolde remained awake for roughly five minutes before she was forced to close her eyes and drop back into a semi-coma state. Her mind stayed alert, but her body was another matter. Starved as it was, it couldn't sustain the effort of full life functions.

Yet.

A shudder went through her.

During the brief time she'd had her eyes open moments ago, there was an increased awareness of her surroundings, and she was able to recall the circumstances resulting in her entombment: Isis had borrowed power from the Six to stop Isolde's rule. But at best, they could only entomb her. Knowing if they killed her, she'd overthrow the Otherworld because there was power in death, too.

How long she'd been contained, she didn't know.

Her eyelashes fluttered enough that she was able to register the stone, inches above her face. She slammed her lids closed again. She sucked in calming breaths and worked to keep the panic from clouding her mind. If she gave into the fear, she'd go completely mad.

As if you weren't mad before.

She ignored the vicious inner voice taunting her. It had always been so. Urging her to do horrific things in the name of feeding it more power. Only once had she been able to circumvent its intentions.

Damian. Her boy.

The monster within her had wanted to consume him too, but she'd fought it. She'd found him a safe haven. Or so she hoped. What had happened to him in the time she was gone? What had he been told?

How much power did he wield?

She wanted to scream at the inner beast to shut up. Damian was off-limits. He always would be.

Ah, but the unlimited magic he would have if he was alive could feed us, the voice reminded her. *He could save us from this tomb.*

Isolde gripped her skirts, feeling her finger poke through to hit bare skin. She almost laughed at the idea of wearing threadbare clothing. She'd not be caught dead wearing anything but the latest fashion in her reign. But now she was, which meant she'd been imprisoned for quite some time.

A single tear escaped from the corner of her eye and trailed to her temple.

The woman. The blood. Thorne blood. Possess her. Live again. Rule again.

Isolde's inner demon had used these two-word phrases in a continual loop through her entire incarceration. Most times, she'd been able to sleep or cancel them out with her own thoughts. Today, having tasted the blood of the Thorne witch who'd dared venture too close to the garden, Isolde's demon was too powerful.

She's ripe. Ready to possess. The Psychic Thorne.

Isolde's eyes flew open. Yes. That's what she'd forgotten until now. The chit had felt her pull, and they'd met by the maze. But when had they conversed? For all she knew, it could've been an hour or a thousand. A day or fifty years. The memory wasn't clear.

But the blood was sweet. So fresh.

Not old, then. The woman was young still. Enough to be of use to her. As her eyes drifted shut, Isolde envisioned the witch. Wavy hair, as red as the summer sunset, hanging partway down her back. A shapely body, a little on the thin side. Her smile lit up the night, and her eyes... Yes, those bold blue eyes held knowledge. Knowledge of the past, present, future. Knowledge of witchcraft. And so... much... *power!*

Tonight, when she sleeps, we can try again.

The poison of the black rose was in the witch's veins. Soon enough, she'd be able to gain control. Isolde only had to stay awake. Bide her time until the woman was asleep and easy to influence. Mainly, she had to find her bloody Book of Shadows. Without it, her complete resurrection would be near impossible, and living this way—half alive in a marble casket—was not an option.

CHAPTER 11

Sebastian stood beside Damian outside the gate of the place he'd long-since dubbed the Garden of Death. Due to the black roses and charred wasteland, that's what it had seemed like to him from the time he was a small child, standing next to his father and absorbing the news of what his duty would be.

Of course, Damian probably had a different name for his mother's grave.

"It pricked her," he told Damian in a hushed tone. As if saying it where no one else could hear would undo the damage done.

"What?"

"A thorn from the other side. It pricked Mack's skin and drew blood."

"Fucking hell."

"My thoughts exactly," Sebastian muttered. "What do we do now?"

"Nothing we can do until Isis decides to answer my summons." Damian scrubbed his face with his hands.

Never before had they been this close in their silent accord or *any* accord for that matter. Never before had Damian allowed Sebastian to see him when he wasn't in complete control. He almost appeared human in his frustration, and Sebastian liked him a little bit more for letting down his guard.

"Is it too much to hope Isolde's learned her lesson? That she might wake and *not* destroy us all?"

Damian shifted to grace him with an incredulous look. His expression gave off a distinct "what are you, stupid?" feel. Sebastian didn't have long to wait for him to follow it up with, *"Have you lost your bloody mind, Drake?"*

"Not yet, but it's a distinct possibility in the near future should something happen to Mack."

Damian's expression softened. "I would feel the same if it were Vivian or Sabrina, I'm sure."

"How much time do we have left, do you suppose?"

"Little. I can feel my mother's life force on the other side. It's stronger than it was." Damian's brows dipped, and he studied the flickering symbols on the gate's frame. "Isolde's pulsing back and forth between sleep and awareness. See here?"

"Is that what the flickering light means?" Sebastian could've done without knowing even that much. He hated being a warden of the property housing an evil entity. Hated knowing he alone was responsible for stopping anyone from entering the gate or mischievous children from climbing the wall.

Or in his case, a mischievous wife.

"What *did* you tell your wife about this?"

Sebastian shook his head and took a step to his left. Damian always gave him the willies when he read his damned mind that easily. "I told her the place was forbidden."

"Not why?"

"Not yet."

"You should, and soon. Knowledge is power. By keeping her in the dark, you may be hurting her chances of surviving."

Sebastian's stomach plummeted to his knees. "I want to take her away from here."

"You can try. But both Sabrina and I felt a resounding boom the moment Mack crossed the boundary to your property. We'd have to test my new theory, but I believe she may be trapped here for now." Damian linked his hands behind his back and turned from where he'd been engrossed in his study of the symbols. "You know, I saw these same carvings recently."

"Where?"

"On the standing stones in the clearing of Alastair Thorne's property."

"In America?" Sebastian did a double-take and stared at Damian. "How can that be?"

"I was there to help them regain their magic. It required a ceremony involving the standing stones. When they rose to their original positions above ground, each one contained a few of these symbols. No one pillar had them all like this gate does."

"Coincidence, do you suppose?" Sebastian asked, tempted to trace the carvings, but not foolish enough to do so.

"Nothing is ever a coincidence in the magical world, Drake. You should know that by now."

"I guess I do." He sighed and strode to the oak tree Mackenzie had used to scale the wall. "It was here."

Damian joined him and glanced up. "Looks harmless enough to a stranger."

"That was the problem, wasn't it? She was ignorant of our big secret." Sebastian shook his head, angry at his own stupidity in not telling Mack about this place and warning her away earlier. Her injury was his fault. "The boom, the trap. How does it work?"

"My mother cast a spell long ago. Normally, it would've died if it weren't sustained by constant magic. However, since Mother didn't die and was instead entombed, any spells remained active."

"What does that mean for today? For Mack?"

"The boom we heard was the arrival of the Psychic Thorne. Isolde charmed these lands so that should the witch possessing psychic ability set foot on the property, the magic wouldn't allow her to leave. At best, I'm worried Mack is now tied to it."

"And at worst?"

"It's not clear to me yet," Damian admitted with a heavy sigh. "I know I'm asking a lot, but be patient, Sebastian. No one wants to keep my mother contained more than I do."

"Because of your daughter." Sebastian didn't need to ask. The goal here was obvious: keep Isolde away from the small child who holds the power of a Goddess.

"Yes." Damian withdrew his cellphone and took a series of pictures of the gate and its sigils. After a quick swipe through the images he'd captured, he nodded and tucked his phone in his coat. "I intend to confer with whoever I can summon. In the meantime, pick Leopold's mind. He was here from the early days and may know something."

"How old *is* he?"

Damian's bark of laughter rang out across the garden. In a flash of light, he was gone.

"MACK, WE NEED TO TALK."

She put down her teacup and gave Sebastian her full attention.

"Sounds serious. Are you having second thoughts about us? Is it because I haven't put out in a few hours? Because we can change that right now if you have time." The fine lines next to his eyes crinkled, and his lips twitched as he tried to remain serious in the face of her teasing. She nearly laughed at his effort. It seemed Sebastian found her entertaining despite the heaviness of the situation in which they found themselves. Shifting, she created space on the settee, next to her. "Tell me."

Sebastian lifted her hand from her lap and turned it over. The long, angry wound from the rosebush had caused the skin to pucker. It also itched like mad. If Mackenzie didn't know better, she'd say an infection was beginning, but an illness of that kind was impossible for a witch.

"We cleaned this right away, and yet…" He shook his head with a deep frown.

She met Sebastian's concerned gaze. Seemed they were on the same wavelength. "I know. It's odd, isn't it?"

"Exceedingly." He gently palpated the area, careful not to press directly on the wound itself. "Does this hurt?"

"It's tender, but not unbearably so. Why do you think it's not healing?"

"I'm not skilled in that area, Mack, but as soon as we're done here, we'll seek out Aunt Gwennie. She may know."

"Whatever you're thinking so hard about, you just need to come out with it, Baz. Is it about the possessed rosebush? Tell me it hasn't taken over the garden. I'll be honest, I'm an air elemental. Fighting rogue plants makes me nervous."

"Actually, it does have to do with the roses, along with the whole Garden of Death."

She snorted a laugh, but regained her composure when she saw he wasn't kidding. "Dude. You're completely serious about the name." With a glance over her shoulder out the window, Mackenzie shuddered. "I suppose it's fitting."

"It's the resting place of Isolde de Thorne."

Her breath escaped and refused to return to her lungs. After what she'd overheard last night, Mackenzie was beginning to think escape was the only option. She wasn't a coward by any stretch of the imagination, but glowing symbols carved into the garden's gate, midnight conversations with an evil Enchantress, and deadly rosebushes made her tremble in her proverbial boots.

"We—my family and I—are Keepers of the Gate, Mack. Made so two hundred years ago by the Goddess." He leaned in as if to ensure she understood the import of his words. "We are the last line of defense against Isolde."

"And I've 'cocked it up' as you Brits would say. Simply by coming here."

"I didn't know what you were, or I'd have kept you far, far away."

"But Arabella did," she said quietly. "Does she have an ulterior motive for the invitation?"

"No. Maybe. I don't know. I think she believed you would be good for me because you challenge me."

"Highly irresponsible on her part, wouldn't you say?" she snapped. Mackenzie wiped her damp palms on her slacks, wincing as the still-tender wound came in contact with the material. She stared down at the festering gash. "You can't leave, because you need to defend this place. I can't leave because…?"

"How did you guess you can't leave?"

"It's what you're here to tell me, isn't it? It's gone too far?" She gestured behind her, toward the window with her thumb. "The glowing carvings. That's because of me."

"Yes. Damian and I both believe so."

"You and Damian. Right." Mackenzie rose to pace in her nervousness. "I'm leaving. Because despite what everyone thinks is inevitable, I am opposed to resurrecting the spawn of Satan to lay waste to the witch community and possibly the rest of the world."

She paused her pacing and faced him. His expression was troubled, but he remained silent in the face of her declaration.

"You don't think I should go, Baz?"

"I don't want you to, but if you can, it would be for the best."

"Will she go back to sleep, do you think?"

"What makes you think she's awake? I didn't say that."

Mackenzie jerked in place. What *had* made her ask? Why had she assumed Isolde was out of stasis? She closed her eyes and visualized the Garden of Death. "I can feel her. Her heartbeat. The panic when she opens her eyes. Her struggle not to lose her shit inside the tomb. It's faint, but I feel it."

"*Good goddess!* Damian said awareness, not awake." Sebastian surged to his feet and grabbed her hand. He half dragged her through the hall and to the main entry. "Don't move!"

He took the stairs two at a time, and Mackenzie was too worried to even admire the flash of ass cheek she saw when his kilt flared out.

"Might I get you more tea, miss?"

She bit back a terrified scream when Leopold materialized

beside her. "Jesus, Leo. You nearly gave me heart failure," she gasped out, with a balled fist pressed to her chest. "Now is not the time to be showing up without a bit of warning."

His rheumy eyes twinkled, and he looked as if he fought a smile. "Yes, miss. Would you care for a spot of tea?"

"No, thank you. I..." She glanced upward, toward where she'd last seen Sebastian. "I'm supposed to wait."

"Very good, miss." Leopold shuffled off toward the kitchen, but a loud "psst" changed his trajectory.

Mackenzie eased sideways and caught a flutter of white lace. As soon as the ancient butler disappeared from view, giggles floated back to her. She bit her lip to stop her own bubble of laughter. Seemed Leo and Teddie were all about the stolen moments, Goddess love them. Mackenzie hoped she had their stamina when she was their age.

If she lived through this current nightmare.

She sobered and chewed on her thumbnail. What Sebastian needed from upstairs was anyone's guess, but Mackenzie was having a difficult time subduing her instinct to teleport.

"Leaving is pointless, Mack."

A cold wave of air fluttered her hair and danced along the exposed skin of her forearms. She tugged down the pushed-up sleeves of her sweater and faced Arabella. "Did you bring me here to resurrect the Enchantress?" Mackenzie's voice resembled that of a croaking frog, and she longed for the "spot of tea" Leopold had offered a few minutes before. Anything to quench her dry mouth.

"Not intentionally." Arabella wasn't pretty by anyone's standards, but she had a striking face. Her features resembled her brother's and, on her, were too masculine for traditional feminine beauty. Yet, her countenance drew one's eye, and her expressions always appeared genuine. But perhaps the friendship she offered Mackenzie had been an act all along.

She surged forward and gripped her sister-in-law's wrist. "Tell me the truth, Arabella. Right now."

"I had a dream. In the dream, my family was happy. Baz was

happy. All because you came here. I wanted to see that happen in truth."

The rightness of the words struck Mackenzie. Whatever Arabella had done, it wasn't to cause trouble. Loosening her grip, she brought her friend's hand to her cheek. "I'm sorry to have sounded so accusing."

A flash of unease tempered the forgiveness in Arabella's dark eyes. "This is on me, Mack. Whatever I dreamed, it was a lie, wasn't it?"

"I don't know, Belle. It's hard to know what's real here, I think."

"You're talking about your midnight journey to the maze, aren't you?"

"Yes. I spoke to…" Mackenzie glanced around, almost afraid to utter the name. Taking a deep breath, she said, "Isolde."

"And it seemed as if she were truly there."

"Yes. And now I'm terrified she was."

"Do you think she manipulated my dreams?"

Mackenzie started to shake her head, but stopped. Why not? If the Enchantress had enough power to tap into her brain, why couldn't she tap into Arabella's? "I think maybe she did."

Anything Sebastian's sister would've said was cut off with his return. "There you are, Belle! I've been searching the entire north wing for you."

"What is it, Baz?"

"I want you to pack your things and go. Take Teddie and Gwennie and get out."

"I thought we went through this last night. Drakes stick together." Arabella's strong chin jutted out. "I'm not leaving you to fight this alone."

"We are all leaving. Mack and me included."

Her eyes widened, and she gasped. "But who will watch for…" She turned toward the terrace. "… for… the Enchantress?"

"Damian can pay people, or Isis can send a guard. I'll not risk my family anymore to this nonsense." He laced his hands together and cradled the back of his head. "I can't."

His agitation was painful for Mackenzie to witness. "Maybe you won't have to if I go, Baz. Maybe it will all go back to normal."

"Try to teleport to your flat, love."

Mackenzie closed her eyes and visualized the living room in her New York apartment. Her cells heated as the magic in her blood fired up. She felt an instant relief as her body broke apart and reformed a second later. When she lifted her lids, she almost threw up. In front of her was the gate to the Garden of Death with its glowing symbols.

Okay, so teleporting was out. She had two perfectly good legs for walking down the main drive. Closing her eyes, she snapped her fingers to return to the foyer of the Drake home. Both Sebastian and Arabella were waiting, optimistic expressions firmly in place.

She hated to dash their hopes. "I couldn't get out. My teleport deposited me in front of Isolde's garden gate."

"Right." The light died from Sebastian's eyes, and it made Mackenzie's stomach hurt to see it.

"What about an old-fashioned human exit?" Arabella suggested, apparently not ready to give up.

"I had the same thought, actually," Mackenzie said, pasting on a determined smile. "Let's go for it, huh?"

Sebastian skirted his sister and stalked to the four-foot round table occupying the center of the foyer. He stuck his hand inside a massive white bowl and removed a set of keys, jangling them in the air. "How do you say it in America? To escape a place?"

"Let's bounce. Let's fucking ride." Mackenzie shrugged. "Take your pick."

He smiled, but it never reached his eyes. "A mashup of the two, then. Let's fucking bounce."

She forced a laugh and threw her arms around his neck. "I'll make an American out of you yet, Lord Kilbride." She drew back and snatched the keys from his hand. "But I'm going to do this alone. If I can't break through the barrier, I don't know what'll happen to the vehicle. It may crash into an invisible wall for all we know, and I'm not risking Arabella's or your safety."

"You're not going alone." Sebastian grabbed for the keys, but she danced backwards.

"Stand by the fountain and watch the drive, Baz. If I make it, you guys can teleport. This lockdown doesn't pertain to you two."

He crossed to her and hauled her close, dropping his forehead to hers. "You're killing me, love."

Not yet, purred a silky smooth voice inside her head. *A voice not her own.*

Mackenzie felt as if she'd been doused with a bucket of ice water. She gasped and began to shiver. Even wrapped in the blazing warmth of Sebastian's embrace, she couldn't shake the cold.

"What is it?" He inched back enough to meet her panicked gaze. "Mack, what's wrong?"

She clenched down on her chattering teeth and shook her head. She'd rather die than let him see her cry. The last time she'd cried in front of anyone, she was six years old and her father had walked out on his small family.

Sebastian shared a worried look with his sister.

"I have to go," Mackenzie snapped. *"Now!"*

CHAPTER 12

As Sebastian watched in stunned disbelief, Mackenzie ran for the door. It only took a quick shove from Arabella to get him moving, but he was too late to catch Mackenzie or prevent her from sliding behind the wheel of the Land Rover.

The locks clicked as he reached for the door handle.

"Mack!"

She swiped angrily at the wetness on her cheeks and shook her head. The vehicle roared to life, and Sebastian experienced a rare sense of helplessness as he watched the distance grow between him and the taillights. The Land Rover screeched to a halt at the end of the drive, kicking up gravel in its wake.

Sebastian teleported and arrived in time to see Mackenzie kicking the tires and raging aloud in her frustration. Some of her words were new to him, and he was awed by her expansive vocabulary. She put hardened sailors to shame with her language.

He waited, resting one hip on the bumper, until she ran out of steam.

When she faced him, the color on her cheeks rivaled her fiery red hair. The blue of her eyes was a murky gray and indicative of her distress. Most witches couldn't hide their emotions one-hundred percent. The changing of their irises from bright to dull always gave them away. Mackenzie's eyes were no exception.

"I won't let her win!" she hollered to the sky. "I can't."

His heart ached to hear the pain in her words. The hoarseness of her cry spoke of her tortured thoughts.

"Mack."

She refused to look at him, instead staring off into the distance.

Uncrossing his arms, he pushed away from the Land Rover and stopped shy of touching her. *"Mackenzie."*

Her head turned, but her gaze was focused somewhere around his knees.

"I need you to look at me, love. To hear what I'm about to tell you."

"I can hear you without looking at you," she muttered.

He bit back a smile. "Feisty to the end, aren't you?"

That caught her attention. "You don't understand, Baz. The second I let my guard down, she wins. How can I be here when it could mean possession or worse?"

A frown drew his brows down, and he lifted her chin with the tip of one knuckle. Possession? Alastair Thorne had mentioned something about Sabrina and her worry regarding Isolde possessing Mackenzie, but Sebastian had forgotten about it in all the excitement. He hadn't gotten that far in wrapping his mind around this mess. His main goal was keeping the Enchantress entombed.

"And what constitutes worse, Mack?"

"Your death."

The air whooshed from his lungs, and he couldn't speak to ask anything else. Hell, he couldn't *think* to ask anything else either.

"She's putting thoughts in my head, Sebastian," she said achingly.

"When I held you a short bit ago? That's why you reacted badly and pulled away?"

She nodded.

"All right." He led her to a nearby stone bench. "Tell me everything."

"When you said, 'you're killing me, love,' she was in my head. She said, 'not yet.'" Mackenzie's lower lip trembled, and she traced the wound on her palm. "I don't want to hurt you."

"You won't." He placed a hand on her knee and squeezed slightly. He wasn't quite sure how to get his point across, but he had to try. "I know you, Mack. You'll outsmart her."

"I'm scared."

"Me, too. But I'm not afraid of you. I'm afraid *for* you."

"Last night..." She frowned and looked around.

"Last night," he encouraged.

"Was it only last night we decided to get married? Already it feels like forever ago."

"Thanks?"

She cracked a small smile. "I don't mean it like that, and you know it. I feel like a long time has passed since the ceremony."

"You're not telling me anything I don't already know."

Her smile dropped, and Mackenzie cleared her throat. "Last night when you asked me about my vision, what I didn't tell you was I saw myself kneeling over you with an athamé in my hand. It wasn't one I'd ever seen, and I don't know where it came from. I felt her desire to kill you, Baz, and it terrified me. There were two faces of me, and a while ago, it became clear one was Isolde."

"The possession." Yes, it made sense. If the Enchantress couldn't get out of her prison, she'd likely try another route to kill her gaolers. "Because of the vision, you now fear what she can make you do."

"Yes."

"Have you seen my actual death, Mack?"

She seemed to look through him for a moment before she shook her head. "No."

Relief made him weak, but he forged on. "Good. Then we have nothing to worry about."

"I couldn't leave the estate."

"What happened when you tried? Obviously no invisible wall, or the Rover would've been destroyed at the rate you were traveling," he said dryly.

"Yeah, well..." A light blush tinged her cheeks. "I felt a burning. It started in my chest and expanded out. A thousand times worse than cells ramping up for magic. This was like a nuclear meltdown, and the closer I got to the end of the driveway, the worse it became until I almost blacked out." She stared in bemused wonder at the entry gates. "I had to stop, or I'd have crashed."

"We'll have to find a work-around. Come back to the house."

They rose together and clasped hands. He led her to the passenger side of the vehicle and secured her inside. After climbing behind the wheel, he gave the gates a considering look. "You'd feel the burning, but if I'm driving, you couldn't faint at the wheel."

Shifting slightly in his seat, he sought her reaction.

Mackenzie's gaze was packed full of worry. "The pain was almost unbearable, Baz. What happens if I pass out and you continue driving, but when I wake, I can't make the burning go away because we are too far from the property?"

"Well, if you're going to be all logical about it," he muttered, throwing the Land Rover into reverse to turn back.

MACKENZIE PICKED UP HER PHONE FOR WHAT SEEMED LIKE THE hundredth time and put it back down. Calling in reinforcements when she might end up getting them hurt in the long run didn't sit well with her.

"Would it be better if I called him?" Sebastian's voice startled her, and she let out a small meep of surprise. He pressed his lips together, but he couldn't hide his desire to smile.

"I'm going to put a bell on you." This house was totally creeping her out at this point. Everything was making her jumpy as fuck. "And how do you know who I'm thinking of calling?"

"The logical answer is Alastair."

Okay, she had to give him that one. "I don't want to bring anyone else into this, but I'm worried we'll need more help. You and Arabella might be no match for Isolde when she takes over."

His thick brows met in the middle as he stepped farther into the room. "Call him if it makes you feel better. I'm not prideful or ignorant enough to believe we won't need assistance. Also, we need to find out what he may have discovered from Isis."

Her shoulders sagged with her relief. Part of her fear had been offending Sebastian. She dialed her cousin and didn't have long to wait for him to answer.

"Thorne."

"Alastair? It's Mack."

"Mackenzie. How are you holding up, child?" His tone was kind and caring, making her want to seek the shelter of his embrace as she had when she was a kid.

He'd come along after her father took off for parts unknown, and he'd made sure she had a home. Alastair had done a fantastic job of raising her until she decided to head out on her own at eighteen. After that, once a week, he'd arrive in New York to check on her and to take her out to dinner. They'd spent hours conversing over wine and pasta. Catching up on the family, her job, and Rorie's condition at the time.

"To be honest, I'm frightened, Alastair. Seems I can't leave the estate without frying my insides."

"I think you'd better tell me from the beginning. One moment."

Mackenzie could hear him in the background, although his words were hard to distinguish. Finally, he spoke to her again.

"I'll be there within the hour. You can explain it all then."

"Thank you, cousin."

"You can thank me by having a tumbler of scotch ready for my consumption." A muffled female voice on his end could be heard putting in her two cents. Alastair sighed, and his irritability came through loud and clear. "And tea. My beloved requires tea, because apparently she is coming with me."

Mackenzie laughed at how put out he sounded. "Tell Rorie we'll take care of her when she gets here."

She signed off and updated Sebastian.

He nodded, and some of the tension around his eyes eased. "I'll admit, I feel a lot better knowing he's coming here. You'd better text him a photo of the terrace so he can teleport freely without worrying about where he lands."

She did as he suggested and snapped pictures of the terrace outside the main salon. After she forwarded them to Alastair, she crossed to where Sebastian stood, noting how tired he seemed and how strained his expression appeared to be.

"Are you okay, Baz? I know this is wearing on all of us, but it must be especially hard on you."

"I can't deny I'm worried about the consequences of Isolde escaping. The fact that she's awake, biding her time until she can wreak havoc on the rest of us, is terrifying to say the least."

Mackenzie dropped her gaze from Sebastian's unnervingly perceptive stare as she thought over her options. Damian's words came back to her. *"If you had a choice, would you take your life to save the others?"* She wondered if it would come to that or if it was now too late.

"What are you thinking, Mack? Based on your green expression, it can't be good."

Turning away, she rubbed her upper arms. "Nothing, really."

"Don't do that. Don't lie to me."

His tone was harsh, and beneath the anger, Mackenzie detected no small amount of fear.

She spun back and placed a hand on his chest, prepared to reassure him, only the psychic attack struck with such force, she cried out and dropped to her knees.

"Mack!"

Sebastian dropped down beside her and gripped her shoulders as she clutched her head, rocking front and back.

"Mack, love, tell me you're okay. What's happening?"

ISOLDE'S EYES SNAPPED OPEN. THE FIRST THING SHE SAW WAS THE handsome dark-haired warlock in front of her. Worry clouded his ashen face, and he looked ready to lay down his life for the woman she inhabited.

She smiled and lifted her hand to trail a finger along his lips. "Hello, lover."

He recoiled, jerking back so fast, his kilt caught on his boot and caused him to careen sideways. He barely managed to steady himself, but he didn't try to touch her again.

"Mack?"

"Mack?" She grinned. "No. Your *Mack* can't come out to socialize at the moment, but I'm at your disposal should you care to entertain me."

Before she could fully appreciate his horror, she was thrown back into her tomb. As her energy waned, she closed her eyes and savored the look on his face. Soon she would be strong enough to maintain hold of the body she'd possessed.

SEBASTIAN BACKED AS FAR AWAY FROM MACKENZIE AS HE COULD GET without actually leaving the room. Without a doubt, whoever was using her body as a puppet wasn't his wife. The cold, calculating look was at complete odds with her normally friendly, open expression.

Surprise crossed her features, and she grabbed her head, releasing a low moan. *"Get out of my head, you fucking bitch!"*

Her arms dropped to her sides as she sat back against the table leg closest to her. Sweat beaded her brow, and her lips had gone pale. The look in her eyes had changed from cunning to terrified, and still, Sebastian was hesitant to move closer.

"Mack?" His voice came out rough and maybe a little ragged. He felt as stunned as she appeared.

"Yes, Baz." Moisture welled in her large blue-gray eyes and slowly spilled over to trail down her cheeks. "I'm frightened," she whispered.

So was he, but he couldn't leave her emotionally broken on the floor. He forced one foot in front of the other until he reached her. He squatted on the floor beside her and, with one trembling hand, caressed her cheek. "It's okay, love. You're okay."

They reached for each other at the same time, and he drew her into his lap. He didn't know how long they sat like that before the door cracked open and Leopold rolled in a tea service. From their place on the rug, Sebastian had a clear view of his butler's socks.

"My favorite animal is definitely the beaver."

He choked on his own saliva, coughing until his lungs ached. When Mackenzie gave him a concerned look, he covertly gestured to the writing on the socks. Her gasp turned into a giggle and then to full-bodied laughter.

Leopold's brow rose haughtily, but the twitching at the corner of his mouth gave him away. Either old Leo had a facial tick, or he was trying not to join in with their merriment. Again, the question of his age flitted through Sebastian's mind.

"If that will be all, m'lord?"

He cleared his throat and tried to regain some small semblance of decorum. "Alastair Thorne will be joining us within the hour, Leopold. Will you make sure we have a bottle of Glenfiddich on hand for our guest?"

"Of course, sir. And for Master Damian?"

Both Sebastian and Mackenzie whipped their heads around to stare at the man leaning his shoulder against the doorjamb leading to the terrace.

"I'm fine with whatever everyone else is having. Thank you, Leopold," Damian said with a smirk.

"Very good, sir."

CHAPTER 13

Now, more than ever, we need to continue with tradition, don't you think? It's the perfect time to stretch and refresh your snacks.

CHAPTER 14

Sebastian helped Mackenzie to her feet and took an extra moment to run his thumbs beneath her eyes, wiping away the evidence of her crying.

She gave him a grateful smile and faced the Aether.

Damian spoke first. "What happened? I received a call from Alastair, instructing me to meet him here."

"He should be arriving in a bit," Mack assured him. She relayed her experience from moments before. Sebastian followed it up with an explanation of her earlier attempt to leave the estate.

Damian's expression indicated he was five seconds away from losing his cool. "And neither of you thought to call me the first time my mother waltzed her way into your mind?"

His barely suppressed rage tingled along Mackenzie's nerve endings, and she shuddered at the knowledge of all the raw power he held inside. His magic far surpassed hers, and if his mother possessed even half of what he did, Mack was in deep shit.

"Actually, we did," Sebastian assured him. "We were scarcely recovered from the first before this second… incident happened."

Damian's sharp dark gaze darted between them. Abruptly, he nodded. "Fine."

Mackenzie squirmed under his penetrating stare. "What?"

"So we're clear, the first time was just a fleeting thought?"

"Yes."

"This time, she hijacked your mind completely?"

She swallowed and nodded.

"Where did you go?"

"Pardon?"

"Where did you go, Mack? Were you in there with her? Did she trade places with you? As in, were you in her body in the tomb?"

"I don't think so, but I don't know for sure. It was like being in a black room with no light," she recalled, struggling to pull forward any memory other than the terror she'd felt.

"Did you smell anything?" Damian continued to push for answers as he fixed her a cup of tea.

His gesture seemed out of place to her, but she appreciated his consideration. The small kindness tempered his harsh rapid-fire questions.

"Smell?" She started to shake her head, but the memory of a faint scent lingered. "Wait. Maybe. Like a blend of lavender and a spice I'm not familiar with."

"Was it earthy?"

"Yes, I believe it was, but there was another mustier scent."

Damian's expression darkened, and he turned away to stare over the yard. "Ruta, or Rue as it's called now, I would imagine."

Mackenzie shared a confused look with Sebastian.

"Where do you think Mack went, Dethridge?"

"I don't know that she went anywhere other than her own mind, but it's possible she traded places with my mother."

The idea of being inside a two-hundred-year-old tomb was repellent and grossed Mackenzie right the hell out. She clamped a hand over her mouth to stop her urge to scream.

Sebastian rubbed her lower back. "Come again?"

Damian turned from the garden and locked gazes with Mackenzie. "It's possible you and my mother exchanged bodies for however long she was able to possess yours."

"Fan-freaking-tastic." She gulped down her tea in one swoop. "Admittedly, I know nothing about this type of thing, but if Isolde is able to pull a Freaky Friday, she clearly has use of her magic."

"Freaky Friday?"

"It's a movie. Never mind." Mackenzie waved a hand in dismissal. "We need to come up with a solid plan to lock down my body. Make it a no-entry zone."

Sebastian's choked cough caught her attention. Heat crept up her cheeks as she realized how her words sounded. A quick glance showed her Damian struggled against a smile.

"Pfft. Men. Always with their minds in the gutter. Am I right, cuz?"

The sweet sound of Spring Thorne-Carlyle's voice floated to Mackenzie, and she gasped her delight. Her cousin was as brilliant as the day was long, and if anyone could figure a way out of the mess Mack had found herself in, it was Spring.

Rushing to embrace her, Mackenzie registered the presence of Spring's husband, Knox, along with Alastair and Aurora. The tension within her uncoiled from the knowledge her family would have her back. One by one, she hugged them tightly, gushing her gratitude for their timely arrival.

Spring hugged Damian. "It's good to see you again."

"None of us expected it to be this soon though," Knox added as the two men shook hands.

"Dire circumstances and all," Damian countered with a grimace.

"Right." Alastair waved a hand, and the bottle of Glenfiddich floated up to pour a dram of his favorite whisky into a tumbler. "Why don't you start from the beginning, and leave nothing out."

Mackenzie and Sebastian took turns relaying all that had happened since she set foot on the Drake estate. Damian remained silent during their explanation, even when Alastair shot him the occasional questioning glance.

"You married Drake?" Alastair's eyes reflected a sadness, and Mack wondered if it was because he'd wanted to give her away in a more traditional ceremony.

"It was an impulsive decision." She glanced down at her lap, where her hand was joined with Sebastian's. He gave her a light squeeze, and Mackenzie knew she'd done the right thing regardless of timing. "I'm sorry we didn't think to include everyone."

A slow, pleased smile spread across Alastair's aristocratic features. "You have nothing to apologize for, child. You followed your heart."

She nodded. "I did."

His sapphire gaze shifted to Sebastian and narrowed slightly.

"I did, too," Baz assured him so quickly Mackenzie almost laughed.

"I believe you, son." Alastair took an unhurried sip of his drink and stared into the crackling flames of the hearth. "What's our next step, Dethridge? I assume you've been working on a plan."

"Not much of one, I'm afraid. I've been unable to get a clear read on any of the unfolding events, and Isis refuses to answer my summons."

"We're going to need reinforcements," Alastair said with a resigned sigh. "I'll call Ryker, Nash, and Quentin before I try to summon Preston."

"Of course with the arrival of the guys, their other halves will follow," Knox said with a chuckle. His grin widened when Spring elbowed his side. "What? You know it's true. I've yet to meet a Thorne female who doesn't dive right into trouble."

"It's because we're the smarter of the pairings and are always there to get you guys out of the messes you create." Her arched brow and smirking mouth dared him to argue.

With a deep, rumbling laugh, he hugged her close. "Whatever you say, sweetheart."

"There's an intelligent man, who knows how to surrender the field," Sebastian whispered in Mackenzie's ear.

"Better for their sex life all around, I imagine," she murmured in return. "I heard a rumor that she once filled his mouth with dirt for being an ass to her."

Sebastian buried his chuckle against her hair.

The blinding headache struck without warning, and she cried out.

Sebastian watched the color drain from Mackenzie's face and released her in an instant. "This is what happened before—"

Mackenzie's head whipped up, and a calculating look crossed her face as she noted the people around her. Her eyes narrowed as she stared at Damian.

A sense of dread started low in Sebastian's gut and spread from there. "It's Isolde."

She shot him a side glance and winked. "Hello, lover."

Rising, she crossed to where Damian sat in a wing-backed chair by the hearth. Her expression softened marginally as she reached out a hand to touch his face. He, in comparison, remained still as a statue, showing no emotion at all.

"My boy," she whispered. She used her thumb and index finger to shift a lock of his hair from his forehead. "You've grown to be a beautiful man, haven't you, Damian?"

He stood and gave her such a look of pity Sebastian's heart almost ached for him. "This is no longer your time, Mother. Leave Mackenzie alone. For all our sakes."

"No!" Her expression hardened, and an ugliness came into her eyes. "This vessel is perfect for my use."

"She's a person, not a vessel," Alastair snapped, surging to his feet.

Aurora said his name, heavy caution in her tone.

Isolde turned on him in an instant, hands raised, ready to strike. Confusion flooded her features, and her questioning eyes bounced back and forth between Alastair and Damian. "You're the Alastair Thorne from my dream," she said softly. "My boy's savior."

"He did save me, Mother. Only last week." Damian stepped between them and ducked a little to capture her attention, which was locked on Alastair. "Because of the spell *you* wrote." His smile didn't quite reach his eyes. "Because of the love *you* held for me."

A sad look stole across Isolde's face. "I had to save you from the Beast. He wanted you then, and he wants you now."

"Yes. But you can stop it, Mother. By going back to sleep."

Her rage was palpable as she knocked his hand away. "No!"

They all felt the slap of her power and jerked in place.

Sebastian's skin began to burn, as if he'd been in the sun too long.

"Isolde," Knox spoke to her, and the tone held the voice of authority.

She spun to face him with a snarl on her lips. Sebastian had the fleeting thought that she looked like a cornered mongrel.

Knox repositioned himself between her and Spring. "If you don't leave Mackenzie right now, I'll fry your ass."

From Sebastian's vantage point, he saw Knox draw molecules together to form a ball of electricity behind his back. Everyone who knew the man, knew he'd been gifted the power of a god by Isis, lifetimes before. That ancient magic was fused with his very soul, and he was reborn with it in every incarnation. Everyone also knew he'd do whatever it took to protect his wife, who had been his soulmate for thousands of years.

Sebastian's heart started hammering at such a rate he couldn't catch his breath. Mack would never survive being electrocuted. Surging forward, he grabbed Knox's arm. "Don't," he whispered. "You'll kill her."

Knox's arctic expression said he was well aware of the consequences.

Unacceptable, as far as Sebastian was concerned. He released Knox's wrist and moved forward until he was within a foot of Isolde. Truth be told, he was wary of getting closer.

"Mackenzie is stronger than you," Sebastian taunted. He didn't know if he was doing the right thing or if she had the power to smite him on the spot, but he had to try to loosen her hold and encourage Mack to fight to return to them. "She is, and she'll eventually destroy you."

Isolde's hands curled, palms up, and fire flared to life. "Not before I destroy *you* first."

"My Mack will never let you hurt me, Isolde," he assured her.

She positioned her hands to attack, but surprise flashed across her face as the flames were extinguished. Her eyes went blank and rolled back in her head.

He got to Mackenzie as she collapsed, catching her before she could fall. His knees suffered rug burns as the full weight of both their bodies crashed to the floor.

"Goddess preserve us," Alastair muttered as he hiked up the legs of his trousers and squatted beside them. "That took courage, Drake. Even I felt a momentary unease."

Sebastian almost laughed at the "momentary unease" comment. Alastair was always calm, cool, and collected in the face of any adversity. Unfortunately, this incident was no laughing matter. If they didn't find a way to contain Isolde, and soon, they were sitting ducks.

As he watched Mackenzie, waiting for her to come around, he smoothed back the scarlet hair from her pale face. Unconscious like this, she seemed so fragile. Of course, she'd scoff at him for even daring to think it. And yet, he knew she *was* strong, because she'd pulled Isolde back down.

"Why isn't she waking?" Spring asked, trying to fight Knox's hold to move closer. "Will you let me go, you over-bearing tool!"

"No. Not until we are sure she's gone."

"I will feed you up a mountain of dirt if you don't let me get to Mack."

"I swear to the Goddess, woman!"

"Swear all you'd like. I'm tending to my cousin, Knox."

With a pained sigh, he released her.

Spring joined Sebastian and Alastair on the floor. "Should we call Aunt GiGi?"

Sebastian looked up to consult Damian and swore. "Where did he go?"

"Hopefully to fire-bomb that damned garden holding Isolde's body," Spring said. "I'm calling Aunt GiGi."

She jumped to her feet and ran out to the terrace, cellphone in hand. Knox was hot on her heels.

When they were alone, Sebastian allowed himself to express his fears to Alastair and Aurora. "This is three times today. I'm terrified for her."

"I know. I can feel it. Try to remain calm, son." Alastair placed a hand on Sebastian's shoulder. "If I can sense it, I know Damian and Mackenzie can as well. She doesn't need anything else to distract her in this battle."

"Where do you suppose Dethridge really went?"

"If he's smart? To get Sabrina out of the country. Perhaps hide her in a Monastery outside the farthest reaches of civilization, where he can fortify the place."

"You're not instilling confidence in me, Thorne." In fact, the idea of Damian running away, downright terrified Sebastian.

A gold light shone out of a widening rift to their left. The Aether stepped through and gave them both a look of such disgust, Alastair chuckled.

"Really, Al? You thought I'd run off with my tail between my legs?"

"You disappeared awfully fast, Dethridge," Alastair mocked. "I mean, I always *believed* you were a stand-up guy, but could be that you've grown soft."

"Sod off, why don't you?" Damian handed him a small ceramic pot with a lid. "GiGi will want this salve when she arrives."

Alastair accepted the jar with a nod. "Thank you, my friend."

"Sebastian."

The serious note in the Aether's voice brought Sebastian's head up.

"What you did took courage, Drake. You put a lot of faith in Mackenzie's ability to defeat my mother. It worked this time, but I doubt it will again." Damian's somber gaze dropped to Mack's still face. "She's a fighter. I pray it's enough, but you need to be prepared for the worst."

"As long as I draw air, I'll fight for her." Sebastian traced her cheekbone. "She'd do the same for me. I know she would."

"Take her to her room," Alastair said in a low, gentle tone. "When GiGi arrives, I'll send her up."

Damian strode for the glowing rift. "You can relax for a bit, Drake. Isolde isn't strong enough to return this soon. She's expended all the energy she can by possessing your wife this close together."

"Then why retry so soon?"

"Wouldn't you if you'd been entombed for centuries?"

Sebastian slowly nodded. "Yes. I suppose I would."

"Take her and go rest now," Damian said kindly. "Also, that salve will help the burns on your face." The portal between their residences sealed shut after he crossed through.

"I don't suppose I'll ever get used to him being nice to me."

Alastair chuckled and helped Sebastian rise with the burden of Mackenzie in his arms. "Don't assume it will last, son. Dethridge is unpredictable at best."

CHAPTER 15

Mackenzie wandered alongside a river, wondering how she'd come to be here when the last thing she remembered was the arrival of her family at Sebastian's home.

So much for being restricted to the property boundaries!

She smiled. The others must've found a way to break her invisible chains.

"Mackenzie."

She turned cold.

Preston's was a voice she recognized, but he shouldn't be here with her now.

Unless she was in the Otherworld.

"It's okay, child."

With dread in her heart, she faced him. "Am I dead?"

"Not in so many terms."

"Stasis?"

"Of a sort." He shrugged.

"Christ, Preston, how about a straight answer?" she snapped. "I'm in the Otherworld, aren't I?"

"Yes. In the space that acts as a holding area. Time is suspended here, as it is on the earthly plane while you're with me."

She processed the information and closed the distance between them, stopping short before touching him. "May I hug you? Can I? I mean, you're not a ghost or anything, right?"

He laughed and opened his arms.

Tears burned behind her lids as he enfolded her in a bear hug. Her returned embrace was fiercely tight. It felt as if he'd been gone forever, although it had been less than a year. "We all miss you so damned much, cousin."

"I miss you all just as much, Mack."

With one final squeeze, she drew back and swiped at her eyes. "Although I love our little reunion, care to tell me why I ended up here?"

"Isis has a message for you to relay to the others. It was easier to bring your soul here while Isolde was active, rather than for me to go there."

"Again?" she croaked. Her throat sported a lump of fear the size of a baseball.

"Again. The Enchantress is one determined bitch."

Preston's use of profanity made her laugh, as he'd most likely intended it should. "She really is. I'm worried for Sebastian."

"Not yourself?"

"I'll come here if she wins, won't I?" In the face of his hesitation, she shrugged. "Baz and his family have more to fear, I think. She'll make it painful for them should she be resurrected. Not only in her attempt to steal their power, but because of her revenge toward them for imprisoning her."

"You're not wrong." He ran his fingers through his hair. "Isolde herself is not necessarily evil. But an evil lives within her, and she's unable to resist its commands."

"Can we separate the evil from the woman?"

He went still.

"What? You don't like that idea?" she asked.

Shaking his head, he grinned. "I'm not sure why no one has ever thought of it before."

"Perhaps they have and knew it was hopeless." Mackenzie had

always possessed a practical side. Throughout her life, it had allowed her to see things from multiple angles and swiftly weigh her options. "Like if they'd left even a smidgeon of the evil behind, it would grow again. Similar to cancer."

"Perhaps." He stared off into the distance with a frown. "But even should we achieve the goal of destroying her demon, what about her mental state after all this time? I suspect the madness has plagued her so long, she may not recover."

"If we can't bind her and have no hope of fixing her, our only option is to end her life," Mackenzie concluded. For the moment, she ignored the relief she felt in her reasoning. Poor Damian. How horrible it must be to go to war against his own mother. To see her defeated not once, but twice in his lifetime. *If she could be defeated.* "We'll need to do something before she's out of her tomb, Preston. She's weaker there, right?"

"Yes and no. She was put into the garden because it was the only recourse at the time. A sleeping spell, using the blood of the Six. The most powerful on both sides of the veil couldn't defeat her completely."

A shudder chased along Mackenzie's spine. "What does that mean?"

"Apparently, somewhere along the way, she'd syphoned magic from not just one god, but two. She was practically unstoppable on earth, and she couldn't be brought here without her causing chaos and destruction."

Understanding dawned on her. "If she'd been brought here, with the type of magic she held, she'd have been able to draw more from those on this side. She could've basically destroyed the Otherworld."

"Yes. The only option was entombment. It took Isis and her small army to make it happen."

"And one psychic witch to innocently undo it all," Mackenzie murmured as she looked out over the glistening water's surface. The twinkling lights seemed peaceful, and she wondered if it would be so bad to live here. "Damian suggested I might do well to end it all."

"Suicide is never the answer, Mackenzie Thorne." Preston

gripped her shoulder, his fingers digging in enough to display his anger. *"Never."*

"What's the alternative?" she cried, spinning to face him. "I can't be her tool, Preston. *I can't!*"

His troubled expression gutted her. Everyone saw the inevitable train wreck she would cause, but not a single person knew how to slow the locomotive. Mackenzie was the engineer who would bring the magical world—and perhaps the non-magical world—crashing down upon them all.

The air around them grew charged, but before she could ask what the hell was happening, Isis joined them with a black-haired man at her side. He was large, dwarfing the exotic goddess, who was of medium height. The man stood a good six inches over Preston's six-feet height. His posture was militant, and his honey-gold eyes, lined with thick black kohl, were cold and calculating. His bearing screamed god, and he seemed familiar to Mack, but she couldn't place him.

Preston was quick to bow his head, so she did the same.

Isis touched Mackenzie's shoulder in greeting. "Hello, child. Preston has explained to you why you are here?"

"He has, Exalted One."

"Good. Set has devised a plan, and I need you to relay it to your relation, Spring."

"Spring?" Mackenzie risked a glance at him.

Set's golden eyes warmed marginally, and he nodded his confirmation of Isis's statement. "She is the beautiful, intelligent one married to the ignorant bear of a man."

Mackenzie frowned and glanced at Preston. Knox was as far from dumb as it got. His IQ was off the charts.

"Just go with it," Preston whispered. His eyes had dropped to the ground, and he pressed his lips in a tight line. If Mack didn't know better, she'd think he was fighting laughter.

"Ohh-kayy." She met Set's narrowed-eyed gaze. "What is your plan, Exalted One, and how may I be of assistance?"

He smiled.

Mackenzie sucked in her breath. She had to admit, it was as if the sun became brighter in the sky and she was seared by its intensity. It was a good thing he didn't reside on earth, because every mortal on the planet would worship the very ground he walked on for the smallest token of his affection.

"I gave her a scroll some months back. I will come to her in a dream and give her the full details of the plan. She will follow my dictate without question or fail, understood?"

"Why can't you just tell me now, so there's no mistake?"

Lightning swift, Set's expression went from friendly to hostile.

Isis answered in his place, preventing the scolding Mackenzie suspected she would've received from the god. "The Enchantress will have access to your memories, child. She will have access to what we have planned and find a way to subvert it."

Mackenzie nodded. She was the weakest link in this little chain. One firm tug from Isolde, and it would break. "I'll let her know."

"Be brave, dearest. You'll be rewarded for your sacrifice."

She wanted to scoff her disbelief. Wanted to scream her fury at the way her life was being waylaid by a crazy enchantress, a couple of all-powerful entities, and a prophecy. Instead, she bowed her head in acceptance. What other choice did she truly have?

"She's waking up!"

Sebastian's voice was the first Mackenzie heard, and she turned her face toward the sound.

"Mack? Can you hear me, love?"

Her lids felt like lead weights as she tried to force them up.

His dark eyes were strained, and lines of worry creased his brow. When she lifted her hand to smooth his forehead, he recoiled.

Although his instinctive reaction hurt her heart, she understood his reason. Whatever Isolde had done while in possession of her body made him a little gun-shy. "It's me, Baz."

His exhalation was pure relief. In an instant, she was cradled in his brawny arms with her cheek pressed to his chest. "Thank the Goddess!"

Mackenzie peeked past his broad shoulder, hoping to catch a glimpse of the room's occupants. GiGi stood a few feet away with her hands on her hips and a wide grin on her face. Mack returned her smile.

"It's good to see you back in the land of the living, child."

She felt Sebastian's wince, and she eased back to apologize for all she'd put him through.

He didn't give her a chance. He pressed his lips to hers in a tender, lingering kiss.

The sweetness of the gesture almost made her cry.

After he pulled back, he bracketed her face between his large palms. "Don't ever scare me like that again, okay?"

She wanted to assure him she wouldn't, but she'd be lying. If her conversation with Isis, Set, and Preston was any indication, he was in for the scare of a lifetime.

"Where's Spring?" she asked in place of answering. "I have a message for her."

Sebastian frowned and shot a look toward GiGi.

Her cousin moved forward and placed a hand on his shoulder, her slender fingers giving the beautifully rounded deltoid a light squeeze. Mackenzie almost laughed when GiGi's eyes took on an appreciative gleam. What had started out as a touch of comfort turned into a quick feel of a beautiful man's muscles.

"Focus, cousin," Mack teased. "Spring?"

"Right." GiGi patted his shoulder then put her hand behind her back like she'd been burned. She gave her blonde head a quick shake and turned her attention to Mackenzie. "She's wandering the maze with Knox. My niece has fallen in love with the gardens here. She was babbling on about the vastness and the selection of herbs the Drakes have."

"That's our Spring." Laughing, Mackenzie scooted to the edge of the mattress.

Sebastian stopped her with a hand on her knee. "I think you should rest, love. You had quite a morning."

"Two possessions and a meeting with the gods. Yes." She still couldn't wrap her brain around the craziness of it all. Sighing, she nudged him aside. "But I have to relay what Set said."

"Set? As in Ra's mouthpiece?" GiGi asked, mouth agape.

"Hulking brute, built like a tank, gold eyes with eyeliner Captain Jack Sparrow would envy, a surly attitude, and a massive hard-on for Spring," Mack replied. "That the one?"

GiGi laughed. "That's the one."

"Yep, he's insisted I speak directly to her and tell her he has a plan of attack."

"Interesting. I can't wait to see what the overprotective Knox will do when he hears."

"Am I missing something?" Mackenzie glanced between GiGi and Sebastian, but he looked just as frustrated as she felt.

GiGi rubbed her hands together, gleeful to be relaying gossip. "Well, when Nash needed to revive Ryanne—"

"Don't tell me!" A shiver of awareness caused the fine hair on Mackenzie's arms to stand at attention.

Both GiGi and Sebastian froze.

Mack's heart began pounding in her ears. Somehow, some way, Isolde was tuned in, and Mackenzie didn't want to be responsible for giving her a clue as to what was about to go down. "I think the less I know, the better."

Her cousin nodded thoughtfully. "Of course, dear."

"Mack, are you one-hundred percent?"

"For now, Baz." She rubbed her arms. "Let's go find Spring."

CHAPTER 16

"What do you suppose Set intends to do?" Knox asked. Spring's young man wasn't thrilled to learn the God would be visiting his wife in her dreams, and Alastair almost chuckled at the heavy irritation in his tone.

"The transmutation spell would be my guess," Spring replied.

Alastair could see the wheels spinning behind her lovely jade eyes. Her intelligent mind was always going, turning over everything she learned to see how best it could benefit her. Or rather, the Thornes as a whole. Her generous spirit encouraged her to look out for the family's best interest at all times, much to Knox's dismay. Spring's willingness to put her life in jeopardy to save another was giving the poor man gray hair.

"I believe you may be onto something," Alastair said. "I assume you still have the scroll Set gave you when we swapped the souls of Ryanne and her sister?"

"I do, but I don't need it." She tapped a fingertip to her temple. "I know it by heart."

"Of course you do." He allowed an approving smile. Spring was the Thornes' jewel. Multifaceted, beautiful, and full of life. And perhaps the favorite of all his nieces, although he'd never say as much to anyone else.

"What remains to be seen is what he wants us to do with it." Knox placed a hand on her knee and absently caressed it.

Alastair was positive he didn't know he did it.

Ever since the two of them had been reunited after Spring's resurrection by Isis, Knox had been unable to keep his hands off her. It was as if he needed to touch her to reassure himself she was safe and constantly within reach.

Alastair felt the same way about Aurora. After nearly two decades in stasis, she'd returned to him, and he worried he'd finally snapped. That he was living in a dreamworld and had conjured his love only in his broken mind. Rorie was always quick to hug or kiss him, assuring him she was real. But he knew she'd say that in his dream state, too.

Her hand touched his, and Alastair smiled. Their connection was strong, and she'd picked up on his worry without him ever needing to speak. He raised their joined hands and kissed her knuckles.

"I would imagine Set wants us to perform a swap of souls. Isolde's for Mackenzie's, but the when and how would need to be determined," Rorie said. She arched a brow and met Alastair's gaze. "Am I wrong, darling?"

He grinned. "I'm sure you have the right of it, my love."

He glanced around the room, cataloging the reactions of everyone. Ryker sat on the arm of the sofa, rubbing his wife's shoulders. Spring and Knox sat beside GiGi, the couple practically fused at the hip. Their gazes connecting in some unspoken communication. Damian had yet to speak, and Sebastian was pacing a hole in his expensive Safavid silk Persian carpet.

Alastair's gaze shifted to the Drakes' butler, Leopold, as the old retainer set about pouring tea for their small gathering.

Leopold's rheumy sapphire eyes flitted to him and down again.

Alastair almost laughed the second he recognized the man. His gaze zeroed in on Damian, and they shared a knowing glance. The wily, old buzzard's presence might be a good thing. The Aether understood the fact, too.

"What has you so amused, darling?" Rorie asked, accepting a cup of tea from the Drakes' manservant.

"Life."

Her eyes cut sideways, and although her dark brows shot up, she held off commenting. She knew he'd tell her in good time, but she wasn't necessarily happy about it. When his empathic ability picked up on her pique, Alastair bit the inside of his cheek to curb his urge to laugh.

"So, *Leopold*, is it?" The manservant's eyes narrowed, and he gave a slight nod in the face of Alastair's wicked delight. "Tell me, *Leopold*, how long have you been *employed* here at the Drake estate?"

Alastair didn't need to look around to know all eyes were on him and the butler.

"I couldn't say, sir."

"Couldn't? As in you're sworn to secrecy, or is it that you've been here so long, you don't remember?"

"Why all the questions, Thorne?" Sebastian stopped pacing. His expression reflected confusion. "What are you about?"

Alastair waved him off, his gaze still locked with that of Leopold. "I'm simply interested in people, Drake. No need to get your knickers in a wad."

Spring giggled, and Damian coughed into his hand.

"Leopold, be a dear and fetch me some brandy, won't you, my good man?"

The butler tugged at his cuffs and straightened his tie. "Of course, *sir*. Right away."

"On second thought, I'll get it myself. I realize with your age, getting around must be a bit more difficult these days."

"I'll give you difficult," Leopold muttered for Alastair's ears alone.

Biting back a laugh, Alastair rose and slapped a hand on the other man's back. He leaned in to whisper, "Nice disguise. Soon, we need to discuss how you came to be here and why you didn't tell me."

Because Sebastian had shifted closer, Leopold remained silent on the subject, instead saying, "If that will be all, I'll bring refreshments to Lady Kilbride."

"Thank you, Leopold," Sebastian said. "Please tell Mack I'll be up momentarily to see how she's fairing."

"Yes, sir."

As the butler put on an act of shuffling to the door, Alastair watched his progress. Right before he exited, Leopold glanced back, met his gaze, and winked.

AFTER HE CLOSED THE DOOR, LEOPOLD DID AWAY WITH HIS OLD-MAN act and sprinted into the next room.

"He recognized me."

Teddie grimaced as she put aside her book and wineglass to stand. "What did he say?"

"Nothing yet. Basically, he taunted me regarding my age. The nerve of that beastly boy!"

"Don't work yourself up, dearest. If he's recognized you, Alastair is simply being his mischievous self." Teddie waved a hand and transitioned back into her standard beautiful body, dispensing with the batty spinster-aunt disguise.

Leopold smiled his appreciation even as he morphed back into the lean, muscled form he'd maintained throughout the years. He drew her close and tucked a lock of silver-blonde hair behind her delicate ear. "We only have a moment or two because I have to check on Mackenzie, but let's make the most of them, love."

ENCHANTED MAGIC

MACKENZIE IMPATIENTLY TAPPED HER FINGERS AGAINST THE WOOD surface of the desk as Arabella perused her family grimoire. "What are you looking for, Bella?"

"I'll know when I find it."

"Don't believe for one second I don't know this was a ruse to get me away from the others for them to discuss what's happening with Isolde."

Arabella smirked and turned another page. "Then I suppose you should simply be patient."

Mackenzie blew out a frustrated breath and rose to explore the room for the second time. She was drawn to the far back wall, but she couldn't figure out why. As she studied it, she wondered if this old place had secret passageways like other English estates she'd read about.

"What's behind here?"

Arabella's head came up, and she frowned. "Nothing. Why?"

"I feel... I don't know... something. Have you ever explored?"

"Of course. I know our home inside and out."

Mackenzie ran her hand along the wall, feeling the pulse of magic behind it. "Are you sure there's nothing here?"

"Yes."

The yellow light she'd previously followed to find this room started as a barely discernible glow and flared brighter as she moved toward the west-facing window. "Bella. There's something here."

Arabella joined her and stared at the corner of the room. Confusion and worry were plain on her countenance. "Mack, I don't see a thing."

Mackenzie could either argue the point or revisit this room later, when no one was around. Because she didn't want to give Arabella heart failure by tearing down a wall in her home, she decided to come back.

Facing Sebastian's sister, she pasted on a bright smile. "Do you suppose they are done with their war meeting by now?"

Before Arabella could answer, Leopold appeared in the doorway.

His thinning hair was rumpled, and his tie was askew. Again, one sock drooped down around his painfully skinny ankle.

"Lady Kilbride, Lord Kilbride wished me to bring you refreshments and tell you he'd join you shortly."

Rushing across the room, Mackenzie took the heavy tray from the elderly butler. "Let me, Leo. You should come in and take a load off. I suspect you've worn yourself out with Teddie."

His blue eyes lit with humor. "She's a wily minx and keeps me on my toes, m'lady."

Arabella slapped her hands over her ears and began humming, and Mackenzie bit her lip to hold back her laughter as she set the refreshment tray on the desk.

"Leo, when I grow up, I want to live my best life—like you."

His deep chuckle triggered a distant memory, but for the life of her, she couldn't recall where she'd heard the familiar sound. "Enjoy your tea, m'lady."

"You don't need any of that m'lady stuff. I'm just Mack."

"Well, Just Mack, enjoy your tea. You'll find your favorite biscuits have been added to the tray."

She couldn't prevent her wide grin. "You made me chocolate, chocolate chip cookies? Goddess, I adore you, Leo! Never retire, okay?"

His amused expression faded by slow degrees as he crossed to where she stood. "One day, I won't have a choice. My duty to the family will be finished."

Unsure whether it was due to his somber mood or a faint premonition about what was to come, Mackenzie shivered. Sadness flooded her heart as she stared up into the craggy face of the man she'd come to adore. When his rheumy sapphire eyes locked with hers, she wanted to cry, to throw herself into his arms and hold on for dear life. Exactly why, she couldn't say, but a sense of importance filled this moment.

"I'll miss you if you leave," she whispered. "You brighten my days."

His smile started small and grew to encompass half his face. "As you brighten mine, my dear."

He let down his guard enough to tug a lock of her hair. "You remind me of your great-great-grandmother. A pure ray of sunshine, she was."

"You knew them? Nathanial and Evie?" She'd always heard they'd settled in America. Somewhere in the Baton Rouge area before they moved to Leiper's Fork, Tennessee. "How? They disappeared around the Witch Wars, didn't they?"

He pressed his lips together and looked out toward the garden. "I can't recall." Leopold shook his head as if to clear his confusion. "No matter, m'lady. I'm sure it will come back to me in due time." He avoided her gaze and shuffled back toward the door.

Arabella joined her by the desk and stared after his departing back. "That was the oddest thing I've ever heard him say."

"Really?" Mackenzie looked at her. "What was he like when you and Baz were small children? Was Leopold more forthcoming?"

"No. Indulgent perhaps. He laughed at our antics, but he always remained reserved." Arabella gave her a curious glance as she picked up the teapot to pour. "Not like he is with you, though. I've never seen him touch another person."

"Not even your Aunt Teddie?" Mackenzie teased.

Arabella laughed as she prepared their drinks. "No. Those two think they are being clandestine, but the reality is, we all know what is going on behind closed doors."

"You're okay with Teddie's and Leo's affair?"

Arabella acted out gagging, and mock shuddered. "I don't care to think about them at all. It's too disturbing for my peace of mind."

"Now you sound like Baz," Mack said with a laugh.

"Well, my brother and I agree on a great many things. Like how wonderful you are for our family."

Because she didn't feel the same way, and because she felt like she was detrimental to the Drake family's well-being, Mackenzie remained quiet as she picked up a cookie and studied it. She broke it in half to test the consistency before popping it into her mouth. The rich taste of dark chocolate filled her mouth as the semi-sweet morsels followed on its heels. Her tongue lapped up a stray crumb from her lip. "Goddess, this is amazing. I guess Leopold prepares something properly."

Arabella picked a cookie for herself. "I have to admit, since you've been here, everything is actually edible. Why do you suppose that is? Are you sneaking down to the kitchens to prepare our meals?"

"It's my charm. I think Leo is trying to impress me."

"Don't let Aunt Teddie hear you."

CHAPTER 17

Dinner was a major strain on Mackenzie's nerves. It seemed everyone was putting on an act of forced cheer, and she absolutely hated it. Part of her wanted to call them out on their weird behavior, but she understood they were trying to make everything as normal as possible. Trying to watch every word to avoid a slip of the tongue that could reveal what they'd discussed when she was banished from their earlier meeting.

She sipped her wine, appetite gone.

"Are you all right, child?"

Mackenzie glanced to her right and noted Alastair's watchful expression. She shrugged and took another sip.

"Mackenzie."

The deep understanding and affection he felt for her were packed into that one name. A sob caught in the back of her throat, and she had to question why she'd felt like crying more in the last week than she ever had in her entire life combined. "I'm fine, cousin," she choked out.

"No, you're not."

The sound of his chair scooting back forced her eyes open. As she watched, he tossed down his napkin and strode to her side of the table. "Come."

The rest of the room's occupants grew silent, and she cast a quick glance around her. Goddess, she hated being the center of attention. Wasn't it odd how much she, one of the world's most popular supermodels, hated to be in the spotlight?

Slowly, she set aside her wine and removed the garnet-colored napkin from her lap. "It's okay, Alastair. You don't need to—"

He cut her off by clasping her hand. "Your stubbornness is one of the things I admire most about you, child. But not right at this moment. *Come.*"

He led her out the double doors to the stone terrace. With a simple wave of his hand, the lanterns around them lit, illuminating the beautiful gardens around them and creating an inviting space. They crossed the expanse of the patio and descended the many steps leading to the grass.

"What are we doing, cousin? If you wanted to talk to me, there was no reason you couldn't have in the dining room."

"I don't want to talk. I'm here to listen, should you wish to, and to show you how to recharge your batteries, so to speak."

"I already practice meditation," she argued.

Stopping short, he faced her. One of his dark-blond brows lifted nearly to his hairline. "Are you determined to resist the entire time?"

His arrogance made her laugh. It always had. "No, I suppose not. Lead on."

His unsmiling mouth twitched, as if he too wanted to laugh. He lingered another moment, brow still firmly in place in that arched, haughty way of his.

Mack laughed a second time and linked her arm through his.

Scenes of the past crowded her mind, and she gasped at the ones that took place yards from where she stood.

The first was of Isolde using her magic to scribble a note. "Deliver yourself to Alastair Thorne," she'd said. The next was of the Enchantress hugging a small black-haired boy. She'd made him promise to hide and not come out for anyone but Alastair. The last was of Isolde in the garden. A malicious grin flitted across her face as she spun to face the small group of witches gathered to confront her. All her attention was focused on the blond man who stood front and center, prepared to do battle.

"Alastair Thorne?" Isolde asked curiously.

He shot a quick look at the older warlock next to him. "Nathanial Thorne."

"You'll not set your sights on my son," the auburn-haired man beside him snapped.

She laughed, and the wicked sound echoed off the trees, lending a macabre air to the scene.

The witches present shared uneasy glances and shifted closer to one another.

Gliding forward, one hip-swaying step at a time, Isolde kept her gaze locked on Nathanial Thorne. "You're incredible. All fierce and proud. Your magic..." She closed her eyes and inhaled. "Your magic is divine." Her eyes snapped open. "Come to me, Nathanial," she ordered. "I want to taste you, lover."

"Shit!" Nathanial shook his head and jerked backward, his fingertips pressed to one brow. "Evie."

Isolde closed her eyes and smiled. The smugness of her expression plain for everyone to see. "She's lovely. I've never seen anyone with her hair color before. So silver as to be white," she said, taking another step toward him and lifting her hand to beckon him forward. "If you join me now, I shall spare her life."

He turned gray, but he stood his ground.

The boy appeared from a rift in the fabric of space between his mother and Nathanial. He rushed toward the man, stopping short of touching him.

Nathanial's father conjured a flaming ball of energy and aimed for the boy.

"Noooooo!" Isolde screamed. Her body jerked, and she started forward, but halted when Nathanial caught his father's arm.

"We don't make war on children, Father. You taught me that."

"He's her son, Nate. He'll grow to be evil like her. Did you forget what she did to your brother Jonah?"

Nathanial's cold-eyed stare collided with his father's. "He's a boy, now under my protection. You'll not harm him."

"Mackenzie! Snap out of it!" Rough hands shook her. "Mackenzie, right now!"

The past disappeared in the blink of an eye.

Alastair's expression was fierce, as if he were prepared to fight all the demons in hell to bring her back to the present.

She raised a trembling hand to her forehead and nodded. "I'm good. I'm here."

"What the hell happened?" He still hadn't let her go, and she was grateful for the support since her knees felt as shaky as the rest of her.

"I don't know. Once I touched your arm, it was like I was teleported back to the confrontation between Isolde and Nathanial."

"Nathanial?"

His sharp tone brought her head up.

"Yes." She rubbed her arms against the chill of her vision and the cool night air. Closing her eyes, she envisioned heat forming and spreading to each of her cells.

"Better?" Alastair asked.

"Yes." Inhaling a deep, calming breath, she met his probing gaze. "There's a connection. To you, I think. Why did she deliver the letter to you? You weren't born for another hundred and twenty-five years or more, right?"

"I think, like you, she had psychic visions. It may well be why you both are linked together." He straightened the cuffs of his dinner jacket, the dark look never leaving his face. Mackenzie had come to realize this was his deep-in-thought expression, as she liked to call it. For most people, it was off-putting. However, she understood he was working through a problem.

"Why do you suppose the replay of that incident came to me now, Alastair?" she asked softly. Falling into step beside him, she tried to reason the importance of the past she'd just witnessed. "They weren't her memories. Nor were they Nathanial's. It was as if I saw everything from an outside perspective."

"I don't understand what you're getting at."

She halted and plucked at his sleeve, careful to release him as quickly as she'd touched him. "If Isolde was in my head and those visions came to me, I'd have her thoughts and feelings to lend them more detail." She frowned down at her feet, trying to find the right words to explain. "This was as if I were watching a movie. I didn't know all the players, but she would've."

"Ah. So you believe someone else—say Isis or Set—fed you that vision when you touched me."

"Exactly."

He nodded slowly, his expression turning thoughtful. "Obviously, if either of them is providing you information, there's an importance related to it. Something took place that you can use."

"That's how I see it, too." She liked she wasn't alone in her thinking. It helped her to believe Alastair understood there was something deeper at play here.

"Come on."

"Where are we going?"

"To the place I was originally going to show you."

With a small shake of her head, she allowed him to lead her. A short while later, they arrived at a small stream.

"What's this?"

He only smiled and bent to remove his shoes and socks.

She followed suit, kicking off her heels and rolling up the flowing material of her pants legs.

With a hand on her elbow to support her, he guided her up onto a small boulder overhanging the stream. The snap of his fingers next to her sounded loud. She didn't have a chance to comment before the night sky around them was lit with hundreds of fireflies. It lent a wondrous glow to the water, and as the fireflies danced and played, the surface of the stream caught their light and made this hidden paradise magical.

"I love it." Truly, she was awed by the beauty. "When I think you can't surprise me, you do."

"I'll take that as a compliment," he said with a deep chuckle.

"Alastair?"

"Yes, child?"

"Thank you."

As he turned his head, the wind picked up and a lock of his hair fell over one brow. Mackenzie could see the young, dashing man he'd once been. Long before the wars, long before responsibility, Alastair Thorne would've been a charming rogue, collecting hearts as he made his way through life.

Their gazes locked. In his, she saw deep affection.

"For what?" he asked.

She shrugged, leaned sideways, and put her head on his rounded shoulder. "For always being there for me. For always making sure I was provided for and encouraging me to chase my dreams. You're the father I never had, and I love you."

He rested his cheek against the top of her head. His voice was gruff when he replied, "You're welcome, Mack. I couldn't be prouder of you if you were my own daughter." He wrapped his arm around her and gently squeezed. "I love you, too, dear girl. And I'll be here to see you through this."

"I'm scared. For Baz. For you and the others."

He remained quiet for a long time in the wake of her confession. "I think you and Sebastian Drake are the perfect match."

Mackenzie snorted and raised her head. "That's what you say when I tell you I'm afraid?"

His chuckle triggered her smile. Remaining serious in the face of Alastair's wry humor was impossible.

"You, Mackenzie Ann Thorne, are a woman to be feared. You're not the one who should ever be afraid."

"How do you figure?"

"You're highly intelligent, you are quick on your feet, and you have the ability to charm the stars from the sky. You're also a force to be reckoned with when you're protecting your own." He made a scooping gesture with his hand, and the water crested, rising up to fill his palm. With a flick of his wrist, he splashed her.

She shrieked when the cold water hit her face.

Alastair teleported a safe distance away and scooped up his shoes. "I look forward to your devious revenge."

The air crackled, and he was gone.

Mackenzie laughed and kicked her feet in the water. The fireflies dipped low and surfed the breeze she created, circling around her.

SEBASTIAN STOOD IN THE SHADOWS OF THE TREES AND WATCHED HIS wife play. When she threw back her head and her lovely laughter rang out, her enchantment over him was complete. To him, she was a faerie princess in the mortal world. Mackenzie Thorne's magic was her beautiful spirit. The rest was just packaging. He couldn't deny he appreciated the hell out of her body, but her soul was pure. Her love for those around her was fierce. She was everything he could ever want.

The only thing hanging over their heads was Isolde.

But for tonight, he didn't intend to let her win.

Sebastian closed the distance between Mackenzie and him. "Can anyone join, or is this a party for one?"

She grinned and held out a hand. "I wondered when you'd show up. I was worried I'd have to send you an engraved invitation or something."

"I'm never far behind you, love." He crowded next to her and placed an arm around her shoulders.

When she turned her face up to his, her eyes held the promise of a love so great, it made his heart stall and his lungs seize. Any words would've been wasted at this moment. The driving desire inside him was to kiss her. Touch her. Worship her body in every way. He lowered his head, and she shifted to meet him halfway.

CHAPTER 18

Mackenzie wasn't sure what woke her, but she didn't immediately get out of bed. Instead, she stilled and held her breath, listening. No sound, no lurking figure, nothing but a faint yellow illumination. The line of light crawled across the floor and up the far wall, beside the hearth. About halfway up, it stopped where it met the chair molding.

With a quick look at Sebastian, who was lost to dreamland, she eased back the covers and grabbed her robe from the ottoman at the foot of the bed. As she got closer to the wall, the yellow light pulsed and became brighter.

Hesitating, she glanced back at the bed and wondered if she should wake Sebastian. Her adventurous nature could potentially be a problem if it wasn't a pot of gold at the end of this mysterious trail. Also, with the Enchantress prone to hijack her body whenever she was so inclined, Mackenzie wasn't sure she shouldn't have a babysitter. She was independent, not stupid.

"Find the book, and all will be well."

She shivered. Goddess preserve her. When this was all said and done, she'd be lucky to get out of it with her sanity intact. How was it she could see trails no one else did? It didn't bode well regardless of the encouraging voice in her head. The true question was whether the entity prodding her into action was the Goddess or the Enchantress. She wasn't sure she could trust either at this point.

Still, the light was inviting, and Mackenzie found it difficult to resist. She ran her hands along the molding lit by the golden glow, feeling for a hidden latch or anything out of the ordinary. A small indentation caught her fingernail, and she paused to examine the spot a little closer. Silently cursing under her breath, she crept back for her phone.

As her hand closed over the device, Sebastian's husky voice surprised her. "What are you doing, love?"

The cellphone fell from her hand, and she slapped a palm over her mouth in an effort to muffle her surprised scream. Crap on a cracker, she was jumpy!

His low laughter woke the butterflies in her belly. How the hell he sounded amused and sexy at the same time was beyond her.

"You scared the crap outta me, Baz! Goddess! Are you trying to give me a heart attack?"

He sat up, and the sheet fell to his waist, stopping at his happy trail. Those divine abs of his caught and held her attention. Her pulse began to pound in her ears for a whole different reason, and she had a very real fear drool was pooling in the corners of her mouth.

"Mack?"

"What?"

"Eyes up here, love."

With reluctance, she met his twinkling gaze. "Right. What was the question?"

Again, he laughed. "You were sneaking around, feeling up the wall. I was getting jealous of the attention you were paying it."

"Uh huh." Her lips twitched, and she dropped to her hands and knees to search under the bed for her phone. "There's a secret passage by the fireplace. I need my phone's flashlight to see what I'm doing."

"Why not use your magic?" He yawned and stretched. Her words finally penetrated his sleep fog, because he went on full alert and swung his legs over the edge of the bed. "Wait! What? A passage?"

Before she could explain, Sebastian was across the room. He snapped his fingers and illuminated the entire room.

Mackenzie took a full minute to admire his bare backside and legit wiped her mouth with the sleeve of her robe to rid herself of the excess moisture pooling there. The man's ass was beautiful—as were those sculpted, muscular thighs. Now that she'd had a glimpse under the kilt, she would bask in her good luck and give thanks to the Fates every day. The first chance she got, she'd kiss Isis's robe for pairing them up, because surely only a goddess would've blessed Mackenzie this way.

"What are you doing, Mack? Come on."

Apparently, as she sat on the floor, ogling his body, Sebastian had found and triggered the lock mechanism for the secret door. It separated from the wall with a flare of red light.

"It was magically sealed so no one could find it?" she asked as she joined him to peer inside the opening.

"It appears so. I never knew it was here."

"Huh." She cast him a wary glance and gnawed on her thumbnail. "Is it smart for us to enter? Like did we just unleash some terrible curse or something?"

Sebastian grinned as he waved his hands down his body.

Mackenzie sighed to see all that gorgeousness covered up.

He cupped her neck and nuzzled the spot just below her left ear. "If you don't stop looking at me like that, I'm dragging you back to bed."

"It might be a better option than walking into a Hellmouth," she muttered, turning her face to seek his lips.

Before she could connect, he pulled back and frowned down at her. *"Hellmouth?"*

"Well, apparently you've never watched horror films."

He didn't bother trying to hide his amusement. "Hellmouth. Right. You may want to put on some sensible shoes so we can explore."

"I was afraid you were going to say that."

"Weren't you going to go on your own before I woke up?"

"Yes and no."

His brows shot up.

Mackenzie shrugged. "Yes, I was going to explore the opening, but no, I doubt I would've gone into the passageway alone."

His thumb caressed the sensitive column of her throat. "I'm fortunate I married such an intelligent woman." His eyes dropped to her lips. "And such a sexy one."

"Are you buttering me up to go into the Hellmouth first?"

"Is it working?"

She laughed and shook her head. "I can see chivalry is dead."

"I'd have to exchange my jockstrap for a purse if I let you venture into the Hellmouth first."

"You don't even know what a jockstrap is, let alone own one. Don't forget, I now know what's under that kilt, darling." Mackenzie stretched up on the tips of her toes to kiss him. "But it was a nice save."

Sebastian captured her mouth in a longer, more drugging kiss. He pulled back with a wide, satisfied smile and lightly swatted her butt as she struggled to overcome her sexual haze. "Shoes."

ALL TEASING ASIDE, SEBASTIAN WASN'T THRILLED TO EXPLORE THE passageway at this point in time. Two weeks ago, before the Enchantress reared her nasty head, yes, he'd have been eager. Now, it felt as if there was a menacing air surrounding the opening.

As Mackenzie scrounged for her phone and changed, Sebastian contemplated what it had taken to open the door. She'd somehow known there was a passage, but it had taken him to open it. Was it only intended for a Drake?

"Mack."

She lifted her head from wiping off her device's screen. "You sound thoughtful. Maybe even worried. What's up?"

"I think I should go in alone."

"Nope."

He looked at the opening and back to her. "You weren't able to open it. I was, with only a single touch."

"So you think I'm not supposed to go in?"

Once again, he studied the opening. With a shrug, he faced her. "I don't know what to think. Tell me, how did you know it was there?"

"The yellow light."

"Like the one that led you to our hidden ceremony room?"

"Yes." She chewed on the corner of her lip as if she wanted to say more.

"You might as well tell me, love."

Mackenzie waved her arms, and twinkling lights encompassed her. When they faded, she was clothed in jeans, a hoodie, and trainers, with her hair in a ponytail. In other words, she was dressed for exploring.

Sebastian sighed. "Okay, we can do this together, but I want to know what led you to the wall first."

"Nothing really. Something woke me—what, I can't say—and there was a yellow trail from our bed to the wall. As I watched, it climbed to the molding and stopped."

"That's not all, Mack. I can tell by the way you're avoiding looking at me."

She heaved out a sigh. "I may have heard a voice in my head."

He went cold. "Isolde's?"

"I don't think so, but I can't be sure."

"What did it say?"

"'Find the book, and all will be well.'"

Sebastian swore under his breath. "As if that's not ominous."

"You asked."

"And you didn't care to volunteer this information prior to me opening the Hellmouth?!" He realized he was shouting, but his concern was pressing.

With a suddenness that surprised him, she busted out laughing.

"What's so bloody funny, Mackenzie?"

"You!" She wiped her tears of mirth as she continued to giggle. "Your use of 'Hellmouth' when you're pissed, to be exact."

Coming to a decision, he pointed at her. "You're not going. You're staying here, and I'm going to wake Spring to watch over you."

"First, I am going, and second, it's the middle of the night. We shouldn't wake anyone." She placed her hands on her hips and returned his glare. "It's rude."

"Then we leave the exploration of this passage for the morning."

They had a stare off. Finally, Mackenzie caved. "Fine. I'll wake Spring and Knox to tell them where we're going. But I *am* going."

"This is the worst fucking idea ever." But he was still going to do it. He couldn't dismiss the chance that one of his ancestors—or possibly the Goddess—was responsible for leading them to this hidden entry. If there was a tool they could use to keep Isolde contained, they needed to find it.

Mackenzie smiled.

The beauty of her happiness froze him in place. He'd seen so many different emotions on her expressive face in the short time he'd known her, and yet, every time she smiled, it floored him. Her glow was a sight to behold, and the mischievousness in her blue eyes was captivating.

"Hurry, love," he ordered gruffly. "Who knows if this door is on a magical timer."

"Be right back."

After she dashed away, he crossed to the bed and quickly tidied up. Opening the nightstand drawer, he pulled out a wicked-looking blade and tucked it in the waistband of his jeans. Not that he expected any trouble that magic couldn't handle, but it was always better to be prepared.

Conjuring a flashlight, he leaned into the opening and looked around. Wooden stairs led down a narrow hallway flanked by wood-slat walls. No handrails.

Lovely.

"Hello?"

Only the sound of his voice echoed back. He didn't know what he'd expected, but he'd probably shite himself something proper if anyone called back.

An idea struck, and he removed an autographed cricket ball from its protective plastic case where it rested on his dresser. He sent a quick apology to James Anderson, England's premier cricket player, and with a quick charm to protect the integrity of his prized ball, Sebastian hurled it into the void of the passage. He leaned forward and thought he heard it bang into something once, but then nothing.

Another thirty seconds went by with no noise. Surely if something was down there, he'd have heard the impact? With a shrug and a mental note to look for the ball when he went exploring, he turned away from the opening.

He was decidedly unprepared for the fierce blow to his back that sent him flying toward the heavy bedroom door. Throwing up a hand to protect his face, he hit the wood hard enough to slam it shut. Spinning back, prepared for a fight, Sebastian gaped in shock when he saw the cricket ball resting on the floor at his feet.

"Bloody hell!"

How the damned thing had returned to him was a mystery—one he wasn't looking forward to solving. Leery of touching it, he stared at the ball and weighed his options. When the bedroom door was flung open, he jumped sideways. For a man who had spent the entirety of his life on this estate without incident, his new nervousness was laughable.

Knox Carlyle filled the doorway, surveying the room as if looking for enemies. His shrewd azure gaze landed on Sebastian, and he grunted. "Seems safe enough. Come in."

Spring shoved by her husband with an eye roll, followed by a smirking Mackenzie. The latter looked as if she thought this whole incident was a lark.

"Knox and Spring insisted on going with us, Baz. I hope you don't mind."

"Why should I mind? Why don't we make this a real party and invite Alastair, Aurora, Ryker, and GiGi?"

"Not the worst idea you've had, Drake."

All four of them turned to face the blond man in the doorway. Alastair tugged on the cuff of each shirt sleeve and grinned. "I hear there's adventure to be had."

"Who told you that?" Sebastian cast a sharp glance at Mackenzie.

"Not your wife, if that's what you suspect." Alastair laughed and shot a curious glance around the room. Although it was made, his eyes touched on the bed, and a knowing smile lingered on his lips. He winked at Mackenzie, whose face flared bright. Leaning in, he whispered something to make her laugh.

When her dancing eyes locked on Sebastian, his irritation with Alastair eased. He couldn't be angry with anyone who made Mackenzie happy. Even if the joke was at his expense.

"Ready for our adventure, love?"

"Yes. You?"

He glanced at the other three occupants of their room. If he were pressed on the subject, he'd admit he was happier they were going, too. "Let's do this."

CHAPTER 19

The stairs were surprisingly sturdy. Not one of them creaked under the weight as their group descended. It seemed to Sebastian the passageway went for miles. There were three other interconnecting hallways, but they chose to ignore them for now, relying on Mackenzie's instincts and the "yellow light" to guide them downward. Around the time they'd come to the first offshoot, she said the trail had appeared to her.

"How much farther, do you suppose?" Spring asked.

Mackenzie snorted. "I don't think you have to whisper, cousin. It's doubtful anyone upstairs can hear us at this level."

"Valid point," Knox said. His harsh grunt followed. "What? I was simply agreeing with Mack that we are too far below stairs to be heard."

"Quit your bickering, children." Alastair's dry tone held a bit of an edge.

Sebastian registered the underlying emotion but didn't look back. It appeared his weren't the only raw nerves. It was good to know the Mighty Alastair Thorne was subject to unease now and again. He had to admit he'd never met anyone as unflappable as the Thorne patriarch. The man had ice in his veins.

"Shhh. Wait." Mackenzie ordered, tugging Sebastian to a halt and holding up a hand to the others. They all froze. "Can you hear that?"

"What?" Knox asked.

"Running water," Spring answered. "I think this passage opens to an underground cavern. There's a vibration from the earth... I feel... *something*." She shook her head. "I don't know for sure, but it's similar to the clearing between our home and the Carlyles'. It's putting off a signal like that of the Standing Stones."

"Ancient magic." Alastair glanced back over his shoulder before addressing their group. "If you had to guess, child, how much farther?"

Spring closed her eyes and held up her hands. The tremble of the ground was so slight, had Sebastian not known she was sending out a magical feeler, he'd have ignored it as his imagination. Still, the mini-earthquake made him acutely aware of a claustrophobia he didn't know he suffered from.

"Perhaps we should return," he suggested.

"Around that bend, we'll hit solid ground." Spring released Knox's hand and pushed her way past Sebastian and Mackenzie. "Come on."

Knox rushed forward, swearing as she disappeared around the corner. When Sebastian and Mackenzie would've gone after them, Alastair held them back.

"What's wrong, Thorne?"

"Spring's right. The pull of the magic is extremely strong. I'm surprised you can't feel it, Drake." Alastair frowned and rubbed a hand along the back of his neck. "It's been cloaked from your family for some time, which is concerning to the extreme. Why would someone build over such a power source unless they were drawing from it?"

"And how is it my aunts never mentioned it?" Sebastian experienced a sense of foreboding. "Mack, I think you should go back."

"Nonsense." She ripped her hand from his and scowled. "I'm the one it showed itself to."

"Exactly. The question is, why? And why now?" He shook his

head, mainly because he had no answers. "I don't know how to explain it, love, but I feel it's trying to lure you. Right now, we can't risk it."

"What about the book? Do you think it may be there?"

"What book?" Alastair's gaze sharpened to match his tone.

"Mackenzie heard a voice earlier when she saw the yellow light illuminating the passage location. It told her to find the book and all will be well."

The blast of Alastair's anger was like a hard shove to the chest. Sebastian staggered back a foot or so at the same time Mackenzie grabbed for the wall.

"What the bloody blue blazes were you thinking?" Alastair demanded. He faced Mackenzie, his narrowed eyes advertising his ire. "That voice could very well be the Enchantress hoping to guide you to her spellbook. With her grimoire, you—possessed by her—would be nearly unstoppable, even for Damian."

"It didn't sound like her." Mackenzie cut her eyes toward the direction Spring and Knox had gone. "I didn't see anything when I touched the wall. Not good or bad. Surely, I would've had a premonition of sorts."

"Would you?" Alastair ran a hand through his hair, and the sight of it concerned Sebastian as nothing else the older man had done or said yet. Alastair was well and truly upset, which meant he was scared. When a warlock with that much power showed fear, it meant whatever they were up against should make a normal witch run for cover. "Mackenzie, I don't think you understand the severity of this situation."

"I'm not naive, Alastair," she retorted. "I think I know more than anyone there is a problem. It's my body that twatwaffle has been trying to possess."

There wasn't really anything to say in response. She was right; she stood to lose the most. The rest of them had a chance of escaping. Yes, it was slim, but still there. She didn't have that option. If Isolde gained total control, then Mackenzie was as good as dead.

Sebastian rubbed the spot between his brows. He met Alastair's worried gaze then shifted his attention to his wife. She stood, hands on hips, glaring at her cousin.

"You've earned the right to see what's down there, Mack. Let's go." Sebastian held out his hand. "Whatever we discover, we handle it together."

Gratitude welled in her large eyes, and the shimmering sight about broke his heart.

"Thank you, Baz."

"Don't thank me yet. I could very well have consigned us to the farthest depths of hell."

A half smile stole some of her solemness. "As long as you're with me, I'm cool with it."

He lifted a hand to cradle her face. "You say that now, but you can't come back after an eternity and yell at me. This was all your idea."

She laughed and glanced at Alastair. "You with us?"

"Of course. It isn't as if I wished to sleep tonight or anything."

"Oh, give over, you big teddy bear. I know you were on watch tonight."

Sebastian laughed. "She's onto us."

Alastair surprised them both when he inserted himself between them and gave her a fierce hug. "You're like my own daughter, Mackenzie. There will never be a time when I don't look out for you. Protect you." He pulled back and stared down into her face. "Kill for you, if I must."

"Dammit, Thorne! That was my line."

Alastair never looked at him, but his lips twitched. "She's like your own daughter?"

Heat rose up Sebastian's neck and into his cheeks. "Only you could twist my words, you wanker."

Turning to face him, Alastair winked. "Come on, son. Let's go see what those other two have gotten up to."

Mackenzie clasped Sebastian's hand again and gave it a soft squeeze.

"Thank you, Baz," she said softly.

Her earnest words wrapped around his heart and made him stand taller. *Goddess, he loved her.* With every minute of every day, he fell deeper under her spell. So much so, that he now feared life without her would be an endless wasteland of days and nights, waiting until the moment he could see her lovely face again. Hear her bubbly laughter.

"What's wrong?" Her voice held a note of trepidation.

"Nothing. In fact, everything is right, perhaps for the first time in my life."

"Now is not the time to declare your undying love, Drake," Alastair inserted. He nodded toward the far wall of the cavern. "Mackenzie's yellow beacon is back."

Mack gasped when she looked up and saw the glowing ball of yellow light, all intention of addressing Sebastian's possible love for her on hold. She hadn't realized she had a death grip on his hand until he reached down with his other one and loosened her hold.

"I may need those fingers, love."

"Oh!" She gave a half-hearted smile but never took her gaze off the magical sphere. "What do you suppose it is?" She took a step forward before it occurred to her to question how Alastair saw it. "How... you... how...?" She looked at Sebastian. "Do you see it, too?"

He squinted into the distance and shook his head.

"Alastair? How is it you can see the same thing I do?"

"I'm not sure. Maybe it's the same way Drake can't feel the magic. We must be more receptive to it."

Her stomach plummeted. In her experience, being receptive to powerful influences didn't bode well. "Do you suppose it *is* Isolde? She was a Thorne by blood, right? Maybe her magical things call to us as they did to her."

Spring popped her head around the corner. Excitement lit her face but changed to confusion as her attention was caught by the golden sphere. "What the hell is that?"

"I don't know if I feel better knowing she sees it or not," Mackenzie said in an aside to the others.

"Actually, I do." Alastair sauntered off, stopping in front of the glowing two-foot ball. With a curious expression, he lifted a hand and ran it along the outside, not quite touching. "The power emanating from this is incredible. It's almost like..." His bark of laughter shocked them all. They stared as if he'd lost his mind. "You can show yourself now, *Leopold.*"

"Leopold? What?" Air gushed from Mackenzie's lungs as the Drakes' butler took the place of the pulsing sphere. "Ohmygod!"

"Not quite," Alastair replied with an amused snort. He held out a hand to the elderly manservant. "Don't be shy, *Leopold,* old boy. Take my hand."

The butler straightened his tie and tugged at his cuffs. "I don't see where that would be appropriate, *sir.* I'm here to serve." With a simple wave of his hand, light flooded the darkened passageway.

"He's a Thorne!" Spring and Mackenzie blurted at the same time. Their eyes connected across the distance in their excitement, and as one, they rushed toward Leopold.

"Who are you?" Spring asked, practically bouncing on the balls of her feet. She paused only long enough to touch Alastair's arm. "Did you know about this, Uncle?" Waving a hand, she didn't give him time to answer. "Nevermind. Of course you did. How exciting!"

"Leo, have you been my guide all this time? The magic in the hallway leading to Sebastian's ceremony room, the beam of light on the wall showing me this passage... that was you, too?"

His lips twisted, and he relaxed his stiff persona. "Yes, my dear. All me."

"I don't understand. Why not just tell me?"

He cast a quick glance toward Sebastian. "You needed to overhear what your presence on the estate would bring. I wasn't certain the family would tell you, and I didn't feel you should be left in the dark concerning your own personal well-being."

"Okay, that I get. You thought I might not believe you if you told me directly. But this passageway?"

"Ah, well, yes. This leads to my private chambers. I had no idea you'd tell the entire household what you found." He grimaced. "I was relying on your curiosity and discretion."

"Discretion? Tell me you aren't interested in moving on from Aunt Teddie." Sebastian shuddered.

A wolfish grin transformed Leopold's face, and Mackenzie caught a glimpse of what he must've been like in his younger years. "No, my wife would hand me my bollocks on a silver platter."

"Wife?!" The loudness of Sebastian's, Spring's, and Mackenzie's shock rang out, echoing off the stone surface around them.

"What about Aunt Teddie?" Mackenzie sputtered, indignant on both women's behalf.

Leo's bark of laughter was loud and full-bodied, completely at odds with the skeletal old man's frame. "Teddie *is* my wife."

Only Alastair didn't appear surprised by any of Leopold's explanations.

"You knew, cousin?" Mackenzie put her hands on her hips and shifted her irate glare between the butler and him. "But that's not all, is it? Spill."

"I thought I was." Leopold's dry tone was so similar to Alastair's, Mack did a double-take.

"You aren't just a Thorne." She peered into the depths of the older man's sapphire eyes. They were no longer the rheumy ones she remembered from their previous interactions. "You're closely related to *him*." She pointed to Alastair.

Spring danced forward and studied both men. Her slow nod gaining more momentum. "Give over, Gramps. The gig is up."

When both Alastair and Leopold laughed, it was almost as if they were twins. Their bark of laughter was so eerily similar, Mackenzie shivered.

"Seriously, who *are* you?"

With a wry smile and a soft shake of his head, Leopold snapped his fingers. Twinkling gold light cloaked him for the five seconds it took him to transform into his true self.

Knox had joined them when he heard their earlier yell, and now his shocked exclamation played in stereo with theirs.

Alastair stepped forward and placed his arm around Leopold's shoulders. "Children, allow me to introduce my great-grandfather. Nathanial Thorne."

CHAPTER 20

They all began to speak at once, but Alastair held up his hand. "One at a time, children."

"You know, it makes us sound like we're squabbling five-year-olds when you call us children," Mackenzie grumbled.

"Duly noted." Alastair gave her an indulgent smile.

She gave him a sour look and compressed her lips to smother a grin. Turning to Nathanial, she studied him with a sense of awe.

He bore an uncanny resemblance to Alastair, with the exception he was a bit burlier than his descendant. But the deep blue eyes, the color of their hair, and even their sardonic expressions were all the same. Of course, Nathanial wore his hair a bit longer, and he didn't seem to be as elegant with his clothing choice, but that could be due to the fact he was dressed as a butler.

"Do we call you Grandfather?"

Nathanial's smile widened, and he opened his arms in invitation. "You, my dear Mackenzie, may call me whatever you wish."

She rushed into his embrace, shutting her eyes as his arms closed around her. "I felt a connection to you from the moment I saw you. I had to fight the urge to constantly hug you."

"A part of you recognized me. I imagine it was owing to your psychic ability." His arms tightened momentarily before releasing her. "And I've wanted to hug you as well. It's good to be able to meet you as myself, dear girl."

Emotions long suppressed crept up on her. She'd been rejected by her own father. Most likely the only deadbeat Thorne in existence. But Nathanial's love for her was clear in his every look. Every smile. "Your responsibility to our family is why you are here, isn't it?"

"To a large degree, yes."

"So, you've never been our true butler and Teddie really isn't my aunt?" Sebastian asked, wrapping an arm around Mackenzie's waist, as if he needed comfort, too. "It explains the godawful scones."

"All good fun, boy." Nathanial's sparkling eyes practically illuminated the cavern all on their own. "And you are correct; Teddie is no blood relation to you."

"Aunt Gwennie?"

"Is really your aunt. She's a formidable woman and insisted on helping us in our cause to keep the Enchantress entombed."

"What is Teddie's real name, Grandpa Nate?" Spring asked, her head tilted slightly and her face full of undisguised curiosity.

Their two-times-great-grandfather smiled his approval at her, giving her a quick hug in turn. "Teddie's true name is Evelyn. Evie to family and friends. She's been my one-and-only love throughout time."

Spring's beatific smile widened as if he'd confirmed some fact she already knew.

Mackenzie shook her head and patted his arm. Maybe she had to touch him to make this seem real, but it felt like she was in the midst of a bizarre dream. "How is it you're this old and still so healthy?"

"The Aether."

"I don't understand."

Alastair stepped forward, cutting off any reply. "How about we shelve this conversation for the moment? I believe this would be better over a brandy and sitting next to a blazing fire."

"You're getting weak, boy." Nathanial's expression was teasing, but he turned and led the way toward the sound of the running water. "Come. I have just the thing."

They followed him in silence, each of them most likely trying to process this revelation like Mackenzie was attempting to do. It wasn't until they were around the stone wall and passing by the iridescent aqua waters of a pool that she registered the beauty of the underground grotto.

"Holy hell! You had no idea this was here, Baz?"

"None." His tone was troubled, and she placed a hand on his arm, halting him.

"What's wrong?"

"I'm not fond of surprises, and we've had quite a few recently. I wonder how many more we're in for."

"Does it bother you Nathanial has been here in disguise the entire time?"

"Yes. No." He sighed and ran a hand over his face. "I don't know. Maybe."

"Want to talk about it?"

His attention was fixed on the others as they crossed the bridge over the shimmering pool. "I'm not sure how I feel at the moment. Confused, mostly." He turned his dark gaze on her and grimaced. "I suppose I should be happy there's a powerful warlock watching over us, but it almost feels like a betrayal of trust. Why not tell us before now?"

"Seems like Gwennie knew. She could've spoken up." Mackenzie wasn't trying to be difficult, but he had to see the responsibility wasn't only on Nathanial or Evie to reveal themselves. "There has to be a good reason they kept it quiet, don't you think?"

"Perhaps."

"You've every right to be upset, Baz. Essentially you were lied to your entire life. When you became laird of your little clan, you should've been made aware of the facts."

His expression softened as he cupped her cheek. "Thank you for understanding. Let's go have that drink. I don't want to miss the origin story."

ENCHANTED MAGIC

. . .

Sebastian was more disturbed by Nathanial's revelation than he cared to let on. The elderly butler had been a fixture in their home for as long as he could remember. As had his Aunt Teddie. Later, when he was alone, he'd examine his feelings on the matter and decide how to get past his sense of betrayal. The lies and subterfuge had to stop, though. Moving forward, they all had to be of one mind to defeat Isolde. If they weren't, the results could be catastrophic.

As they crossed the bridge to join the others, Mackenzie kept casting him worried glances, as if she sensed his underlying anger. Perhaps she did. His beautiful wife was in tune with most things. Maybe due to her abilities, maybe just because she cared, but either way, he appreciated her empathy.

He captured her hand and gave it a little squeeze. His way of assuring her he was fine for the moment. She returned the gesture. Her way of supporting him.

Before the dedication gala for Georgie Sipanil, Sebastian had only met Mackenzie a handful of times in passing. He'd been struck dumb by her loveliness, but she hadn't so much as cast a glance his way. Then, right when he was feeling his lowest about GiGi and Ryker's reunion, she showed up at Alastair's estate and served to remind him how much he'd desired her from the second they met. Since that day, she'd danced through his dreams, conjuring fantasies of the two of them locked in a passionate embrace.

Last night, as they made love, he recognized snippets from those previous dreams, making him wonder if they hadn't been fated from the start. To think, if he'd let down his guard before this weekend, they may have been together sooner. How much of his life had been lived from behind his reserved wall?

"You ready?"

Sebastian lifted his head at Mackenzie's softly spoken question. "Sorry. Woolgathering." He took a steadying breath. "Ready."

She smiled and would've turned had he not tugged on her hand and spun her back to face him.

"You're the best thing that's ever happened to me, Mack. I love you."

Happiness shone back at him from those incredible, expressive eyes of hers, and her smile widened. "I'm glad. I feel the exact same way about you, Baz." She gripped his shirt and tugged him forward until there was no space between them. Stretching up, she placed her lips on his.

Taking advantage of the moment, he kissed her. Theirs wasn't the savage, passionate kisses from mere hours before; instead it was one of love and promise. He wrapped his arms around her waist and lifted her until they were at the same level.

She ended their kiss, placed a palm on either side of his face, and locked gazes with him. "I can't see past this week, Baz, and it scares the life out of me. But never give up hope. I'll always find a way back to you."

His heart seized. Hers was a premonition of sorts—he could tell by the serious, sad quality in her eyes—and that glimmer of warning was all he needed to resolve to fight to the death to keep her with him. Whatever the cost, he'd pay it. A small shiver shook her body, and his arms tightened with his desire to ward off her demons. "And I you, love. Always."

She rested her forehead against his. "Thank you for loving me, Sebastian Drake. My time with you was all I ever imagined and more."

Moisture stung his eyes, and he struggled to hold back his tears. He, too, had felt the ache of loneliness in the past, as he somehow sensed she had. "It's absolutely my pleasure, Mackenzie Drake. Thank you for loving me."

She dropped a quick kiss on his lips and grinned. "We'll readdress pleasure when we get back to our room later."

"No doubt about it. I say we lock ourselves away and discover all the pleasure there is to be had."

Her hips pressed forward, and his eyes nearly rolled back in his head from the exquisite feel of her delectable body against his. He eased her to the ground, sliding her front down his as he touched her everywhere.

He buried his nose in the hollow of her throat and gave her a small love bite. "Want to skip this little party and return upstairs?"

"Hell. Yes!"

"Are you two coming?"

They both groaned when they looked up and saw Spring at the far end of the bridge with her hands on her hips.

"Apparently not anytime soon," Sebastian said in an aside to Mackenzie.

She laughed and threaded her arm through his. "Should I leave you here to cool off, darling?"

"No, I'll picture Leopold's, er, Nathanial's pickle socks. That should do the job nicely."

Sebastian didn't fail to notice Spring's knowing smirk as they met up with her.

"Based on my cousin's glowing face, I have a good idea what is now beneath that kilt of yours, Mr. Drake." Her laughing gaze bounced back and forth between Mack and him. "Knox definitely has to get one of those."

"I'll set him up with my tailor."

CHAPTER 21

*E*veryone remained quiet as Nathanial described the summons from his parents at the behest of Isis. He told them of his leaving his youngest siblings under Evie's care in America and returning with his brother Andrew to the battleground where the Six were to fight the Enchantress. Once there, he'd caught the attention of Isolde and probably would've been her next victim had Damian not shown up when he did.

"I brought Damian to Evie, so she could look after him as she'd volunteered to do for my siblings Chase and Lottie. It seemed I was gone only moments, but when I returned here to help, the devastation was complete." Deep sorrow was reflected back at them from his darkening eyes. "My father was killed with Isolde's first strike. Drew, in trying to protect him, was gravely injured."

Their group remained silent as Nathanial ran his hands up and down his face as if trying to wipe the memory away.

Mackenzie could almost see the scene in her mind, maybe it was a residual memory from when Isolde had possessed her, but it seemed as clear as the brightest day. Bodies lay strewn in the garden. Pillars were overturned, and small fires dotted the landscape around them. Isis looked the worse for wear, and Isolde knelt, bound by a thick chain. It pulsed a dark, glowing red, indicative of the deep magic used to hold her.

"How many were lost?" she asked in a low tone.

Nathanial sat down across from her, resting his elbows on his thighs and dangling his large hands between his knees. His haunted eyes gutted her.

With a light shrug belying the horror he'd witnessed, he said, "I never learned the true count, but it was great. Souls from the Otherworld were obliterated."

"What does that mean, obliterated?" Sebastian asked sharply. His fierce frown emphasized his worry. "As in no more? Can Isolde do that?"

"She can, and she did to feed her power." Nathanial looked from one to the other in their small group. "Obliterated, in this case, means no way of reincarnating. The energy of the soul is no more. Think of it like a nuclear-bomb explosion; it destroys everything within a certain radius. I found out later, the only ones who survived were protected by the Goddess's quick thinking."

Spring gasped and looked at Knox. Her husband's face grew pale as he returned her look. These two were true soulmates, and the import of a soul destroyed meant future lifetimes with an empty hole in place of their heart. No true love to guide them or make them stronger. No feeling whole. Ever.

Mackenzie reached for Sebastian's hand. "We can't let her be resurrected again. We can't."

"Don't even think it, Mack," he growled.

"Baz, if I'm the only pawn she has, I have to be removed from the board." She directed his attention to Spring and Knox. "Their souls have been entwined for thousands of years. One isn't whole without the other. Can you imagine having that torn away?"

Sebastian placed a hand on her jaw and directed her gaze back to him. "Yes, Mack, I can."

She pressed her lips into a tight line and swallowed her urge to rage at him. He was telling her he didn't want to be without her, but she couldn't risk her family being forever unhappy and alone. It came down to her happiness with Sebastian, or everyone else's as a casualty of her actions.

"It's no contest, Baz. I can't do this to them."

His eyes cooled, and he dropped his arm to his side. "Of course. I understand how tight the Thornes are."

"It's not like that."

"Isn't it?" His expression hardened. "I don't consider myself a selfish person, Mackenzie. I would never put my happiness above the others. But forgive me if I don't want to see my wife sacrifice her life due to a half-baked idea that may not work."

Frustrated with his stubbornness, she pulled away and crossed her arms. None of her family spoke, but they each looked at her with censure.

"What?" she snapped. "You all think we should take our chances? Did you not hear Grandpa Nate's account of the fight? Souls *obliterated*." Anger and restlessness drove her to her feet to pace. "Obliterated! Do you think I could live with myself if any of you were to die because I'm to be the key to that psycho bitch's prison? *Do you?*"

"Mackenzie." Alastair's understanding, love, and compassion were all rolled into her name.

She closed her eyes and swiped at the moisture on her cheeks. Until that moment, she hadn't realized she was crying. Fury at herself for giving into the useless emotion vibrated in her voice when she said, "I can't do this, cousin. I can't. I'm not strong enough."

"We're here to help you, sweet girl."

"You don't understand. None of you do. I'm strong enough here..." She pounded a fist against the center of her chest, indicating her heart. "But I'm not strong enough magically or mentally. She's weakened after a two-hundred-year slumber, and yet she's more powerful than I am. She's gotten in my head multiple times already."

Sebastian surged to his feet and wrapped her in his tight embrace. "We *will* win, Mack. We have something she doesn't: allies. People who love us. People determined to see she *doesn't* win."

She hugged him back for a brief moment, soaking up his

comfort, courage, and strength before jerking away. "But at what cost to our loved ones, Baz? Seeing Spring and Knox separated forever? Seeing your own sister die? Seeing my family cut in half?"

He had no argument, because deep down, he had to know she was right.

"I need a moment alone," she said.

Nathanial stood and caught her arm as she moved to pass him. "Mackenzie. Don't go far. Please."

She shot him a glare, furious to have her movements curtailed. "And why's that? Are you going to stand there and order me not to 'sacrifice' myself, too?"

"No, dear heart, I'm not. I think that should be a decision we make together, when the others are present, but I've noticed Isolde can sneak into your mind easier when you are in a highly emotional state. If you're alone and she gains control, there's no telling what she can do."

The wisdom of his words sank in. Mackenzie took a calming breath and focused on his hand on her forearm. With the exhale came visions of Nathanial's past: On the riverboat when he heard the news he'd been recalled home to battle the Enchantress. His goodbye to Evie. Young Damian, looking up at him with trust and all-seeing eyes. And finally his return to England, to the devastation Isolde had created. The last images were in line with what she'd imagined when he told the story, and it broke her heart to bear witness to the scene.

She met Nathanial's kind, understanding gaze. "I don't want to hurt anyone. Please don't let me." She lowered her voice for his ears alone. "Please, Grandpa Nate. Don't let her win. If you have to..." More tears rolled down her cheeks, and she angrily swiped them away. "If you have to, you know, promise me you will."

He kissed her forehead. "I promise, Mack. She won't use you to hurt our family. Not while I'm alive."

"Thank you."

"You're welcome, dear. Try to calm yourself now." He ran his thumbs under her eyes and smiled softly. "There's pictures over on the shelf that you may care to see. Pictures of the family. Of Alastair as a boy." He leaned in close. "I'm sure there's one of him with a gap-toothed grin and a dripping ice-cream cone that you can use it to poke fun of him later."

"I adore you."

Nathanial grinned. "What can I say? I'm exceedingly adorable."

She crossed over to the shelves as he turned back to the others, who had been talking quietly amongst themselves. The entire time she wandered and explored Nathanial's chambers, she felt Sebastian's sad gaze trailing her. Deep within her, she knew he viewed her potential actions as giving up on them as a couple. But she needed to find a way to show him any steps she took to stop the Enchantress were meant to keep his family safe, as well as hers.

"Grandpa Nate?"

Nathanial held back to speak with Mackenzie as the others filed by them to cross the bridge. He gave her a signal to wait and called out to the others. "There is an elevator to the left. Save yourself the trek up the stairs."

As one, the group spun back to face him. He found it difficult to hold back the laugh at their disgruntled expressions.

He shrugged. "Yes, I could've told you before you came down, but where's the fun in that?"

Spring gave a chirp of laughter.

Mackenzie simply shook her head and stared at Nate. "You really *are* Alastair's twin. It's eerie."

"Who do you think taught him how to make the most of life?"

As Nate watched her beautiful, animated face turn serious, his heart grew heavy. Poor Mackenzie bore the weight of the world on her shoulders and was having a difficult time coping with the eventual possibility that she'd fail in the fight against Isolde.

"What is it, dear?"

She shot a glance toward Sebastian, who stood on the opposite side of the bridge. "Will you find a way to make sure he doesn't suffer should the worse happen to me? I don't want him to be alone as he was before I came."

"I can't make him fall for someone else, Mack."

"I know. But maybe you and Damian can remove his memories of me. Make him whole so if he meets someone, he's not haunted by what went down here."

Nate lifted her chin with his knuckle. Her earnestness spoke of her pure soul and honest intentions. Mackenzie wanted nothing more than for those around her to live their best life and be happy. "I don't think Isolde could've chosen a witch any more opposite than she is."

She gave him a tight smile, and Nate felt a pang. Like her, he'd had to make tough decisions. One had cost him his father's life and his brother's respect. Another had made him miss out on knowing this generation of his family.

"I wanted Damian to do something similar for me once."

"You did?"

"Yes. I asked him to take away Evie's memories regarding the death of our children. I wanted her to believe they lived somewhere else in the world, happy and healthy, because no parent should outlive their children. That rawness never goes away."

"And did he?"

"No. No, he magically tied me to a chair and made me listen to his lecture for a solid hour on the foolishness of my request."

Mackenzie's lips twitched, and humor came back to her eyes. "Damian did that?"

"Indeed. He felt I was dishonoring our children by even making such a request. He was right, but you see, I couldn't bear Evie's pain. I told myself it would be better if, whenever she thought of our sons, a false memory of a happy phone call or letter supplanted the truth."

"She would believe they'd already been to visit or were at least planning to?"

"Yes." He closed his eyes for a moment and allowed the haunting memories from long ago to wash over him. "Damian was right. It was a foolish request. Evie deserved better than lies and half truths."

Nate sensed his wife's presence a few seconds before she placed her hand on his lower back.

"And it's a damned good thing you didn't take my memories, because if I'd ever found out, I'd have skinned you alive, Nathanial Alastair Thorne."

A smile tugged at his lips, as it always did when she scolded him. "Ah, Evie, my heart. You're just in time to be properly introduced to Mackenzie."

His vision blurred as his two favorite women hugged. After he dabbed his eyes, he tugged at his cuffs and cleared his throat of the overwhelming emotion.

"He's what you would call a big softie, dear," Evie said with a fond look back at him. "My Nathanial."

"I confess, I'm going to miss the antics of Teddie and Leopold," Mack told them. "I don't think I've ever laughed so hard in my life as when Baz and I found the pickle sock on the bedroom floor."

Evie's light, breathy laugh—the one that always squeezed his heart and made his dick stand up to take notice—rang out. "He has an entire dresser drawer full of those socks. Each has some sarcastic saying or another."

Reaching down, she lifted his pant leg. The quote on the purple sock read, *"Don't worry. It only seems kinky the first time."*

Nate shrugged and turned his ankle to model the sock. "Should we show her your favorite embroidered pillow, Evie, my love?"

Mack's smile was open and engaging, and Nate was happy to have her mind off the subject of the Enchantress for the time being. He nodded to Sebastian as he joined their small group.

"What's it say, Grandma Evie?"

Evie arched a brow and conjured the pillow with Nate's image pressed upon it. Underneath his grinning mug, it read, *"I'd totally sit on this man's face until I came or he suffocated, whichever came first."*

Mackenzie's laughter echoed off the grotto walls and triggered theirs.

"Now I know where Mack gets her naughty streak," Sebastian said with a low chuckle.

Grinning, Nate clapped him on the back. "You have no idea just how naughty 'Aunt Teddie' can be, son."

A sickly pallor came over Sebastian's visage. "Please, please don't call her that in front of me. I'm not sure my stomach can handle the idea of her 'naughtiness' in Teddie form."

Evie snapped her fingers, reverting to Baz's elderly aunt. A puke-green evening gown opened in the front and plunged down to a heavily wrinkled belly button, giving her skin a sallow hue. She placed her hands over pancake-flat, sagging breasts and gave them a quick boost up. "I don't know what's wrong with young folk today. How do you think babies are made, Baz?"

Sebastian turned paler when she winked at him, and he pressed a palm to his stomach. "I. Can't. Even."

Not to be outdone, Nathanial waved a hand and transformed into Leopold wearing a seventies-style suit in leopard-print material. He hefted Evie/Teddie into his arms and strode toward the door to their underground apartment. "I'm taking you to bed, Evie, my love. And when you sit on my face, I trust you'll come *long* before I suffocate."

Sebastian's audible gag sounded behind them, and Evie's breathy laugh rang out, doing what it always did and sending blood straight to Nate's groin.

CHAPTER 22

The next morning, Sebastian paid a visit to Ravenswood. Before he could knock, the door swung open to reveal Damian standing in the opening.

Sebastian's brows shot up, and he glanced beyond the Aether, into the hallway. Sabrina peeked around the stairwell, curiosity lighting up her little face. He shot her a quick wink.

"Drake."

"Dethridge."

Damian's lips twitched. "I suppose you are here to discuss Leopold and Teddie." He stepped back and waved an arm as an invitation to enter.

"I'm curious why no one thought to tell me he was a Guardian."

Guardians were selected by the gods, goddesses, and the Aether to watch over whatever they deemed important enough to monitor. In most cases, they stood in as representatives or moderators and relayed the wishes of those powerful entities. Most were brought back after their death and locked to a certain location. Some voluntarily transitioned before their demise. But again, they were forced to watch over a specific place for whatever reason the gods or goddesses deemed necessary.

"I'm not sure. Obviously, you and I weren't on speaking terms, but after your parents passed on, it fell to Gwennie, Evie or Nathanial to tell you. I can only assume Isis had her reasons for them to remain quiet on the subject."

Irritation sparked inside him, and Sebastian tamped it out. It did him no good to be upset, because what was done was done, but it didn't sit well that he hadn't known what was going on under his own roof. "Thank you for your honesty. I'll leave you to enjoy your day."

"Join me for a cup of coffee."

For the second time that morning, Damian surprised him.

Sebastian nodded and followed him into the sitting room.

"Come join us, beastie. No sense lurking outside the doorway."

Damian's indulgent smile held a world of love for his tiny daughter, and Sebastian felt a kernel of envy. Not that he wanted Damian's life, but because he wanted something similar with Mackenzie. He wanted to have children with her, mischievous little beasties of his own to run about, taking joy in and laughing at everything life had to offer, like their mother.

"We'll stop her, Baz. We have no choice for both our families' sakes," Damian said in a low voice so his daughter didn't overhear.

Sebastian nodded and gave him a grim half smile. "I pray you are right."

Sabrina skipped up to him and gave him another curious look.

"Hi. I'm Sebastian. We didn't have a chance to talk at the wedding ceremony, but I greatly appreciate that you took part. It made Mack happy."

"She let me make my own dress."

He flared his eyes wide and smiled. "She's fun like that, isn't she?"

Sabrina nodded. "I'm sorry for what my Grandma is going to do to her."

The blood in Sebastian's veins froze, and it seemed his heart had to pump twice as hard to push it through its chambers. A dull thudding started in his ears.

"Beastie," Damian said with a heavy warning tone. "What did I tell you about blurting things of that magnitude to strangers?"

"But he's not a stranger, Papa. He's Cousin Baz."

Both men exchanged a shocked look.

"What do you mean, my love?"

Sabrina dropped her gaze to the floor, shrugged, and picked at the hem of her frilly pink dress.

Damian knelt beside her and wrapped an arm around her to tug her closer. Taking her tiny hand in his, he lifted it and placed it on his cheek to gain her attention. "Sabrina. Don't be shy now. I won't be angry and neither will Baz, but you need to tell me what you've seen."

"It's all in the book, Papa. The one Mack will find." She smiled and leaned close. In a not so quiet whisper, she said, "Grandma's magic book. Not the one you keep in the room behind the wall."

"Mack said something last night…" Sebastian struggled to recall her exact words. "'Find the book, and all will be well,'" he said softly. Glancing up, he saw Damian was now focused on him as if his next words were paramount. "She told me she'd heard a voice in her head. It said, *'Find the book, and all will be well.'* At the time, I thought it was ominous as he—uh, heck," he corrected with a quick glance in Sabrina's direction. "Do you think that's Isolde's book, Damian?"

The girl tapped her father's cheek to gain his attention. "Not that Grandma, Papa. Grandma Drake."

"I'm confused." Sebastian looked at the father/daughter duo. They wore matching thoughtful looks, and he was left to wonder what the hell they were turning over in those ever-active brains of theirs.

Damian shrugged and lifted Sabrina. "I suppose we are going on a treasure hunt." He grinned at his daughter and flared his eyes wide. "Run tell your mama we are escaping this joint."

"Vivian's here?" Sebastian faced the door as if just by saying her name, she'd appear. He didn't know how he'd feel about seeing her after all this time and paused to examine his innermost feelings on the matter. Nothing. No resentment, no lingering jealousy. He sighed his relief. It seemed if they could defeat Isolde, he'd be entirely free of the past and open to moving forward with Mackenzie without a cloud hanging over them.

"She is." Damian's tone was grave, almost sad in nature.

"Ah. You still haven't repaired the rift?"

Damian absently touched the front of his shirt and drew Sebastian's gaze to the outline of a ring on a chain beneath the white material.

"It's none of my business, Dethridge. Forget I asked."

"No, it's all right. She agreed to move back for Sabrina's sake. But apparently, I still only deserve her suspicion and disdain."

"I'm sorry." Sebastian found he meant it. He hated they were at odds. Looking back, he could now admit he'd never seen a couple so enamored with each other after their first meeting. Vivian was exquisite with her peaches-and-cream complexion, wide blue eyes, and stark-white hair. She'd always reminded him of a Christmas angel that sat on top of a tree. Damian, on the other hand, was the direct contrast to his wife. Dark. Dangerous. No one would ever mistake him for an angel unless it was the fabled Lucifer.

"Because I can feel you mean it, I'll say thank you." The Aether sighed heavily and patted him on the back. "But one problem at a time, *cousin*."

"So you believe Sabrina, then?"

"She's never wrong. It's disturbing some days."

Sebastian found himself chuckling at Damian's put-upon expression. "Well, all that remains, in that case, is for us to find Grandma Drake's book."

SEBASTIAN AND THE DETHRIDGES—VIVIAN INCLUDED BECAUSE SHE insisted on meeting Mackenzie—decided to take the scenic route back to the Drake estate. And by scenic, it meant Damian wanted to teleport into the far garden to check the wards for the Garden of Death were still firmly in place.

As they strolled across the expanse of lawn toward the gate, Damian made clopping noises for his daughter's benefit. From her piggyback perch, the girl giggled and patted his shoulder.

"What's she like, Baz?" Vivian's sweet voice didn't trigger the old emotion he'd once held for her, and for that, Sebastian was grateful.

"Who? Mack?" At her nod, he grinned. "She's amazing, Viv. Intelligent. Funny. Full of life." He looked down at her. "I think you'll like her. It's impossible not to."

"She's all Sabrina can talk about these days." Vivian reached up and caressed her daughter's pink cheek. "I think this one has a case of hero worship."

"There's much to admire about Mackenzie," Damian said with a tight smile.

Vivian's expression turned chilly, and she looked away from him.

Sebastian's gaze collided with Damian's. Because he couldn't offer up his regret for their troubles, he sent a silent message, knowing the Aether would receive it. Damian gave a brisk nod and looked toward the enchanted gate.

"This is where we all part ways." He swung his daughter down. "I'll meet you on the terrace shortly."

"Aww, Papa. I want to see the Death Garden."

Sebastian snorted. "Seriously? That's what you named it?"

"Why? What do you call it?" Damian asked a bit defensively.

"The Garden of Death."

They shared a laugh. Vivian simply shook her head at their silliness and clasped her daughter's hand.

"We'll see you at the house, Damian," she informed him coolly, setting off in that direction.

Sabrina looked over her shoulder, her expression forlorn.

"I believe your daughter has a morbid curiosity, Dethridge."

"I worry she'll grow to be like Wednesday Addams."

Sebastian laughed. "Look at you with your pop-culture reference."

"I'm hipper than you know."

"You were referring to the black and white version of the show, weren't you?"

"Stuff it, Drake."

CHAPTER 23

Mackenzie rose from the lounger as Sabrina arrived with an ethereal-looking blond woman in tow.

Vivian.

It had to be, because Damian wouldn't trust his daughter to just anyone. Seeing her in all her loveliness, Mack experienced a twinge of jealousy. Here was the woman once engaged to Sebastian. The one no longer in love with her own husband and who could potentially look to rekindle what she'd once had with her neighbor.

Mackenzie frowned at her dark thoughts. She wasn't normally prone to jealousy or suspicion. The only question mark hanging over her future happiness with Sebastian was that of Isolde's resurrection. Shaking off her mood, she pasted on a welcoming smile and descended the wide stone steps to greet the newcomers.

Vivian stopped a few feet away, a wary expression in place. "You must be Mackenzie."

"Yes. And you must be Vivian," she said with a cordiality she didn't feel.

"Yes."

Okay, seriously awkward as far as introductions went, and Mack almost laughed at their formality. She dropped her gaze to Sabrina, giving her the genuine smile she'd been unable to manage for the girl's mother. "Hello, beastie."

The child's excitement bubbled up, and she pulled away from Vivian to fling herself into Mackenzie's waiting arms. "We're here to hunt for treasure, Mack!"

"Really? How exciting!" She laughed and lifted Sabrina so she was eye level. "What kind of treasure? Gold doubloons? No, wait, those were Spanish. Hmm, let me think." She bit her nail in pretend contemplation. "I know! A leprechaun's pot of gold."

Sabrina's eyes were wide and sparkled with her joy. "Nope. That's Ireland, silly."

"Hmm. Right. Okay, so if it's not doubloons and not a pot of gold, it must be jewels from a highwayman's take. Am I close?"

"Nope." Dark ringlets bounced as Sabrina shook her head. "Not close."

Mackenzie glanced at Vivian, who was watching her daughter with an indulgent smile. "What say you, Vivian?"

"Apparently, we are here to find her grandmother's book."

Mackenzie froze, not sure she'd heard correctly. Her smile dropped from her face. "What?"

"Grandma Drake's book, Mack. Cousin Baz came over and told Papa you said you needed to find it."

Unsure if the budding betrayal was what she was supposed to feel at this moment, Mack nevertheless did. She'd told Sebastian about the book last night, but she hadn't expected him to go running to Damian first thing this morning.

"I see." She set Sabrina on her feet and tapped her nose. "Then I suppose we should wait for Baz and Damian, huh?"

"We don't have to. I can show you the room."

"How?"

Sabrina tapped Mackenzie's temple. The picture of a tall furniture piece appeared in Mack's mind. Channeling the image, she looked around the room—not one she'd ever seen before—but the sun shining through the far window was in the same position in the sky as it currently was.

Lifting her head, she stared at the east tower, seeing for the first time an extension above the roofline. The room had a stained glass window depicting an entwined couple dressed in medieval garb. The sun caught the woman's auburn hair, and it flared bright. If Mackenzie didn't know any better, she'd say the woman resembled her in profile. She squinted up at the building. The black-haired man holding her looked remarkably like Sebastian, too.

"*There,*" a voice inside her head purred. The twisted satisfaction coursing through her veins gave Mackenzie pause, and she shifted to stare down into Sabrina's horrified eyes, briefly wondering if her own held a matching horror as Isolde possessed her. The vicious headache struck.

"Please don't hurt my mama, Grandma," Sabrina whispered.

Mackenzie grabbed onto Sabrina's fear like a lifeline. She struggled to regain control of her body even as Isolde fought like hell to remain in charge.

"Vivian... take her... go... *now!*"

Vivian ran forward and snatched Sabrina into her arms, teleporting to Goddess only knew where.

Still, Mackenzie fought for supremacy over Isolde. "Not... this... time... *you bitch!*"

She grabbed her head, feeling if she didn't, it would split wide open like a watermelon at a Tennessee family picnic. The pain was excruciating, and she wanted nothing more than to give in to relieve the pressure.

Footsteps pounded the pavement behind her, and she managed to hold up a hand. "Don't!"

"Mackenzie."

The soothing sound of Alastair's voice reached in and eased a smidgeon of the pain.

He touched her arm. "Mack, stay with me, child."

She glanced up and met his calm sapphire eyes. They were a

little deeper blue than normal, and she realized the color represented his worry.

"It's so... hard to stop... her," she cried.

"I know, but I also know you can do it. You're stronger." He lifted her chin and locked gazes with her. "Stay focused on me, child. I'm here with you now. Keep looking at me and breathe."

Each inhale was labored. Each slow blink of her eyes brought with it the fear that when she opened them again, he'd be gone. Isolde screamed inside her head, and the voice was no longer seductive and purring, but more like nails on a chalkboard, bordering a high-pitched screech.

Then silence. Blessed silence.

Mackenzie loosened her grip on Alastair's forearms in slow increments. She took stock of her surroundings and saw her family and Sebastian's lined up on the terrace, all terrified this might be the moment when everything changed for them.

"I can't do this to them, Alastair," she croaked. "I just can't."

"*You're* not. *She* is."

"They're afraid of me now."

"No. They're horrified for what you are going through." He gripped her hands and gave her a small shake. "Trust me, child. I'd know."

She gave him a single jerky nod. "We'll need to tell Damian and Baz."

Alastair tipped his chin to something behind her. "They already know. They've been here the entire time. The Aether always knows when his daughter is in danger. It's part of their bond."

SEBASTIAN AND DAMIAN TELEPORTED TO THE LOWER GARDEN RIGHT outside the terrace steps the second the sigils engraved in the wood of the gate lit. Upon seeing Mackenzie standing there, her arms wrapped around her head, Sebastian started to rush to her, only to be halted by Damian's magic.

"Let me go, Dethridge. I need to help her."

"You can't. Let Alastair take care of it."

"Goddammit! Let me go!" Sebastian struggled against the spell holding him in place. He fucking hated that the Aether had so much power. Not only was it unsettling to be a helpless victim to Damian's whims, Sebastian's stomach churned at the idea Mackenzie was feeling something similar as Isolde's intended target.

"No," Damian said quietly. "I'm asking you to wait, Baz."

"No, you're forcing me to, and that's a different thing altogether," he retorted.

"If I let you go, will you let Alastair handle it?"

"It's not like I have a choice either way."

Damian sighed deeply and gave a short nod. With no outward sign from the Aether, the bonds holding Sebastian released him. He stumbled forward, barely catching himself in time to avoid a faceplant.

It went against every instinct to stay where he was, and the second Mackenzie turned their way, he was off and running. When he would've embraced her, she stepped back and held up a hand. The fury on her face caused his stomach to tighten more and unease to dance along his spine.

"Mack?"

"Isolde almost gained control because of you." She punched him in the chest.

Sebastian grunted from the painful impact. "What the bloody hell did I do?"

"You told Damian about our conversation, and Sabrina gave me the location of the book. Or more importantly, she gave Isolde the location of the book!"

They both froze, staring at one another.

Sebastian imagined his face reflected the horror on hers. "Where is it, Mack?"

She gestured to the east tower. "That room with the stained glass window frame." She turned as she pointed, and her mouth dropped open. "Where did it go?"

Sebastian eased closer and ducked slightly to make his face level with hers, trying to stress the import of his next words. "There's no room in the east tower with stained glass, Mack."

"But there was. I saw it. Sabrina did, too."

He gathered her close and looked at Damian over her head, but the Aether never met his look of inquiry. Instead, he was focused on where Mackenzie had pointed.

"You see something there?"

"You don't?"

Those who had gathered on the terraced joined them and looked upwards. Their expressions were as confused as Sebastian felt. Apparently, they didn't see it either. "Show of hands, how many people see an east tower room with stained glass?"

Only Damian raised his hand.

"Must be an Aether thing," Mack said dryly. "But since we know it's there, I suggest you take Damian and go in search of the book, Baz. I no longer believe it's good for me to get a hold of it, and because the Enchantress now knows where it's located, it should be hidden elsewhere."

"I'm not sure I understand exactly why she wants a spellbook belonging to my grandmother," Sebastian said.

Spring raised her hand and moved forward like an eager pupil in class. "Maybe there's a spell in it that can destroy her."

Mackenzie's eyes flared wide. "I think you're right." She turned back to Sebastian. "Last night, I wasn't sure if the voice in my head was good or evil. What if it was good? What if there is something in the book I'm supposed to find to combat Isolde, but now she knows, it's too late for me to find it?"

He nodded slowly. "And because she's always hanging around, she got wind of it and now wants to prevent anyone but her from finding it."

"Yes."

Damian put a hand on Sebastian's shoulder. "Then you and I go find this magical book. We'll read through it and see what we might discover."

"Might I suggest you take Spring with you?" Alastair graced his niece with a wide, admiring smile. "She has the ability to figure out what incantation would work best."

"Thank you, Uncle."

Their group walked into the house, Damian and Sebastian in the lead, toward the main staircase. Just as they entered the foyer, the main bell rang, and Nathanial—disguised as Leopold—swung open the door.

"Hugh?" Sebastian experienced a wave of irritation. As if he didn't already have enough things on his plate, now he had to worry about this imbecile mucking up his plans. "What are you doing here?"

"Can't I visit a friend? What? What?"

Sebastian bit his tongue to keep from blurting the fact he didn't consider Hugh a friend to any degree any longer.

"Mackenzie!" When the other man caught sight of her, a sly look passed across his face before he replaced it with his attempt at charming. The overall effect was a snake oil salesman. "I'd have thought you'd have thrown Baz over by now. The ladies love him, but it's a well-known fact he doesn't commit. Doesn't commit."

Mack locked eyes with Sebastian, and he was relieved to see the humor lurking in hers. His own had to be reflecting his annoyance with Hugh.

Right when Hugh made a grab for her hand, Damian stepped into his path. "Hugh, is it? Hugh, we're having a bit of a family crisis at the moment. I'm sure I speak for everyone when I say, no one has it in them for a social call." His humorless, cold eyes chilled Sebastian, and they weren't even focused on him. "You'll need to come back another time."

"Preferably when you're invited," Nathanial added.

"I say!" Hugh sputtered.

Sebastian imagined he was about to object to being spoken to by a manservant, the rotten snob. Stepping forward, he gestured toward the door. "My apologies, Hugh, but Damian is correct. I'll be in London again in a few weeks. Perhaps I'll make time to visit."

"But I came all the way here. Surely, you don't intend to turn me out? 'Tisn't done. Not done at all."

"Listen, it's not safe for you to be here right now."

Hugh's pale-gray eyes lit up, and he touched the side of his nose. "Oh, intrigue? I say, I'm smashingly good at the spy game."

"I doubt that," Nathanial muttered from beside Sebastian.

Hugh whipped his head around and glared. "What?"

"He said he didn't doubt that," Mackenzie said, stepping forward to wrap her arm around Nathanial's. Her smile was so wide and welcoming, Sebastian wouldn't have believed it if he hadn't seen it, especially knowing she'd disliked Hugh immensely from their first meeting. "Leopold told me the first day I arrived, he's long been an admirer of yours, Hugh."

Damian coughed into his hand, and it sounded remarkably like the word "bullshit."

For the second time that day, he felt a kinship with his new cousin.

"I could use a spot of tea after traveling all this way. Long way, indeed."

Mackenzie's eyes narrowed marginally. "Of course, Hugh. Leopold makes the most delicious scones you've ever tasted. I bet you can't eat just one."

From behind Hugh, Evie's face turned scarlet red in her effort not to laugh.

Sebastian faced her. "Aunt Teddie, do you and Aunt Gwennie mind entertaining Hugh while Damian and I settle our business matters?"

"Of course, dear boy. We'd be delighted to. Perhaps Mr. Thorne will wish to join us?"

"I think that's a clever idea, Uncle Alastair," Spring added with a wide smile.

Hugh blanched the second he realized whose presence he was in. Everyone was wary of the infamous Alastair Thorne.

"I'd be delighted. It wouldn't do to leave our *uninvited guest* to entertain himself." Alastair turned his hard-eyed stare on Hugh.

"Although, why anyone with any ability whatsoever would drive when he could clearly teleport, is beyond me. You wouldn't be seeking an excuse to crash our family gathering, would you, Mr. Cunningham?"

Hugh looked like he wanted to lose his lunch. To catch the attention of a warlock as powerful and as reportedly temperamental as Alastair was frightening to a normal member of the magical community.

"You know who I am?" Hugh squeaked.

"I do." And Alastair's tone said he wasn't impressed.

Damian leaned close to Sebastian. "He's a bloody master at intimidation."

"You're telling me. Remind me to tell you about the auction last year." Sebastian snorted when Alastair's gaze cut to him. "Apparently, he's got superior hearing, too."

"I'll see myself out. Wouldn't dream of disrupting your family gathering, Mr. Thorne." Hugh ran a finger inside his collar as he dried his upper lip with his shirtsleeve. "Pardon the visit."

For once, he'd left off repeating himself, and Sebastian was grateful.

Somehow, Hugh dug deep enough to retrieve his courage and reach for Mackenzie's hand, lifting it to plant a kiss on her knuckles. "Mackenzie, I hope when you're in London again, you'll do me the honor of dining with me."

"Not happening." Sebastian inserted himself between them. "She's my wife now."

The disbelief on Hugh's face bordered on comical.

His gaze darted between the two of them, finally settling on Sebastian. "Never thought I'd see the day, old chap. Indeed, I didn't." He pasted on a smile and nodded to Mackenzie. "My offer is always open should you tire of Baz. What? What?"

Sebastian growled, and Hugh jumped back, releasing Mack. She cried out and turned her hand over. Blood beaded up on her palm and she stared at it in surprise.

"Beg pardon, Mackenzie. I must've caught you with my ring."

Alastair rushed forward and grabbed Hugh's wrist before he could leave. "We'll be taking your ring, Mr. Cunningham."

"What? Why?"

"I believe you know why." Knox crowded Hugh from the opposite side as Sebastian shuffled Mack and Spring back away from the others. "We can't allow you to possess even a drop of Thorne blood. Accident or no."

"I d-don't understand." Hugh's face turned ruddier than normal, and sweat beaded his brow.

"Oh, I believe you do." Alastair ripped the ring from Hugh's finger. "It seems you'll be staying here after all, Mr. Cunningham."

Damian shot Sebastian a look rife with meaning. He nodded in return.

"Mr. Thorne, if you'll excuse us, Damian, Spring, and I really need to have that emergency meeting we discussed earlier. I trust you can take care of handing Hugh's ass to him on a silver platter?"

Alastair grinned, and the promised retribution in his expression lent a great deal of evil to the smile.

"Right," Sebastian murmured. "I shouldn't have even asked." He drew Mackenzie aside and did a quick inspection of her wound. "I'm sure GiGi can take care of this in nothing flat. Make sure there wasn't anything poisonous on that ring. We all know Hugh cut you on purpose."

Gwennie stepped forward and placed a palm on his wife's shoulder. "I have a quick incantation to show if there was anything harmful on the ring. Once we know for sure, we'll treat Mackenzie properly."

"Thank you, Aunt." He kissed her butter-soft cheek, feeling a sudden swell of affection. Too many times in the past, he'd allowed irritation or impatience to rule him when it came to his aunts and to Leopold. Now, he genuinely regretted he hadn't understood the sacrifices they'd made prior to today. He felt like an ungrateful prat. When he had a few minutes of one-on-one time with Gwennie, he intended to tell her exactly what she meant to him. "I'll be back down shortly."

He, along with Damian and Spring, rushed up the staircase, determined to discover the whereabouts of the secret east tower room.

CHAPTER 24

To Alastair, there was no mistaking Hugh Cunningham's intentions. Although the man appeared like a bumbling fool and tried to convince them he was innocent of any wrongdoing, the intent to harm lurked under the surface. The question was whether Hugh was targeting Mackenzie on purpose or whether he had a bone to pick with Sebastian and decided to use Mack as a tool against him.

With a mere wave of his hand, Alastair tossed Hugh onto the nearest chair. It rocked back under his weight, and Hugh scrambled to keep it from tipping over.

Alastair pinned him with a mere look. *"Don't move!"*

The air around them vibrated with his fury, and the occupants of the room, not related by blood, cast him a wary glance. He didn't bother to reassure them. A ruthless reputation benefited him at times like these.

"Cunningham, you've just declared war on my family with your foolish move," he said in a low, lethal tone. "Why shouldn't I kill you on the spot?"

Someone behind him echoed Hugh's shocked cry.

Alastair ignored it.

"Well, boy?"

"I didn't. I wouldn't. A faulty ring design. Faulty ring."

He raised a brow and narrowed his eyes. "You expect anyone to believe that?"

Hugh looked five seconds away from strangling on his own fear. If the fool wasn't close to wetting himself, Alastair was Morty's uncle and he would need to up his game.

"Yes. No. No. I..." Hugh swallowed audibly. He turned beseeching eyes to Mackenzie and Arabella. "Please don't let him kill me."

Based on their matching flinty expressions, Hugh was getting no sympathy there.

Alastair almost smiled.

"I'll ask you one time, Cunningham. If you don't come clean, I'll stop playing nice." He could practically smell the man's fear. For sure, he could feel it.

"What do you want to know?"

"Why were you after Mackenzie's blood?"

Hugh paled, if possible. His eyes darted sideways as if noting the exit doors.

"Cunningham!"

The force of Alastair's anger slapped Hugh, and his head jerked.

"I want to wake the Enchantress." The confession seemed to cost him, and he slumped in his seat, looking defeated.

"How do you even know about her, and what does my blood have to do with it?" Mackenzie demanded as GiGi finished healing her wound. "And why, for the sake of the Goddess, would you want to do something like that?"

"She is everything," Hugh said simply, turning his face up toward Mackenzie. "And you are the only one worthy enough to make it happen."

She shook her head and squatted beside his chair. "No, Hugh. She's evil, and she'll murder to possess more and more power. You have to see how wrong this is."

Alastair gave her credit for trying to reason with Hugh, but he knew a zealot when he saw one. A small sliver of unease danced along his nerve endings. "Mackenzie, come away now, child."

She looked back at him, but before she could move, Hugh had his arm around her throat and a knife pressed to her breast.

Rage clouded Alastair's vision for a split second, but he shoved it away. Now was not the time to give in to his fury, but oh, how Cunningham would pay.

"Hugh, please don't do this," Arabella begged. "If you ever cared about my brother, let Mack go. She's his everything."

MACKENZIE'S HEART THUDDED AT ARABELLA'S WORDS. ALTHOUGH Sebastian had told her he loved her, she'd doubted his feelings were as powerful as hers. Yet hearing Arabella say differently made Mack's soul sing.

Instead of fighting her captor, Mackenzie decided to humor him. "Hugh, take the ring and go do what you must. None of us will fight you."

"The hell you say!" Alastair sneezed. His shock and anger whipped around the room, causing anything not nailed down to tremble under the force of his emotion. GiGi and Ryker were quick to fist their hands and fend off the wave of locusts sure to descend on the estate as a direct result of Alastair's swearing.

GiGi placed a calming hand on her brother's arm. "Al, rein it in."

Mackenzie met her cousin's violet-blue gaze across the short distance. It appeared GiGi was the more level-headed of the two siblings at the moment.

A wave of affection for Alastair crashed over Mackenzie. He'd reacted as if she were one of his own children, and she loved him all the more for it. When his dark sapphire eyes locked on her, she smiled her understanding, knowing he could feel her love for him.

He looked pained, yet decisive. "Take what you need and go, Cunningham."

Hugh's grip around her neck tightened slightly, and Mack

worried he'd cut off her ability to breathe in his nervousness. "I'll take Mackenzie."

"Wrong answer, you fool," Alastair snarled. *"Commoro!"*

With one simple command, he'd locked Hugh in place, incapacitating him.

"Uh, cousin, his arm's still locked around my neck," Mackenzie croaked out.

An arctic smile curled Alastair's lips. "Then I'll have to detach it, won't I?"

Hugh whimpered.

"That's one way, but I don't wish to have blood all over my lovely blouse. Can you unfreeze his arm long enough to pry it away?"

"Mackenzie, my dear, I thought you were the adventurous one of this generation. Why are you spoiling my fun?" Alastair ran his hand from Hugh's elbow to his wrist, using magic to unlock the joints of Hugh's arm long enough to release her.

"This is Dolce & Gabbana, cousin. Blood isn't so easy to remove from silk."

"We're witches. You could conjure another," he argued, humor heavy in his tone. "Or better yet, buy another."

"This one has sentimental value, and that's all I'm saying on the matter. Now…" She turned to face Hugh, and with every ounce of strength she possessed, she clocked him with her fist. "That's for being a dirty, rotten piece of shit!"

"Bravo, child! I knew you had it in you."

She shook out her hand and sent Alastair an amused glance. "You taught me well. Now, what do we do with him?"

GiGi stepped forward, hands on her hips and a determined glint in her eye. "I have just the idea."

Alastair laughed even as Ryker groaned.

"Don't laugh, Al. It only encourages her mean streak," Ryker said.

Although GiGi narrowed her eyes, she didn't look at her husband.

He stepped forward and wrapped a hand around her waist. "And what, pray tell, my dearest love, is your idea."

"Your only love. And I say let's take him out to meet the Enchantress he adores so much."

Mackenzie gasped, shocked her aunt would do something so cold-blooded. Yet, even as she felt appalled at the idea, a small part of her clung to it. She found herself nodding. "Yes. I think you're right."

Alastair cut her a sharp glance. His face took on a thoughtful look as he turned his attention back to Hugh.

Only Arabella and Gwennie seemed disturbed by this new plan.

"If you'll beg my pardon, Lady Kilbride." Nathanial shuffled forward in his old, butler disguise. "I must insist we wait until Lord Kilbride and Master Dethridge return to make any drastic decisions as to Mr. Cunningham's demise."

Hugh let out a choked sound and began sweating more profusely than he already was.

Mackenzie was hard-pressed not to laugh. She didn't know whether Nathanial's pretense as Leopold was still intentional at this point or whether he'd forgotten to change into the powerful Guardian he was. For sure, his comment threatened to give Hugh imminent a stroke.

"I'm not sure if you know my cousins well, Leopold, but I can promise you, when GiGi and Alastair get something in their heads, it takes a stronger person than either Baz or me to remove it." Mackenzie shrugged and pressed her lips together, careful to avoid eye contact, or she was sure to start laughing. Any sign of humor at this point would be entirely inappropriate, but since Alastair had Hugh frozen in place, the situation seemed well in hand.

"Exactly, my dear. And I second my lovely sister's plan. After all, if anyone should be sacrificed to bring Isolde back, I think it should be one of her disciples, don't you?" Alastair raised a hand, and Hugh's body levitated a foot above the floor.

Arabella charged forward, stopping short of touching Alastair. "Mr. Thorne, the danger involved in resurrecting Isolde is immense. I don't think this is the best course of action, sir."

"I disagree, Ms. Drake. You see, Isolde's body is at her weakest right now. She doesn't stand a chance against us when we are united."

"Yes," GiGi agreed. "We've had plenty of experience with enemies, Arabella. The time to strike is when they are not prepared."

Mackenzie placed an arm around Arabella's shoulders. "Trust them, Bella. They know what they're doing. Alastair and GiGi are powerful all on their own. If they combine their magic and that of anyone else present, the Enchantress is toast."

A small niggling doubt played in the back of Mackenzie's mind, but she wasn't positive it wasn't put there by Isolde. "And on that note, I'm going to take myself off. You all can plan this without giving her..." She tapped her temple. "...any idea of what's going to happen."

"Teddie, be a darling and go with her. Perhaps the two of you can share a cup of tea while the rest of us talk." Alastair shot Evie a meaningful look.

"Of course, Mr. Thorne. Of course." She looped her arm through Mackenzie's. "Come, dear. Let me tell you about the time my nephew was in short pants."

Mackenzie laughed. "Short pants? How *antiquated* a word. Ouch!" She rubbed her side where Evie had pinched her.

"That's what sassy young women get for talking back to their elders."

"So you're where the Thornes get their mean streak."

"Bloody hell! It has to be here somewhere," Sebastian muttered. "How can you see the window from downstairs and still have no ability to see the door from up here, Dethridge?"

"Maybe because your house is a damned maze," Damian retorted on a growl.

"Every other magical thing in this place calls to the Thornes. You're their relation, and the Aether to boot. The fucking book should call to you, for shit's sake."

"You know, Drake, I'm ab—"

"Gentlemen!" Spring spun around and put her hands on her hips. "If you two are going to bicker like a pair of toddlers, then I'm leaving you here."

"I beg you pardon, Ms. Thorne." Sebastian shared a sheepish look with his nemesis turned ally.

"You can call me Spring since you've married Mack and we're family now." She nodded to him then faced Damian. "Now, as the Aether, you have the power to reveal the room. Why are you stalling?"

Sebastian's heart began a resounding thud in his ears. Surely he'd misheard?

"Stalling?" He glared at Damian. "What gives, Dethridge?"

A small smile tugged at Damian's lips as he studied Spring. "You truly are as brilliant as Alastair claims, aren't you?"

"Probably more so," Spring said matter-of-factly, without any vanity. "Again, I ask, why are you stalling?"

"Honestly? I'm worried we are playing into my mother's hands by finding this book." He ran his fingers through his hair and gave a weary sigh. "I can admit it to the two of you, but I'm not sure I know how to deal with her when the time comes."

Spring hugged Damian.

Sebastian was at a loss as to which of the two of them were more surprised, him or Damian.

"What was that for, and how do I get one of those?" Sebastian joked.

Spring's light, musical laughter was like a blanket of joy wrapping around them. The sound brought with it happiness and a sense of well-being. How she managed to do that in such trying times was in question.

"I know about tough decisions, Damian," she told him in a more serious vein. "I'm not sure how much either of you know about my story, but I've been to hell and back. My presence here today proves anything is possible if the will is strong enough." Her eyes took on a soft light. "Knox was forced to kill his own mother to save me. He didn't even care for her as you did your mother, and yet he lives with the guilt of what he had to do."

"And I'd do it all again. A million times for you, sweetheart." Knox's voice came to them, although the man himself wasn't visible.

Spring simply grinned in the face of Sebastian's surprise. "I know you would, darling. Now show yourself. No sense cloaking yourself when we all know you're here."

With a shimmer of light, Knox appeared. He was leaning against the wall, his burly arms crossed over his chest and his loving gaze locked onto his beautiful wife. "Like Damian said. Brilliant."

"It didn't take a brain like mine to know you weren't letting me out of your sight, you overbearing brute," she teased. She sent him a laughing look. "And you didn't even growl or threaten to rip Damian in half when I hugged him."

"I thought about it." Knox shoved off the wall and strode to where she stood, beaming at him. He brushed back the hair from her neck and placed a light kiss at the hollow of her throat. "Oh, how I thought about it."

"Pfft. Now, tell Damian the story of when we were in the woods by our clearing. I think it might help him make a decision."

"I've already made it, Spring. Your young man can hold onto his secrets." Damian clapped Knox on the back. "There was never any doubt as to what I needed to do when or if my mother returns. I want my daughter to grow up and experience what you two have." He shot a look at Sebastian. "What you and Mackenzie have. With Isolde awake, none of that is possible. She'll destroy the magical community for revenge."

The hallway grew disturbingly quiet after his comment. Each of them understood what they faced should they fail to stop her.

"Then let's quit fiddle-farting around, as my aunt GiGi would say, and get to finding the passage to the secret room. I want to have time to study that book." Spring wrapped her arm through her husband's and smiled up at him.

Sebastian felt a pang in the region of his heart. Mackenzie looked at him with that same exact expression. He needed to be able to help her through this so they could build on their relationship as this young couple before him now had done.

He met Damian's somber gaze, and this time, the pang was one of fear. The Aether knew something and was hesitant to say. Sebastian couldn't bring himself to ask either. But he knew. As sure as he was standing here, Fate had a vastly different plan for Mackenzie and him than it did for Spring and Knox.

Sebastian closed his eyes and inhaled a deep, fortifying breath. "Let's get this over with. I need to get back to Mack." If only to tell her how much he'd come to love her in the short time he'd known her.

That was the funny thing about love. Time meant nothing. Whether it was one day or one million, he'd always feel the same. Love wasn't measured by minutes; it was measured by the depth of emotion from that first moment, that first meeting of souls. She'd woven her way into his, and he would never be free of her. He didn't want to be.

CHAPTER 25

It took no time to find the room after Damian made up his mind to reveal the stairwell leading to the addition above the east tower. Once there, they were all drawn to the cabinet where the book was hidden. The pulse of magic from the grimoire was stronger than any object he'd come in contact with recently.

Spring had been correct to call him out about leading them astray a few minutes ago. Seeing the warmth and compassion in her eyes had gutted him. As had the fierce emotion between her and her husband. The love Knox felt for her was as clear as the brightest sunlight on a cloudless day, and it showed when he'd dissolved the cloaking spell and stepped forward with an indulgent grin.

That love was something Damian could understand and respect. He felt the same for Vivian and Sabrina. Yet, here he'd been playing games with all their lives—his own family's included—although not intentionally. All because he was trying to find a way *not* to murder his own mother. All because the little boy in him still cared for the woman she'd been during the first formative years of his life.

The one continual thought burning in Damian's mind was how much he adored his child. How he'd kill for her. But his own mother hadn't been so strong. She'd given into the lure of ultimate power, evil as it had been. She'd seduced innocents to get what she wanted and had thrown away those who cared for her, Damian and his father included.

Now, time was at a premium for Sebastian and Mackenzie. Damian's stalling as he sought another solution, had cost them precious minutes together. The reality was, there would be none after today. Or at least not quality ones for the lifetime lovers they should've been allowed to be. He'd stolen potential memories from them.

Sebastian would have one more thing to hate him for, other than Vivian. And Damian experienced a measure of sadness because a part of him had always known the two of them would've been great friends had life dealt them different hands.

The kicker was that Sebastian already suspected. The wary expression on his face in the hallway had spoken volumes. As did the resignation following closely on its heels.

Damian swallowed down the apology forming on his lips as he once again met the knowing gaze of Sebastian. Instead, he pointed to the cabinet. "There."

"I don't see anything but a wall." Sebastian put a hand out in front of him, just shy of the wood visible to Damian. "Is it inside the stone?"

"No. Stand back."

Spring and Knox were posted on either side of the main door to the room, a mismatched pair of sentinels overseeing the discovery.

Sebastian joined them and crossed his arms over his chest. He, too, reminded Damian of a warrior of old. His watchful, somewhat distrustful, expression similar to that of Knox. Only Spring wore a look of barely suppressed excitement.

Damian figured she'd probably hate that he found her vastly amusing in her childlike wonder. She was a refreshing mix of innocence and worldliness, without pretentious airs. "Are you ready to put that incredible mind of yours to use, Spring?"

"Always." She shot him a cheeky grin.

He was helpless not to return her smile. Turning back to the cabinet, he studied the door. Etched into the surface were runes similar to those on the garden gate, but the order was reversed. He placed his palm flat on the wood and was unprepared to be knocked flat on his back.

"Holy shitballs!"

He looked up into Spring's astonished face. "You could say that again."

"Holy—"

"Don't," he said, disgusted by his own gullibility regarding the linen press' wards. "I'll be tempted to toss you out that bloody window."

"Over my dead body," Knox growled, shifting forward to lend him a hand. "Don't even kid about it."

"My apologies." Damian groaned as he rose to his feet. "Well, *that* was unexpected."

Sebastian leaned against the wall, laughing like an escapee from bedlam.

"Found that amusing, did you?" Damian brushed off his clothing and tugged down the cuffs of his dress shirt. "No doubt, had the situation been reversed, I'd feel the same. *But* I'd like you all to focus for the moment and figure out how we are going to open the wardrobe to get to the book. Because if *I* can't do it..." He shrugged.

Three heads swung from him to stare at the location of the grimoire. He had little doubt they couldn't see it, but he imagined they desperately wanted to.

"It looks to be an early 19th-century mahogany, line press wardrobe, roughly two inches taller than Sebastian." Damian ventured closer to the furniture piece and immediately detected the repelling force field he'd failed to earlier due to his distraction over Sebastian and Mackenzie. "It's not going to let me touch it. If I had to guess, it's protected with some of my mother's blood."

Sebastian weighed what Damian had revealed. If asked, he'd have said there was probably nothing known to man that could knock the Aether on his ass. He'd have been wrong. How his great-grandmother had known of magic strong enough to stop the Enchantress in her tracks would be something he'd never discover if he couldn't even see the linen press holding her grimoire. But perhaps she had nothing to do with it at all. Maybe the all-powerful Goddess herself or one of her Guardians had placed the spellbook there.

"So you don't think it was my grandmother who put it there?" Sebastian asked.

"No, I do. I also believe she charmed it with Aether blood to protect it."

Spring stepped forward, her hand raised. In an attempt to protect her from getting the shock of her life, Sebastian grabbed her wrist. "I wouldn't, Spring. His mother's blood also contained Thorne blood, if I'm not mistaken."

"But some entity revealed this to Mack, which means it believed she could access it. As someone from the same line, I should be able to open it, too."

Spring's reasoning was sound, yet he didn't care to risk her getting hurt.

Damian appeared to agree because he said, "I think we should let Sebastian try it first."

Sebastian moved closer to where the linen press was located. "Tell me what to do."

Spring answered first. "If it's blood magic, you need to find the original spell to reverse it. As a Drake, you might need to use some of your own to counteract whatever shield your grandmother put in place. Grandpa Nate or Grandma Evie might know what she used if they are the Guardians."

"But Nathanial wasn't around then." Damian shook his head. "None of us were."

"What do you mean? I thought he was *the* Guardian?"

"He took over from the last one in exchange for his life. That's how it works. Nathanial made a deal with Isis. If she brought Evie back to stand by his side, they would agree to watch and be here when the prophecy unfolds."

"The ultimate power couple," Knox said softly. "The Goddess would've supercharged them. Like she did for us, sweetheart."

Spring nodded, catching what he was saying. "So, we have two extra powerful couples on the property. Between the four of us, we should be able to keep Isolde from rising up to create havoc."

"Or to stop Mackenzie." Sebastian didn't miss the grim realization that took over their expressions. "I know we keep ignoring it, but the fact she's been possessed and is likely to be again, isn't easily dismissed."

"I'm sorry, Baz."

When Damian met his stare head-on, Sebastian was convinced he meant it. "Thank you."

He tilted his head from side to side to ease the knotted muscles and turned the subject back to retrieving the spellbook. Because what else could he do? If he let his mind dwell on what might happen, he'd lose it. As it was, he was wrapped tighter than a corner-shop sandwich.

"Spring, it's common knowledge you have the Thornes' grimoire memorized from cover to cover." Sebastian shot a quick look in Knox's direction. "I imagine you've done the same with the Carlyles'. Are there any ideas or incantations either of you might think of that could be helpful?"

"My dad might know," Spring said. Her voice hung up when she mentioned her father, and she didn't meet anyone's eyes. "We could call on him or ask Isis to send him to help."

Knox enfolded her in a tight embrace, and she placed her hand over his heart. "We could try, sweetheart."

Sebastian turned away to give her a moment to compose herself.

Preston's death had been sudden and particularly vicious, last year. He'd gone to confront his cousin when she'd tried to poison Aurora. It had earned him a bullet to the heart and his remains burned beyond recognition. It had taken DNA to identify him, and the Thorne family now had an open wound the size of a crater where their hearts should be.

"First, let me try something." Sebastian gestured to the armoire.

"How close am I, Damian?"

"Another foot to your right. If you reach straight out, you should connect with the handle."

He took a fortifying breath and positioned himself in front of the unit. "Here?"

Damian nodded, a slight smirk on his lips. "Knox, you may want to cover your wife's eyes. You wouldn't want her to see what's beneath Drake's skirt when it flies up over his head."

"You're a bundle of laughs, Dethridge," Sebastian said dryly. "If this stops my heart, tell Mack my last thoughts were of her, won't you?"

"Drama, drama, drama. Get to it, mate."

"Why don't you tell me again how comfortable it was for you to be knocked on your arse?"

Damian laughed at the retort and waved a hand toward the invisible chest. "It's not opening itself, Baz."

"I feel as if I should at least try the old 'open sesame' before I electrocute myself."

The wooden door creaked on its hinges at the same time the cloaking spell faded away to reveal the linen press.

"Are you fucking kidding me?" Damian was the picture of outrage.

Sebastian began to laugh, and for a moment, they all stared at him in shock. One by one, they joined in. When he could speak again, he said, "I suppose my gran had the same sense of humor I do."

"Your gran can go to the devil!" Damian's smile belied his words. "Now, reach in there and get that book."

CHAPTER 26

"What's going on here?" Sebastian noticed Mackenzie's absence the second he returned to the drawing room. "Where's Mack?"

"Having a cuppa with Aunt Teddie," Arabella replied. "I suspect our aunt will add a bracing dash of brandy for what poor Mack just went through."

His stomach tightened, and his gaze darted from one person to the other. "What did she just go through?"

Alastair uncrossed his arms and moved closer to him. "Seems your friend, Hugh, decided to hold a knife to her throat."

"What?"

"Don't panic, son. She's none the worse for wear." Alastair's grin seemed out of place until he said, "She punched Mr. Cunningham in the face for his troubles."

Sebastian nearly choked on a disbelieving laugh. "I'm going to check on Mack. I'll be right back." He started to leave the room but retraced his footsteps to stare down at Hugh. "It's a good thing you didn't hurt her, Cunningham. I'd have torn your heart from your chest." Not giving the sniveling prick a chance to respond, Sebastian hauled off and punched him in the face. "I hope that hurts you more than Mack's did, you wanker."

"We'll make a Thorne of you yet, Drake." Alastair's laughter followed him from the room.

Sebastian found Mackenzie seated at the kitchen island, across from Evie. The women looked deep in conversation, so he didn't interrupt, and instead, prepared himself a cup of tea from the pot on the counter.

Without speaking or looking at him, Evie shoved a decanter of brandy toward him. He found his lips twitching as he fought a grin because, in all honesty, he liked this woman much better than the aunt she'd pretended to be. He refrained from saying so, in case he hurt her feelings.

When the conversation between Mackenzie and her great-great-grandmother wound down, he finally spoke. "I'm sorry about Hugh, Mack. If I'd thought he was anything but a harmless coward, I'd never have left you in a room with him."

"You had no way of knowing what he'd pull, Baz. Hell, I'm psychic and never saw it coming." She gave him a tender smile. "Don't tell me if you found what you're looking for, but if there is anything worthwhile, please get on it. I really want this horrid Enchantress trapped forever and unable to cause any more damage."

Nathanial arrived in a burst of twinkling lights. "I think you'd better come quick. Alastair and GiGi have decided to sacrifice Hugh to the garden. Damian, Spring, and Knox have agreed to the plan. Only your sister and aunt believe it to be a terrible idea."

"To the Garden of Death?" Sebastian asked hoarsely. "What the hell are they thinking?"

"It appears you agree with your family." Mackenzie downed the last of her tea like a shot of alcohol—which it most likely was—and got to her feet. "I suppose we should see if we can prevent a murder."

He swore under his breath when it registered she wasn't joking. "Your family is off the rails on a good day, Mack. I wouldn't consider this a good day. They always react without thinking things through."

"First, they *always* think things through." She propped her hands on her hips and glared. "Just because it's not what *you* would do, in all your conservative English glory, doesn't mean they're wrong. Let's not forget, it was *your* sister who thought it was smart to bring me here. The only witch alive who could be used as the Enchantress's tool. Talk about not thinking something through!"

Sebastian had no comeback. Mackenzie was right. Of course, he didn't have to like that she was, but he had no valid argument at this point. "In that case, let's go find out what the plan is and see if we *can* prevent that murder. For sure, this wouldn't be sanctioned by the Witches' Council."

She bit her lip and looked down.

He had the feeling she was about to make a snarky comment. "It was the Witches' Council remark, wasn't it? I didn't realize how absolutely ridiculous it would sound until it was out of my mouth."

Really, Sebastian should've known better than to bring up the Council, considering how many times the Thornes flouted or outright broke their laws. He'd met Mackenzie for the first time some months back because she took part in one of her family's schemes, as GiGi and Ryker had somehow convinced Sebastian to do. A more breathtaking woman he'd never met, but when he'd discovered Mackenzie wasn't just a pretty face and that she held a degree in nanoscience, he was smitten. Her superior intelligence allowed her to convert a magical potion into a sleeping gas, effectively rendering the Council members unconscious while the rest of the Thornes performed a ceremony to bring Ryker's sister back from the dead. All in an effort for Trina Gillespie to testify against her murderer.

He'd been trying to schmooze her into having dinner with him ever since.

"I'm surprised you even went there, Baz, knowing Alastair and how much he detests the WC." Mackenzie turned sparkling eyes up to him, allowing her grin.

"It doesn't mean he shouldn't follow their guidelines."

She shrugged. "You say guidelines, we hear ridiculous mandates."

Sebastian shot her a sour look as he reached for her hand. "Come on."

They caught up with the Thornes by Isolde's gate, and Sebastian breathed a sigh of relief to see the sigils void of light. If they'd been flickering, he'd have more to worry about than stopping Alastair and his half-baked scheme. Because without a doubt, this wasn't straight up revenge against Hugh. Of course, they weren't beyond retaliation, but Sebastian would bet all the money he owned this was to level the playing field or remove the Enchantress from it once and for all. Even without knowing what they'd come up with, Sebastian was familiar enough with this crew to know they were diabolical in their thinking. A Thorne's half-baked idea was still likely to be better than anyone else's fully planned course of action.

"What's this about, Thorne?"

Alastair never looked up from his study of the symbols carved into the opening as he said, "Mr. Cunningham has decided he wants to be the ultimate sacrifice for his beloved Enchantress. We thought we'd oblige."

Okay, so perhaps Sebastian was wrong and it *was* about revenge. "No. Just, no."

"Darling Baz." GiGi sauntered forward and patted his chest. Behind her, Ryker growled. Her violet-blue eyes gleamed with humor, but she showed no other sign she found her husband's jealousy funny. "I'll amend that for Ryker's sake. Dear Baz..." She paused to glance inquiringly over her shoulder. Ryker nodded his acceptance. When she turned back, her grin was firmly in place. "... We're doing this with or without you."

Sebastian glanced down at Mackenzie, but she wasn't looking at her aunt. Her focus was on Hugh. A heavy frown drew her brows together, and she squeezed his hand in reaction to whatever she was thinking.

"What is it, Mack?"

In a voice barely above a whisper, she said, "He seems extremely calm, doesn't he? Why wouldn't he be fearful?"

"Zealots rarely are, my dear child," GiGi said with a dismissive wave of her hand.

But Sebastian understood what his wife meant. Even a person committed to a cause has a moment of nervousness. Hugh should be perspiring at the idea of being sent into the garden. Instead, his visage was filled with a suppressed excitement, as if he were *eager* to enter.

"This is a terrible idea." Releasing Mackenzie's hand, he walked forward until he was close to Hugh. "Do you know anything about the Enchantress and what she can do, Cunningham? I mean, truly do? Or anything about what she's done in the past?"

"Yes. She is a goddess in her own right. She deserves to reign supreme."

"You're a fucking idiot if you believe that. She was mad then, and she'll be even more deranged and dangerous if she wakes again after being trapped all these years." Sebastian had to try one more time to get him to see reason. "She will kill everyone you've ever loved, Hugh. No exceptions."

"You're wrong. She'll be thrilled I've done this for her. I'll be rewarded with a place at her side." Although doubt entered Hugh's expression, he remained stoic and determined to bring this about. "My family will once more be respected in the witch community."

"You've always been a fool, Hugh. This cements it." With a sigh of disgust, Sebastian faced Alastair. "What is your idea, Thorne? I mean the full plan."

"We open the gate, throw Hugh into the center of those possessed roses—as he requested earlier—and while they're distracted by him, we open the tomb and kill the Enchantress in her weakened state."

"As *he* requested? When did this come about, and since when do you think a witch with lesser intelligence than yours has a good idea?"

Alastair shrugged with his usual nonchalance. "What he actually said, was that he'd gladly give his life to bring her back. I was merely happy to make it happen. Of course, the destruction of Isolde was an added bonus."

He had to admit, it didn't seem horrible, except for the death of his school chum. Sebastian cast a side glance at Hugh. Had the man not been bouncing on his toes, ready for action, Sebastian supposed he'd have had more reservations.

Stepping back, he said, "Do what you must."

"*No!*"

They all turned to Mackenzie.

"No. This is a terrible plan. I won't let you do this to him."

"Mackenzie, child, listen to me." Alastair crossed to her. "This is the only way to stop her that any of us can see. Drake's grandmother wrote in her spellbook to say she believed, ultimately, this would be necessary at some point in time." With a thumb over his shoulder, he gestured to Hugh. "Cunningham would've killed you in his place, Mack."

She shook her head, looking horrified. "I don't care. I won't be responsible for his death."

"You'll be responsible for a whole lot more deaths if you don't get on board with this, Mackenzie," Damian snapped.

The air around them kicked up, and the sigils on the gate flickered.

One by one, they all turned to stare.

"Bloody hell. She's awake." Damian cast an uneasy glance around. "But only just. We need to do this quickly."

The wind whipped into a frenzy and bent the branches of the trees around them. Leaves, by the dozens, rained down on their heads.

"Mackenzie, stop. This is the only way." Alastair grabbed her shoulders and gave her a small shake. "I told you once, if it comes to my family or another's, it's no contest."

"You can't do this. I won't let you," she cried.

Alastair gave a short nod to Sebastian. "Get her out of here. *Now.*"

The wind strengthened to storm force, and dark clouds gathered overhead as Mackenzie fought Sebastian's hold. In the end, it took him and Ryker to contain her.

"This is wrong, Sebastian," she screamed over the winds. "Don't do this."

They teleported her into the main hall, and Sebastian was relieved to be out of the building elements. He wasn't quite sure why Mackenzie had suddenly become hysterical when she was always level-headed and even-tempered before. Perhaps it really was the thought of Hugh's demise, but he somehow doubted it.

He gripped her face between his palms. "You said yourself your family knows what they are doing. Don't second-guess them now, Mack. We need a win here."

She forcefully shoved his hands away. "You're a fool. You're *all* fools."

"Oh, shit," Ryker muttered as he grabbed for Sebastian's arm. "It's not Mack."

When a satisfied smile took the place of her rage, Sebastian had serious misgivings.

She placed a hand on her hip and struck a pose. "How do you know for sure, fellas?"

"You're not Mack," Sebastian stated past the dryness of his mouth.

Ryker positioned himself to fight, but they were both too late. Isolde flung her arms wide and sent them crashing into the wall. The impact hurt like a bitch, and try as he might, Sebastian couldn't move.

"*Isolde.*"

She spun around to face Evie, who was no longer disguised as Aunt Teddie. "Ah, a *Guardian*. You're too late to stop my resurrection—or the death of poor little Mackenzie Thorne. By the time her family realizes she's now occupying the body in my tomb, it will be far too late. No. More. Mackenzie." Isolde ran her hands down her new body. "But I'm grateful for my new vessel. I imagine you'll find it difficult to destroy one of your own."

"I wouldn't bet on it." Evie drew energy from the atmosphere around them, creating a weapon with her hands.

Sebastian wanted to call out, but even his vocal cords were suspended. He shot a frantic look at Ryker, locked on the far wall. The other man looked none too happy about the situation. They were going to be forced to watch these two powerful women go head to head.

Alastair waited until the freak storm created by Mackenzie fizzled before he turned to the gate. "What the devil does this mean, Dethridge? Why are these still illuminated this way?"

"She's awake and prepared, would be my guess." Damian's response was grim. He withdrew a stick pin from his shirt pocket and pricked his thumb. After he pressed a drop of blood into the center of the sun disc hieroglyphic, he faced them. "Let's dial this open and get this over with. Spring, are you ready?"

"I am." She positioned herself between Alastair and Damian. Her job as an earth elemental was to redirect the rose runners from them and toward Hugh.

Alastair glanced back. "Knox, start gathering the elements you need to electrocute Isolde. Damian will assist you after GiGi and I remove the lid."

Nathanial placed his palm flat on the gate, and he began to chant some ancient spell in a language long-since extinct. Only Guardians had access to an incantation this powerful in nature.

Alastair shot a sideways look at Damian.

The Aether watched the lights all snuff out with a cold, detached air. It couldn't be easy for him, knowing he'd be ending his mother's reign for good this time.

Alastair didn't know what he'd do in Damian's position. Most likely the same thing, but for sure, he'd have his doubts. Unfortunately, they were out of time and options. Isolde needed to be stopped.

The sigils lit a fiery red, beginning at the bottom and running both clockwise and counterclockwise to meet at the top in an explosion of light. They all threw their arms up to shield their eyes. When the light dimmed, the gate swung wide.

Alastair had half expected the rose runners to be waiting to strike, but they were curled around the marble tomb in the center of the garden. He'd heard about the decimated ground, but he was ill-prepared for the sight of such bleakness. The entire garden looked like the dead area of a nuclear explosion.

Spring was just as shocked as he was if her horrified gasp was an indication.

A clear blue, film-like barrier shimmered over the opening and separated them from the squared-off tract. Alastair had never seen anything of its like before. "How do we breach it?"

"It's an added measure to prevent entry. I'll remove it." When Nathanial turned to face them, misery was etched his features. "You should know, this isn't only the resting place for the Enchantress. This was the final grave site for those who were lost in the battle with her. A rosebush was planted for each of the fallen witches and warlocks as a memorial to their bravery. To their obliterated soul." He swallowed and cast his eyes down. "My father's included."

"But they are all dead," Spring whispered achingly. "All the bushes but the one."

"Yes. It appears the Enchantress was using the life force from the other plants to feed hers, never knowing it couldn't breach these warded walls to get her the blood magic she needed to wake."

"Mackenzie changed all that when she climbed the wall," Damian said. "Her presence attracted the plant runners, and when it sliced her, it brought Isolde enough magic to wake."

"Curiosity killed the cat, and all that," murmured Spring, as she stared grimly past the blue barrier at the ravaged land. "Let's get this over with."

Alastair couldn't shake the feeling something was wrong about this whole scheme. He searched the faces of the people around him, looking for a sign they sensed it, too.

Damian's attention locked on him. His dark eyes were fiercely intent. "What is it, Al?"

"Does this seem, for lack of a better word, *off* to anyone else?"

"How so?"

"I'm not sure, but I have a bad feeling."

CHAPTER 27

The words were hardly out of his mouth when Hugh charged Nathanial. The two of them crashed through the shield, into the garden. The moment they did, the rosebush unfurled, branching out in all directions, hurling toward them.

"Goddess, preserve us!" GiGi charged forward, but Damian blocked her path.

"No. Nathanial is the only one who can cross."

"We can't leave him in there to fight Hugh alone. Those runners will tear him to shreds!"

"GiGi, if you try to walk through that barrier without the help of a Guardian, you'll be eviscerated."

She looked at Alastair, but he had no answers or clue as to what to do. Spring, bless her quick-thinking soul, ran for the oak tree. "Knox, give me a boost up."

"Hell, no!"

She didn't take the time to answer but lifted her arms, palms up. "Rise, my babies."

The ground rumbled, and the roots of the tree became mobile, digging their way up from the earth to provide steps for her to climb to the top of the wall.

"*Goddammit, woman!*" Knox took the steps two at a time, and the rest of them followed the couple up and over.

Three plant runners were poised like vipers, and they bobbed in a back-and-forth pattern, prepared to strike.

Right before Alastair could get to him, Nathanial lifted Hugh and threw him bodily into the threatening vines. Hugh's screams echoed off the stone walls surrounding them, lending to the eerie setting. As much as he didn't care for the little weasel, Alastair still shuddered at the agonized sound.

However, what disturbed him the most was when Hugh stopped his horrified cries and began to laugh.

"What. The Fuck?" Spring asked from beside him.

"You're all so predictable." Hugh grunted when another thorn pierced his flesh. "Do you really believe this wasn't her plan all along?"

"Fuck!" Damian blasted fire from his hands straight at the tendrils amassing around them. "We have to get to Mackenzie. That's what the lighted sigils and freak storm were about."

"Dear Goddess!" GiGi cried, and her fear was like razor blades down Alastair's skin, or perhaps it was his own terror for the woman he considered a daughter.

"She's possessed Mack." Later, he would blame the black smoke from the fire surrounding them for his hoarse, breaking voice, but for now, Alastair didn't care. He had to get to Mackenzie. "Nathanial! The gate!" They all ran for the entrance at once, with Spring and Knox taking up the rear to magically halt whatever plant runners Damian's firebombs had missed.

Once they cleared the exit, they left Nathanial to seal the door as they each teleported to the yard closest to the house.

Mackenzie wasn't gone as Isolde had lied and told the others, but she was definitely locked out of her own body. It had happened the second Sebastian released her hand and approached Hugh. One moment she was there, and the next, the Enchantress had taken over. There had been no pain like before. No warning headache. Just a hard tug, like she'd been sucked through a vacuum tube.

She'd tried to fight it, and in her struggle, she was able to kick up the wind and clouds. But no one had recognized she was gone. Alastair certainly hadn't, and neither had Sebastian or Ryker until the moment before Isolde threw them across the room.

And now, from this distance where she resided, she could see Sebastian's fierce struggle to break the Enchantress's magical hold while Isolde was distracted by Evie.

Mackenzie's fear for her great-great-grandmother was multiplying as she caught glimpses of Isolde's thoughts. That bitch fully intended to play the "don't hurt your great-great-grandchild" card.

With a fervent hope Evie would set aside any sentimentality and do whatever needed to be done, Mackenzie concentrated on regaining control. It was right then she heard the small voice of Sabrina address her own grandma.

"Please don't hurt Ms. Evie, Grandmother." The little dark-haired girl crossed the room. Her pixie-like face was pleading as she stared at Isolde. "Don't hurt any of them, and I'll go with you."

Behind her, Isolde could hear the garbled sounds from the words Sebastian Drake tried so hard to speak. The chivalrous fool was trying to warn the girl off. He, however, didn't know what both the child and Isolde did: this young girl had the second sight, and she had already seen how Isolde's takeover would end. If Damian's daughter had decided to set foot on the battlefield, the girl knew exactly what would happen and the part she'd play. Looking into the dark eyes, so like her father's, Isolde saw a knowing that Damian had never possessed at the girl's age.

"All right, girl. Come here to me, and I'll let them live."

Sabrina shook her head. "No, you won't. You'll try to take my magic."

"Of course I will, but I'll let them go. I promise."

Again, the child shook her head. "The Darkness made you say that, Grandmother. But I need *you* to promise. If you do, you can beat it."

A wave of dizziness swept Isolde, and she grabbed her head.

"Don't listen to her, you fool! She's collaborating with the Aether to stop you," the Evil insisted.

"Grandmother. Please." The girl took a step forward. "You can beat it. I know you can."

From the corner of her eye, Isolde saw the Guardian lift her arm to strike. She countered with a mere flick of her hand, breaking the other woman's forearm.

The Guardian cried out and grabbed for the pulsing green energy ball from her useless hand.

Sabrina stepped into the space between them, with her back to the other woman. Her wide eyes held only a trace amount of fear, but it was enough to tempt the Evil. It had never wanted anything more than to crush the innocent before it.

Another wave of dizziness struck, but this time, excruciating pain accompanied it. Isolde pressed her fingers to her temples.

"Mack?"

"Yes, it's me, Sabrina." Mackenzie smiled to show her sincerity and ease the girl's fear. "We only have a few minutes, but I want you to teleport home now. Find your mother and have her get you far, far away from here. Right now."

"You have to come with me."

"I can't, sweetie. There's no telling when or if your grandmother will come back. I need you to get to safety."

"We can fight the Darkness together. You and me."

Mackenzie wanted to cry in the face of such bravery. Here, in front of her, stood a six-year-old child ready to take on the worst evil imaginable. "Okay, sweetheart." She held out her hand to Sabrina. "Let's go."

"Mack!" Sebastian called her name, and she turned to see him sagging against the wall. He looked haggard and drained.

"It'll be all right, Baz. Find the others and get Evie help for when Isolde comes back." Because Mackenzie had little doubt she would, but Mack hoped to give them all a head start first.

They made it as far as the yard when she felt her grip on her mind loosen. Mackenzie couldn't stop Isolde's takeover this time. The Enchantress had grown too strong to subdue.

But she could at least warn Sabrina.

"*Run!*" Opening her fingers, one at a time, she attempted to release the girl's hand. "Please run," she begged.

She had the satisfaction of seeing Sabrina make it out of her reach before she was lost to the darkness, only able to hear the events around her.

An ear-piercing scream rent the air, and Mackenzie desperately fought to take her body back from Isolde.

"*Papa!*" Sabrina hollered for her father a second, then third time.

The sound tore at Mackenzie's soul. The sheer terror in the girl's voice was difficult to withstand, as was the wave of power that slapped her backwards into a wide, solid tree trunk. The pain stole her breath, and Isolde's hold slipped for a split second. Mackenzie was able to glimpse her surroundings in that instant.

Damian had arrived, and the rage radiating from him was enough to set her knees to trembling. His hands were already lifted to strike, and Mackenzie wondered if his was the magic that had sent her body flying. Her initial thought had been Sabrina defending herself, but now she suspected Papa Aether had arrived to protect his daughter.

"Go, beastie," Damian ordered.

"*Please hurry,*" Mackenzie begged.

Confusion flashed in his eyes as he stared at her. "Mack?"

"For the moment." She gasped as a tearing pain in her abdomen doubled her over. "Goddess, preserve us. She's determined!"

"Good Christ, Mack!" Sebastian had appeared at Damian's shoulder and began to cross to her. His intent to help her was obvious, as was the worry clouding his face.

She held up a hand. "*No!* She's here. Just under the surface." A cry was ripped from her as a slashing pain tore through her a second time. "I can feel her scratching to get out."

Vicious, vile words spewed from Isolde and flooded her mind. The Enchantress threatened, promising she'd make Sebastian suffer if Mackenzie didn't surrender her body immediately. Nausea rose up and burned the back of her throat at the images of destruction Isolde used to break her.

Across the distance, she met the Aether's wary obsidian eyes. "Damian, it's time."

He gave her an understanding nod, and she was pleased he recalled her instructions should she not be able to stop Isolde.

Mackenzie's gaze sought Sebastian's. "I love you, Baz."

Horror dawned as he registered her intent. He surged forward only to be knocked off his feet by a sweep of Damian's arm.

"Commoro!" The Aether's magical command locked Sebastian in place on the ground.

The guttural shout from her husband and Sabrina's terrified cry were the last things Mackenzie heard as Damian struck. A blazing-hot shockwave scorched her insides, not once, but multiple times. Unable to withstand the agony, Mackenzie screamed and surrendered her body to Isolde. Her only hope was that the Enchantress wouldn't be strong enough to survive his assault either.

Isolde only had a moment to savor her successful control of the psychic witch's body before the searing pain of the lightning strikes penetrated her consciousness.

The fierceness on her son's face as he flung bolt after bolt was a sight to behold. He was pure savage intent. The part of her not controlled by the Evil felt pride in his determination to protect his daughter and friends. But that was the part that couldn't withstand the torture he was inflicting on her.

Looking down at the charred remains of her arms, she gave control over to the Beast.

"Damian!" It cried out. "Stop… please stop." It began to weep and rock. "She's gone. Please… stop," the Darkness wailed.

"Dethridge, it's Mack," Sebastian shouted. "Stop this now!"

Damian paused, hand lifted to throw another crackling bolt, uncertainty in his eyes.

His hesitation was all the time the Evil needed.

It teleported to where his daughter stood and grabbed the child by the throat. "I'll break her neck with one snap," It warned.

A muffled sob escaped the girl. She knew her father couldn't win against the threat to her person.

The Evil laughed.

But Isolde heard the cry and had a momentary pang of conscience when Damian lowered his arms.

"Mama, she's your granddaughter. A true innocent."

Isolde's gaze lowered to the solemn girl, and in the tiny face, she saw the image of her son when he was her age. The large, all-knowing eyes stared back. Yes, the fear was there, but so was courage.

The Beast snapped and snarled, trying to gain control again.

Mackenzie's soft, pleading voice filled her head. *"Don't hurt her, Isolde."*

Again, the Evil roared its displeasure.

Isolde was mesmerized by the guilelessness and purity of Sabrina. Although it was a struggle, she seemed to recall that was the child's name.

"Grandmother, don't do this."

With her heartbeat drumming in her ears, Isolde was able to silence the Beast inside her for a moment. She eased her hold and stroked her hand down Sabrina's dark, silky hair. Something akin to love filled her chest and made it ache. She wondered if she had it in her to sacrifice again, like she'd done with Damian when he was a small boy.

"Hide, my dear. Use the cloaking spell, and go as far and as fast as you can. I cannot control it forev—*ahh!*"

The punch of pain she experienced from the knife entering her back surprised her enough to loosen her hold. The Evil hissed its fury as Isolde lost her grip on Sabrina completely. She looked down at the arm banded across her chest, somehow knowing immediately whom it belonged to.

"Nathanial Thorne. The savior of small children," she said.

"I couldn't let you hurt her, Isolde, just as I couldn't let my father hurt your son all those years ago," he said almost regretfully.

"But you made a mistake, Nathanial."

The arm holding her tightened even as he began to withdraw the knife for a second plunge of the blade. "I don't think so."

She smiled and closed her eyes, allowing the Darkness to resume its plan for destruction.

CHAPTER 28

When Mackenzie's burnt body collapsed at Nathaniel's feet, he felt deep, gut-wrenching sorrow. He'd only known the young woman a short time, but he'd fallen in love with her quick, sharp wit and bubbly, fun personality. She had truly been a beautiful soul.

He knew she wasn't dead. Not yet, anyway, but it wouldn't be long. Her body, driven by the Enchantress, would struggle to heal, but something would have to give, and it would be Mackenzie who lost out and paid the ultimate price for Isolde's insane drive to rule supreme.

"Finish it, son," he ground out, looking at Damian.

The lost expression on his face reminded Nathanial of the first time they'd met, when Damian, as a young boy, had teleported him away from the imminent battle between the Enchantress and Isis backed by the Six.

"Damian, please," Sebastian hollered. "Please don't kill her."

Sebastian looked as tortured as Nathanial had ever seen him. Even the death of the young man's parents hadn't had this effect on him.

"I'm begging you. Don't kill Mack."

"Finish it, Damian," Nathanial ordered roughly. He felt his own grief building, and he needed to retain control of his emotions until the Enchantress and her brand of evil were gone for good.

What happened next was instantaneous. The Aether lobbed another bolt of lightning just as his daughter ran to Mackenzie's crumpled form.

"No, Papa!"

Nathanial tried to scoop her up and get her away, but he wasn't as fast or agile as the girl.

Damian couldn't retract the lethal blast he'd thrown at Mackenzie, and as a result, it hit its target along with Sabrina and Nathanial.

"*Sabrina!*"

Somewhere in the distant part of his brain, right before he lost consciousness, Nathanial heard Vivian's bloodcurdling scream and Damian's tortured shout.

Mackenzie found herself in the Otherworld for the second time in her life. But *this* time, she wasn't alone. Across from her stood Isolde—the Enchantress who had caused her no end of grief—and Nathanial. They all stared at one another as if unsure what to do.

"Where is this place?" Isolde asked, with a wondrous look around.

Mackenzie's gaze darted around, touching on all the beautiful things she'd witnessed on her first visit: the crystal-clear water, the startlingly green grass, a stone bench under the tallest, fullest oak tree she'd ever seen. She loved it and hated it, because it meant she was dead. There would be no Preston to save her now.

"I think you know, Isolde." Mackenzie moved closer to Nathanial. A small part of her wanted the comfort of his protection, but a larger part wanted to protect *him* from the Enchantress. Silly, because he was the far more powerful of the two of them.

"The Otherworld," Isolde guessed.

"Actually, a holding area in the Otherworld. It's my understanding Isis uses it to determine what the next course of action is for a soul." Mackenzie felt only slightly more confident when Nathanial's large warm hand encompassed hers. "Last time I was here, I met with Isis and Set."

"Set?" Isolde laughed. "That burly creature is here? Of course. It will be good to see him again."

Rage detonated like a bomb inside Mackenzie's brain at the other woman's casualness. Isolde was acting as if there would be a joyous reunion with old friends when, in fact, there would only be pain in Mackenzie's heart until the day her family joined her here.

"Why? Because you want to try to possess his body, too? Maybe steal some of his magic to destroy more lives? Because you haven't done enough? Haven't hurt your son and granddaughter to the max?" She curled her hands into fists and huffed out a breath.

Isolde's breathtaking face froze in a cold, hard mask of indifference, but her eyes gave her away. They weren't flat and full of madness as they had been the other time Mackenzie encountered her in the garden. They were tortured and shimmered with tears.

In a sick way, Mackenzie wanted to go to her and offer comfort.

"Mack." Nathanial's hand tightened over hers. "She's not possessed by the Evil here."

"What?" She looked back and forth between them. "What are you saying? And where did it go?"

Before he could answer, a flash of gold filled the clearing, and Sabrina joined them. Her large obsidian eyes were curious as she looked around her.

It felt as if Mackenzie's heart cracked in two the second Sabrina arrived here. Six was too young to die. She should've been able to run around like a normal child. To play games and cause trouble. To grow up and fall in love. To have many more years of a loving family surrounding her.

Isolde knelt and held out her arms. "Come here, child."

Mackenzie ripped her hand out of Nathanial's and rushed forward, placing herself between grandmother and granddaughter.

"*You don't touch her!* You don't…" The words caught in her throat. "*Three lives!* You… you took three… lives!"

She dropped to her knees and bowed her head as the wretched sobs wracked her body. Her own family would be okay now, but the idea that Sabrina, that beautiful innocent little soul, was a casualty was too much to bear.

Oddly, it was Sabrina who took charge of the moment. She approached Mackenzie and patted her on the crown of her head. "Don't cry, Mack. It's not over. You'll come back to play with me soon."

Mackenzie lifted her face to stare into the wise eyes in front of her. "I don't understand."

Sabrina smiled and used her sleeve to wipe the moisture from Mackenzie's cheeks. "You and me. We'll still be friends and play in the garden."

"Oh, honey, I want that very much, but I don't think that's going to happen."

"GiGi and Papa will heal your body. It's what they do."

"How do you know about GiGi and Papa?"

Sabrina giggled and patted her shoulder like the old soul she was. "I know everything, Mack. Like you."

"She has the second sight, Ms. Thorne."

"*Drake.* My last name is now Drake," Mackenzie snapped at Isolde. "Something else you robbed me of."

"You will live with Cousin Baz and be my friend, Mack," Sabrina assured her. "And we'll make leaf dragons and dancing elephants any time we want."

"I would love nothing more." She hugged the girl tight and choked back the tidal wave of grief. "That is a beautiful dream, sweetie."

Nathanial stepped forward. "Not a dream, child. She can make it happen as soon as Damian and GiGi heal you."

Mackenzie drew back and stared from one knowing face to the other. "I still don't understand. She's with us here. In the Otherworld. We're…" She covered Sabrina's ears. "…dead."

A sparkling glow lit the girl's eyes, and her smile blossomed, making her the picture of mischievous intent. "I can still hear you, Mack."

Unable to help herself, Mackenzie hugged her tight and laughed. "Your father was right. You're a little beastie."

Sabrina cocked her head as if to listen. "I have to go now. Papa's calling me back."

Isolde rose to her feet and slowly approached. "You'll tell him I'm sorry for all the pain I caused him? For being a horrid mother?"

Sabrina rushed over to embrace her. "He knows, Grandmother." She pulled away to approach Nathanial and held up her arms for him to lift her. When her face was level with his, she hugged his neck tightly. "Thank you for saving me, Grandpa Nate."

"You're welcome, my dear. Tell your father I love him and if I had to do it all over again, I would. Tell Evie, I'll see her soon." His voice was gruff, but Mackenzie knew it covered his deep emotion, his undying love for his wife and adopted son.

"I will. I promise."

"Good. I'll have our home ready and our boys here to greet her. You make sure she knows that, too."

Sabrina patted his cheek. "Papa's calling me."

"Then you must go, child."

"Wait!" Isolde gripped her sleeve, her eyes hungrily scanning Sabrina's face. "I would never have let it hurt you, darling girl. Just as I couldn't let it hurt him."

"I know."

"Damian must salt and burn the body in the tomb. He must also shatter the ruby stone of the necklace. The one buried with me."

Sabrina nodded slowly, as if processing all she had to remember. Just like before, a gold light flared bright, blinding them to everything for the time it took her soul to return to the earthly plane.

"Does this mean I'm the only one of the three of us going back?" Mackenzie asked softly. "Did I interpret her words correctly?"

"It appears so," Isolde said, equally as soft. She put on a brave face and lifted her chin. "I'll be here to face whatever punishment

Isis and Set have for me. Nathanial will see it's carried out. And you, my lovely Mackenzie, will return home to live out your days in harmony if Sabrina's prediction is correct."

As they waited for whatever came next, Mackenzie thought about the events leading them to this moment and tried to recall all the premonitions she'd had. She tried to process everything, but her mind still seemed cloudy.

"Isolde."

The Enchantress turned from her place down by the river. "Yes, dear?"

"The vision of me holding a knife to Sebastian's chest—that incident never took place. Did you implant that thought?"

"No. You truly had the premonition, and it *did* happen. On your wedding night. I possessed your body while you were sleeping. But you were too strong. Your love for Sebastian unwavering." She smiled, and it was tinged with deep sadness. "I've never experienced a love like that." She shook her head and met Mackenzie's stare. "You fought me and won that night. I honestly don't know why you don't remember."

"Because a woman's special day shouldn't be marred with horror or strife," Isis said from behind Mackenzie.

The three of them bowed their heads, offering their respect to the Goddess and God who entered the clearing.

Mackenzie's mind was reeling from all she'd learned in the last few minutes. "You took the memory away, Exalted One?"

"I had Evelyn do it while you slept."

"I see." Her irritation spiked. "Enchantress, Goddess, Guardian. You all like to play with the rest of us as if we aren't living, feeling human beings, but mere pawns on your damned chessboard. Did you ever think I might have needed that bit of pertinent information?"

The kohl-lined, sky-blue eyes of the Goddess narrowed, and Mackenzie knew a moment of unease. Here she was, reprimanding Isis, when she should be minding her tongue and expressing gratitude she'd found favor with her. The Goddess had been kind enough to bestow on her a lovely memory of her wedding day, and Mackenzie had just spat on that favor.

"I'm sorry, Exalted One. Forgive me, please."

"No."

Mackenzie's heart dropped like a stone to the pit of her stomach. Great, she'd just screwed the pooch. Next stop, the Underworld, where she'd live in fiery hell for eternity.

"No, you are correct, beloved. Too many times we play games with the lives of mortals." Isis tilted Mackenzie's chin up to meet her steady gaze. The Goddess's eyes were thoughtful as they studied her. "You were right to speak up. To remind me to give free will to my chosen ones. There is nothing to forgive."

"Thank you for your kindness to my granddaughter, Exalted One," Nathanial said with feeling. "She'll remember this and be more mindful of her tongue in the future."

Isis laughed and crossed to pat his chest. "You're very much like Alastair, aren't you?"

A cheeky grin flashed across his face. "He's very much like me. After all, I was born first."

She tossed back her long black hair and gave him an arch look, but there was no denying the affectionate gleam in her eyes or the slight smirk on her full lips. "Charming scoundrels, the both of you."

"Truth," Mackenzie agreed. She sent a warm, loving smile toward Nathanial. "But we love them for it."

"Truth," Isis repeated as she faced Mackenzie. "Enough time has passed. You must return, beloved."

"Thank you for this chance."

"Don't thank me yet. You and Sebastian Drake have one more trial to face."

"That sounds ominous."

"Doesn't it, though?"

CHAPTER 29

From his study, Sebastian watched Mackenzie as she played tag with Sabrina Dethridge and Spring in the lower garden just off the terrace. The sight was bittersweet. Seeing Mackenzie laugh, the joy in her compelling blue eyes, brought him both gladness and pain. Gladness that she'd lived to draw a breath and play. Sadness because she'd come out of the battle vastly different from who she'd been before.

Alastair stood next to him, observing his family at play. "From all accounts, once a witch has been possessed then subsequently exorcised, she'll never be normal again. Her mind is broken."

His grim expression burned itself into Sebastian's mind. Mackenzie would never again be the woman he'd met and fallen in love with. She was like a broken doll, and her mental capacity was that of a small child. It would take a miracle to restore her back to the functioning adult she once was. And although in the magical community a lot of things were possible, miracles were always in short supply due to the fickleness of the gods and goddesses.

"What do you suggest I do?" Sebastian asked raggedly.

"I don't know, son. We can make her comfortable at my estate. She'll want for nothing."

"She's my *wife*." He rubbed a hand over his heart.

Alastair remained silent, allowing Sebastian to decide the best course of action.

He released a harsh breath. Interacting with her every day for the last month had been pure torture and would continue to be. There would be no way for him to tease her, cuddle her, or make love to her as he once had. It would be vile and the lowest sort of low to take advantage of her mental state. The mere thought of intimacy with her like this left him cold and sick to his stomach. Yes, she possessed the sexy body of an adult, but in her mind, she wasn't, and this new situation was as undesirable as standing naked in a frozen pond. It had the same effect, leaving him numb, without any desire to touch her at all.

Whether she stayed or if he were to send her back to the Thornes, he would remain celibate. He wouldn't betray his marriage vows by taking a lover on the side. It seemed Sebastian was destined to exist in a lonely half-life. How ironic that he'd found the one person to ease his solitary existence, and now she was off-limits because of her condition.

He turned desperate eyes to face Alastair. "Do you think Isis would intervene?"

"She hasn't answered my request for an interview." His gravelly voice spoke of Alastair's worry on that score. Rarely did Isis not appear for her favorite human.

"I'll care for her as I've promised. Should anything happen to me, I'll entrust her well-being back to you." Sebastian rubbed his thumbs across his burning eyes.

"Drake."

Alastair's severe tone told him he wasn't going to like what came next.

"What?" he snapped.

"You don't owe her anything. You were married for all of a minute."

"Would she leave me?" Sebastian shook his head. "I'll tell you now, she wouldn't."

Silence filled the space between them as he struggled with what to do.

"It's funny because she understood me better in the short time we were together than anyone. Even the woman I grew up with and was engaged to didn't know me like Mack did." He closed his eyes against the stinging moisture building behind his lids. "I love her, Alastair. I love her so bloody much. Why did this happen?"

"I don't have any answers for you, son." Alastair surprised him with a hug, and Sebastian fought the desire to weep like a small boy in a father's arms. After a long moment, the older man released him with a pat on the back. Grave eyes met his. "I'll let the rest of the family know she's staying here. If you need anything, don't hesitate to ask."

Sebastian swallowed past the lump lodged in his throat and looked back through the glass to the garden below. Mackenzie laughed in delight and clapped her hands as Spring magically produced a yellow daisy.

Alastair cleared his throat. "Her powers will need to be bound. She's still a Thorne, and as such, has unlimited magic. She may not understand the consequences should she get angry at someone. It's also possible she could be dangerous should her mind deteriorate further."

Sebastian cast Alastair a sharp glance. He hadn't thought of her indulging in a child's temper tantrum, but the possibility existed.

A few heartbeats passed in which he studied her lovely face. "What do we tell the outside world? She's a public figure. I can't imagine she can just drop off the face of the earth after a career like hers."

"A news release of an accidental death would be best. She must remain hidden at all costs from this point forward."

"Like a dirty family secret," Sebastian ground out. He fisted his hand against the glass and hit it lightly, wishing he could punch his balled-up fist through it and every other window in this miserable place.

"You needn't say she's passed. You can put out the tale of a stroke or brain trauma." Alastair gripped his shoulder and squeezed. "The choice is yours. You'll be the one who deals with the fallout."

"Goddess, this is impossible!" Sebastian swore long and loud. With a hard scrub of his face, he turned from the beautiful and heart-wrenching view of the two stunning women and the girl laughing in the garden. "Should a member from each of our families perform the binding ceremony together? If I unexpectedly pass first, the binding will stay in place, and vice versa."

"It's a wise decision."

"Then that's what we'll do."

Their gazes locked, and Sebastian was the first to look away. Those shrewd eyes of his missed nothing, and it was disconcerting as hell.

"I'll go find a spell from our grimoire. Feel free to make yourself at home, sir."

"I already have a foolproof spell, but I'd be grateful if you could round up the ingredients and find us a safe space to cast."

"Of course. I'll meet you in the solarium at half past." He didn't wait for Alastair's response. He couldn't. The air was too thick in this room, and he needed to be outside—in the garden—breathing the same sweet air as his wife. If that was all he could have, he'd take it.

"Sebastian."

He paused in his escape but didn't turn. "Yes?"

"For what it's worth, son, I'm so sorry."

"I know. Me, too."

"She truly loved you, you know. From the moment she saw you, according to GiGi. Mack only pretended disinterest because she didn't want to make it easy for me to matchmake the two of you. Apparently, she wanted you to fall in love without interference."

Mackenzie had said much the same thing on their wedding night. Pain unfurled in Sebastian's chest and made it difficult to inhale. If warlocks could have heart attacks, he'd swear that's what he was experiencing now. Hands clenched, Sebastian gave a single, sharp nod and fled. He could run as fast and as long as he wished, but he'd never outrun the demons that would forever be his closest companions.

Ducking into the solarium, he dropped to his knees and let out the sobs that had been building. His body convulsed as he tried to muffle the sound. Goddess, he loved his wife. More than he'd ever thought possible to love anyone.

"Why?" he cried. "Why did it have to be her?"

He didn't know how long he sat there, hugging the frilly pillow from the settee, nor did he care. When he heard the click of the door opening and shutting, he swiped a hand over his face and placed the pillow back on the sofa. Before he could stand, Mackenzie knelt in front of him. She gently touched his puffy, still-damp lids and traced her fingertips along his face.

He recoiled from her touch. This was a familiar gesture of his old Mack. A lead in to a kiss or caress. But this Mackenzie in front of him wouldn't know how the memory affected him.

"Why are you crying, Baz?"

In her child-like innocence, she broke his heart all over again. He tried to smile, but failed miserably. "I'm sad, Mack."

She tilted her head, and with wide-eyed curiosity, she studied his face. "Why?"

"Someone I love very much has gone away. I miss her."

"She'll come back."

The confidence in her voice almost made him lash out in his anger and hurt. Sebastian wanted to shout and tell her she knew nothing. He bit his tongue against an outburst.

"No, love. She won't."

"She will! I know it," Mackenzie insisted. "Leo will help her."

"Leo's passed on, Mack." He shoved back his frustration along with the pain associated with losing Nathaniel and Evie, who had joined him in the afterlife shortly after his death. "He's beyond helping anyone now."

At first her face crumbled, but then she gave him a look of pity and began to braid her hair. "You're wrong. You'll see."

"I truly wish I were, love." They sat in silence for a moment as

Sebastian worked through the explanation he wanted to give her regarding the upcoming ceremony.

"You don't need to take my magic, Baz."

He jerked. The clarity in her blue eyes surprised him. While the innocence remained, there was knowledge, too. As if she saw something he didn't.

"Mack, do you see the future?"

"Sometimes."

He closed his eyes, not daring to hope. "Have you seen anything recently?"

"I saw you and Cousin Alastair. You were both sad. Not as sad as you were when I came in here." She patted his chest directly over his heart. "You don't need to take my magic," she said again.

His hope fled. He was being ridiculous to believe she could, in any way, see the future still. Taking her hand in his, he toyed with her slender fingers, absently noting the dirt under her nails. Although an air elemental, she loved to dig in the soil with Spring.

Mackenzie didn't allow him to touch her more than a minute before she removed her hand from his and started the process of plaiting her hair over again.

"Mack, sometimes, when someone is very young, they don't know how to deal with all the world's problems. There is a need for the adults in their life to remove the temptation for them to strike back if something hurts or angers them. Do you understand?"

She shook her head, and a stubborn expression hardened her lovely features to stone. "No, Baz. If you take my magic, I'll be mad at you. Because then I can't make flowers dance with Spring or play dragons with Sabrina."

His heart lurched. All she wanted was the simple, fun things to amuse her. "I can do that for you."

Large eyes wide and fearful, she shook her head.

"Mack, I'm trying to help you, love."

"No!"

"Listen to me now—"

Before he could finish his sentence, she teleported.

In stunned disbelief, Sebastian stared at the empty spot where she'd been.

Goddess! There was no telling where she'd gone! He jumped to his feet, yanked open the door, and came to an abrupt halt.

She stood on the other side, grinning.

The relief he felt was immeasurable.

"Don't do that again, Mack! You—"

She was gone in a blink.

"Bloody hell!"

"You shouldn't swear, Baz. It isn't nice," she scolded in a sing-song voice.

He spun to see her on the seat he'd vacated. "This isn't funny, Mackenzie."

A mischievous grin lit her face, and she touched a finger to her lips.

For a brief second, she was his Mack. The one tempting him into trouble. The one he would follow to the ends of the earth for just one kiss.

But she wasn't that Mack, not really.

The constant conflict of memories and reality would break his heart over and over again on a daily basis. He quickly realized he wasn't emotionally equipped to handle it. Maybe it was selfish on his part, but he understood what he needed to do for his own peace of mind.

"I have to send you to live with your family, love. You're going to live with Alastair in his beautiful house."

Her face fell, and tears pooled in her eyes, spilling over her cheeks. "I won't be bad again. I promise."

MACKENZIE DIDN'T KNOW WHAT SHE'D DONE THAT WAS SO TERRIBLE, but it hurt to see Baz mad. She was willing to do anything to be close to him. To see the incredible light surrounding him. Because even if it was dim right now, it was still brighter than anyone else's, and it attracted her like the beautiful butterflies flitting around the flowers.

"Please, Baz. Don't make me go away." She was sure she'd die if he did. "You can take my magic."

"Come here, Mack."

She stepped into his tender embrace and felt a smidgeon of her fear melt away—*until he spoke again.*

"Alastair's home is the safest place for you. You can see Spring more often, and she'll make the flowers dance for you."

Biting her lip, she closed her eyes. She heard his heart pick up its pace, and she wanted to bury herself in his hug forever. "I don't want to leave you, Baz. You're my forever friend."

He sucked in a deep breath, and the movement felt nice against her cheek. It didn't take away her budding heartache, though.

"I'll always be your forever friend, love. *Always.*"

"Please let me stay." Her tears dampened his shirt, and she hoped he wouldn't get angry again. "I'll be good. I promise."

"Mack, it isn't about you being good or bad." He set her away from him and cupped her jaw. "You don't belong here anymore."

He didn't want her. Just like her father hadn't wanted her. It pounded through her brain and into her heart, making it speed up faster than his had been a second ago.

She knew something terrible had happened in the weeks before she woke up, but no one would tell her what she didn't remember. They talked in hushed tones when she was near, and they gave her pitying looks. Sebastian's sister couldn't stand to look at her.

But the worst was the haunting look in Sebastian's eyes. It never seemed to go away when he looked at her. Maybe that's why she wanted to stay, because her vision of the future could chase away his sorrow.

"If you make me go, you'll always be sad," she whispered, trying one last time to change his mind.

"If you stay, it will be much worse," he whispered back.

She dropped her eyes to the ground, unable to look at him another second without sobbing. "You don't like me to teleport, but I'd like to go to my room now."

"I'll walk you."

"I don't want you to." Tears poured from her eyes, and she glared at him. "I don't want you to because you're mean, and if you send me away, you'll never give me the rose in the maze."

He frowned. "Mack, what are you saying? Are you talking about a future event?"

Mackenzie ran. She couldn't answer his questions, because this terrible ache in her chest was too great. Her head hurt, and her brain felt like it was being crushed. As soon as she turned the corner, she visualized a place in her mind. Her cells heated to the burning point, and when she opened her eyes, she was in a strange place. Not the one she'd envisioned.

"Hello, Mack."

CHAPTER 30

*D*amian had been on the terrace when Mackenzie and Spring were playing tag with his daughter. The doors to Sebastian's study had been open, and he'd heard every word of Sebastian and Alastair's conversation. Every unspoken thought.

A miracle.

It just so happened, Damian knew someone who could make one happen. He strode to Sabrina's hiding spot—the large oak Sebastian had toppled in his anger the first day Damian and his daughter had met Mackenzie.

"Beastie, we need to talk."

Her eyes lost their joy. Resignation took its place. "I have to give her back, don't I?"

"Give her back?"

"To Cousin Baz."

"Did you take her away?"

Sabrina's eyes welled with tears, and she nodded. "Don't be mad at me. She said she wanted to play with me."

He squatted next to her and tugged a curl. "When did she say that, my love?"

"In the Otherworld. I said she'll live here and play with me, and she said she'd love nothing more."

Damian sighed. Of course, a six-year-old child would take Mackenzie's words at face value. "So when you helped me to revive her after her cousin healed her body, you did this? You made her your same age inside her mind?"

She nodded, a hopeful expression forming on her tiny pixie features. "Then we could be the same."

"But you're not the same, Sabrina. Mackenzie is a grown woman. You can't put a child's mind inside a grown woman. It causes her loved ones heartache."

"I know." Her voice was small and woeful. "I just wanted her to always be my friend."

"She will always be your friend." He tugged her into his arms and stood up. "But we have to fix what you've done."

"Because Cousin Baz is going to send her away?"

"You saw it, too?"

She nodded, and her lower lip quivered. "I don't want her to go away."

"Let's go make sure she won't."

Sabrina's happy smile filled Damian's heart to full. He hated to squash it, but she needed to understand she couldn't mess with people's lives or alter their path.

"Beastie, when Mack's mind is restored, you will tell her and Sebastian what you've done. You owe them an apology."

"Okay."

"They may be very upset with you and not want to see you for a while. You understand that could happen, don't you?"

Her arms tightened around his neck, and she buried her face against the side of his throat. "I'm sorry, Papa."

Her choked sob killed him. Damian had to struggle to keep it together in the face of his daughter's pain. He cleared his throat. "We'll make it right, my love. And I bet you, Mack is the forgiving sort."

Damian saw confusion flare in Mackenzie's face when she arrived in the Garden of Death. Fear quickly followed.

"This is the bad place." The wobble in her voice reminded him of Sabrina whenever she was scared.

"Not anymore, Mack. See?" He pointed to Sabrina by the fountain. "We've made it safe."

"The Enchantress?"

"Is gone." He felt a pang as he remembered the message Sabrina had relayed from his mother. "She won't ever hurt anyone again."

"I'm going away," she whispered. *"That* hurts."

"It's why I brought you here." He gave her a direct look, tempering it with a gentle smile. "Sabrina and I want to make sure that doesn't happen and that you stay where you belong."

Mackenzie lifted hopeful eyes his way. "I can stay? Here? With Baz?"

"I promise."

"Oh, thank you!" She flung her arms around his waist and held tight. "Thank you, Damian. Thank you!"

As he returned her hug, he looked over her head at Sabrina. His daughter played with the hem of her dress, her head hung in shame. Their strong emotions warred with one another. Sabrina was heartbroken at the potential loss of her friend, and Mackenzie was elated at the possibility of remaining at the Drake estate. What did it say about Damian when he was tempted to let his daughter have her friend? He knew the loneliness associated with growing up different. He'd been much older than the children born to Nathanial and Evie after their marriage.

But right was right, and he had to fix what wasn't meant to be wrong in the first place. "Come, Mack. We need to have a small ceremony."

She pulled back, and her face showed her budding distrust. "What ceremony? Do you want to take my magic, too? I told Baz he could have it if I can stay."

Her words caused Damian's stomach to knot. Were they wrong to believe the Evil had been defeated? "Baz wants your magic?"

"He said I could hurt someone if he didn't take it away."

Torn with indecision, he looked back toward Sebastian's house.

"It's okay, Papa."

Damian turned his head sharply and stared down at Sabrina. He hadn't heard her approach. "What's okay, beastie?"

"The Darkness is gone. It's not in Baz."

"You're positive?"

"Yes." The certainty was clear in her dark gaze.

"Okay, then. Let's restore Mackenzie's mind."

"Can I lift the stones, Papa? Please?"

He grinned at her eagerness. "Do you think you're powerful enough?"

"I had no idea you had standing stones here, Dethridge. You were positively fascinated with mine."

Damian whipped around at the sound of Alastair's dry tone. At first he didn't see him, but movement on the wall by the tree drew his notice. Alastair's arms were crossed, supporting his weight atop the ledge. He looked as if he were being neighborly and ready to have a casual conversation with a friend. If he hadn't been eight feet in the air, Damian might have believed he stumbled across them. "Al."

"Damian." Alastair's tone held an amused note, but he didn't crack so much as a small smile.

"Don't tell me. You happened to scry for Mackenzie's whereabouts and decided to lay in wait, like a spider in its web, to see what I intended to do about Sebastian's little problem." The suddenness of Alastair's grin made Damian laugh. "You old fox! Did you guess what had happened, or did you know all along?"

"I saw you on the terrace earlier. You looked like you'd been hit with a hammer, and I decided to find out what had caused you to react that way."

"Hmm. Clever."

"No, I'd say you were, to figure out what Sabrina had done. The rest of us would never have known."

Damian smiled in acknowledgment of Alastair's praise. "Why don't you inform Drake his wife will be home in time for supper? Sabrina and I have this handled."

All humor faded from Alastair's countenance. "Thank you, my friend, for what you're about to do."

His gratitude pulsed in the air between them and made Damian feel terrible for not uncovering Sabrina's act weeks ago. "It's the least I can do. Oh, and regarding these stones, no one knows of their existence except the three of us. The last time I had access to them, I was a small boy."

"Ah, right. Because Isolde was buried here, you couldn't access them without giving her their power source."

"Yes. As it was, it created that bloody evil rosebush."

Alastair chuckled and disappeared, presumably to let Sebastian know all would be well soon. Or to torture him. One never knew with Alastair Thorne.

Bit by bit, Mackenzie felt the neurotransmitters inside her brain knit and spark to life. Her head ached from the force of the Aether's and Sabrina's combined power as they healed her. Right when she was sure she couldn't take another second of the restoration ceremony, it stopped.

Although her eyes were closed, she heard the footfalls of another person.

"Is she all right?"

Spring. She must've discovered where they'd gone.

"She is," Damian said.

"When will she wake up?"

"In another few hours or so. Her body and mind need rest. A hard reset, if you will."

"You used the reverse transmutation spell." Spring didn't ask, she stated. If Mackenzie could've laughed, she would've. Her cousin had total recall of anything she'd ever read or seen. If she said this was from the scroll Set had given her, Mackenzie would believe it.

"We did," Damian confirmed. "When we initially brought her back from the Otherworld, Sabrina split her mind in two halves, leaving Mack in a child-like state. Apparently, she wanted a playmate."

"All this time, she could've been her normal self?"

"Yes."

Mackenzie heard a small sniffle, and she wanted to reach out to pull Sabrina close. Although she couldn't move or speak, she could feel, and so she thought hard of forgiveness and love with the hope Damian or his daughter would understand she had no ill will for either of them.

A small hand clutched hers, and Mackenzie sensed she'd gotten through to the child.

Spring wasn't done asking questions by a long shot and peppered Damian with questions about how the processes worked to put Mackenzie's mind back together.

He sounded more than happy to discuss the details. "By using the reverse transmutation spell, we were able to fuse the two halves together again to make her whole."

"Well done." Her cousin's light laugh washed over Mackenzie and brought relief. Spring's approval meant it was the perfect spell to use in this instance.

Mackenzie listened to them deepen the discussion to various incantations and charms they'd come across over the years, each warming to the subject. She must've dozed off, because when she again became aware of her surroundings, she registered the softness of a mattress beneath her.

The next thing she recognized was Sebastian's scent. He'd always smelled like sunlight and warm maple syrup on pancakes. She needed to remember to ask if anyone else had likened his personal essence to breakfast food in the past. A smile tugged at her lips.

"Are you back with me, Mack?" he asked in a low voice.

"Mmm. Almost."

"Almost?"

"I'm still groggy and suffering from a magical Aether hangover."

He chuckled, and it was the sweetest sound she'd ever remembered hearing.

His skillful fingers stroked back the hair from her face and created a wonderful sense of being treasured. Like the first time they'd met and touched, she was bombarded with a kaleidoscope of images. These weren't dark or ugly, the way the others had been. These made her happy, and she was inspired by the vision of their future.

He shifted to lift up on his elbow. She could feel his stare.

"What is it, love? What did you see?"

She blinked up at him. "How did you... never mind. Of course you'd know."

"A premonition?"

"The promise of our lovely future."

"Mmm. I like the sound of that."

For what felt like the longest time, they locked gazes. Mackenzie had no doubt they both understood the import of her words. She was fully healed, and theirs would be a bright, happy life.

"What time is it, Baz?"

"Midnight."

Her eyes flew wide. "Midnight! It was still morning when we were in the garden."

"Are you going to complain about a twelve-hour nap, love, or are you going to wake up and let me kiss the hell out of you? Because I've missed you, Mack." His voice cracked as he leaned over her. His eyes were dark haunted pools filled with a budding hope. "Goddess, how I've missed you. I never thought we'd have this again."

She trailed her fingertips over his brow, down his cheek, and across his lower lip. "I'm sorry."

"You have nothing to be sorry for. None of this was your doing. It's my family who needs to seek *your* forgiveness."

"No, Baz, they don't."

"We brought you here without telling you about the danger right off. Arabella could hardly look at you these last weeks. Her guilt was eating her up inside."

"She couldn't have known." But secretly, Mackenzie believed his sister should've considered the possible outcome of bringing her to the estate before she did it. However, Sebastian didn't need her to hammer home the point. He certainly didn't need the added stress of accusations and blame heaped on top of what he'd been through.

Digging her fingers into his thick mane of black hair, she pulled him closer. "Let's not talk about this tonight. I only want to hold you. Tell you I love you." She nipped his lip. "Make love with you."

"Good. I'd high hopes you wake in an amorous mood," he teased. "I put on my kilt for the special occasion. I know how much it turns you on."

"You know, you're still a practiced flirt." She arched a brow but couldn't hold the severe look without laughing. "But I've come to admire that about you. As long as your suave act is only ever for me."

Mackenzie offered her lips up to his.

His kiss consumed her and made her feel as if their souls had been fused into one. As if they now shared one beating heart, one mind. She didn't mind in the least.

He drew away and stared down at her as if he wasn't quite sure this was real.

"I'm back, Baz."

"I'm worried I'm dreaming. That your clever brain is still…" He closed his eyes and swallowed audibly.

She imagined it would take him a while to get over his fears, but she'd continue to do what she could to allay them. First was to distract him from his dark thoughts.

"I get it, darling. You really love me for my brilliant mind, and not my good looks." She grinned when her words registered for him and his eyes flew open.

"Funny woman."

"I thought so." When he would've kissed her again, she placed her index finger over his mouth. "You know, the only thing that would make this moment better, is if you're wearing socks with some raunchy saying."

Sebastian paused for the length of three heartbeats. With a wide smile, he sat up and propped one foot in front of him so she could see the writing on his sock. *"I'm the kind of dirty you can't wash off."*

"You really are my soulmate."

"I also got you some." Sebastian lifted a pink pair from the nightstand.

"'Proud member of the Illuminaughty.'" She hugged them to her and laughed. "As long as you're the President, I'm down for a lifelong membership."

He tackled her back on the pillows with a roguish grin. "I was hoping you'd say that."

EPILOGUE

ONE MONTH LATER...

From her vantage point by the big oak tree, Sabrina watched Mackenzie and Sebastian as they entered the boxwood maze. They were holding hands and laughing as they disappeared behind the tall hedges.

Her papa had been right when he said she'd feel better after she helped heal Mackenzie. Not only did Mack still laugh and create leaf dragons for Sabrina, but now Cousin Baz would never send her away to live with Alastair.

Mackenzie had pulled Sabrina to the side today to thank her for all she'd done for them and to tell her, within the next year, there would be a baby for Sabrina to help spoil. But Mack needn't have bothered telling her, because Sabrina already knew. She'd seen the part the Drake baby girl would play in relation to the baby boy Sabrina's mother would eventually have. They would always be a family unit: the Drakes and Dethridges.

"You did a good thing, beastie."

"I know, Papa."

"Are you still upset Mack won't be your constant playmate?"

"No. I have other things I need to do now."

"Oh?" He smiled down at her, all his love for her on display, and it chased away the last of her sadness. "Care to share?"

"It's a secret between me and Isis." Sabrina sensed his concern right before the frown formed between his brows. "It's okay, Papa. You're going to love it."

"Am I?" He tweaked her nose. "I tell you what. I'll let you keep your secrets for now, but we should be off. You know how cross your mother gets when we aren't home for the midday meal."

Sabrina took the hand he offered, but stopped him after only a few steps. "Mama will forgive you soon, Papa."

All the teasing left him, and he went still. "It's not a subject I wish to discuss with you, Sabrina. What happens between your mother and me, that's not for you to worry about, okay?"

"But I'm not worried. And when baby Nate comes, you'll both be happ—" She bit her lip. The Goddess had warned her not everything should be revealed.

"Some things need to play out for your family and friends without your interference, little one," Isis had told her on the day Grandpa Nate died.

Sabrina lifted her face skyward, worried she'd upset the Goddess. She felt her papa tug her hand. When she looked at him, he was smiling in the way that always made her sure everything would be all right.

"Baby Nate, huh? Well, that may be far off if we're late again." He knelt on one knee and quirked his head. "Hop on, and I'll get us home in a jiffy."

WHEN THE DETHRIDGES TELEPORTED FROM THE GARDEN, PRESTON Thorne dropped the shield cloaking Isis and him. "How did you know it would play out this way? You were rolling the dice by depending on a six-year-old to do the right thing."

Isis shrugged. "Not really. Sabrina is a bright child. She also knows right from wrong and will always be able to see reason. She's Damian's child, after all."

"You could've helped them all with this earlier." He gave her an admonishing look. "Saving them all the heartache. Saving Nathanial and Evie."

"Yes. But then Mackenzie and Sebastian wouldn't have appreciated what they have, and the Guardians' time on earth was done. Nathanial needed a hero's exit."

Preston heaved an internal sigh. The capriciousness of the gods would never cease to amaze him.

Isis sauntered down the garden path, waving a hand here or there and giving a boost of life to the plants around her. "Nothing good ever comes easy, my dear." She paused and cast him an enigmatic smile. "You'll find out for yourself soon enough."

"What have you done?"

"Nothing... yet. But I've decided you deserve happiness."

Preston didn't dare hope her words meant what he suspected. "You intend to give me life?"

"You have life. But yes, I'll return you to the earthly plane. *After.*"

"Ah, so you aren't done playing your games," he said, barely keeping the irritability from his voice.

She shot him a sharp look. "Careful."

"Because it wouldn't do to piss off a goddess?" He grinned to soften his snark.

"Because even with your surly temper, I enjoy having you as a consort. I'm surrendering my joy to give you yours."

Preston approached her and lifted her hand to drop a kiss on her knuckles. "I've been honored to serve you, Exalted One. I always will be."

He thought he detected a shimmer of sadness in her exotic blue eyes. "Nathanial and Evie will assist me now. Moving forward, you'll have your chance to live out the remainder of your days with your true love. Consider it a reward for serving me well."

"But I don't have a true love," Preston reminded her.

She graced him with a wink and a half smile. "Not yet, but you will."

FROM THE AUTHOR...

Thank you for taking the time to read **ENCHANTED MAGIC!**

Subscribe to my mailing list for news on current releases, VIP exclusive content, and contests each month. Your information will always be kept private. www.tmcromer.com/newsletter

For fans who like to interact, my reader group entitles readers to "fan only" contests, as well as an exclusive first look at covers, excerpts and more. Cromer's Carousers is the most fun way to follow yet. www.facebook.com/groups/cromerscarousers

Love & Lemon Drops,
T.M. Cromer
www.tmcromer.com

ALSO BY T.M. CROMER

Books in The Thorne Witches Series:
SUMMER MAGIC
AUTUMN MAGIC
WINTER MAGIC
SPRING MAGIC
REKINDLED MAGIC
LONG LOST MAGIC
FOREVER MAGIC
ESSENTIAL MAGIC
MOONLIT MAGIC
ENCHANTED MAGIC
CELESTIAL MAGIC

Books in The Holt Family Series:
FINDING YOU
THIS TIME YOU
INCLUDING YOU
AFTER YOU
THE GHOST OF YOU

Books in The Stonebrooke Series:
BURNING RESOLUTION
THE TROUBLE WITH LUST
THE BAKERY
EASTER DELIGHTS
HOLIDAY HEART

Books in The Fiore Vineyard Series:

PICTURE THIS

RETURN HOME

ONE WISH

CPSIA information can be obtained
at www.ICGtesting.com
Printed in the USA
BVHW041329200121
598221BV00010B/549